MAYBE IT'S NEGOTIABLE

The two human figures in the silent holo were a vaguely blond, young-looking woman and a delicate-looking boy of about eight who somewhat resembled her. They were relaxed, enjoying their leisure, casually playing some kind of game, tossing back and forth a small ball. The two were laughing as they played, but no sound reached Harry's ears.

He turned to confront an elderly man who could only be Mister Winston Cheng himself. The tycoon was readily recognizable from public images. Cheng gestured toward the vaguely ghostly figures.

"There they are, Mister Silver—may I call you Harry?"

"Suit yourself."

"There they are, Harry. My granddaughter and her son. My only living descendants of that generation."

"Handsome people."

"Less than a standard month ago, Winnie and his mother were as you see them in this recording. Today I do not know if either of them is still alive.

"Mister Silver—Harry—my advisers agree that there are few citizens of the Galaxy, living or dead, who have seen as many of the berserkers as you have. That is one of the reasons why you are here today."

The great man's voice had settled into a monotone. "Harry, you must know what I'm about to ask of you. Whatever the nature of the power that took my granddaughter and her son, I'm going after it—or them. If rescuing Winnie and Claudia alive proves to be impossible, I will do the next thing that needs to be done, and make their killers pay. I intend to have you as a member of that team."

Baen Books by Fred Saberhagen

Rogue Berserker
Berserkers
Berserker Man
Berserker Death

Vlad Tapes

ROGUE BERSERKER

FRED SABERHAGEN

ROGUE BERSERKER

This is a work of fiction. All the characters and events portrayed in this book are fictional, and any resemblance to real people or incidents is purely coincidental.

A Baen Book

Baen Publishing Enterprises
P.O. Box 1403
Riverdale, NY 10471
www.baen.com

ISBN 10: 1-4165-2069-4
ISBN 13: 1-978-1-4165-2069-6

Cover art by Kurt Miller

First Baen paperback printing, June 2006

Library of Congress Control Number: 2004021811

Distributed by Simon & Schuster
1230 Avenue of the Americas
New York, NY 10020

Pages by Joy Freeman (www.pagesbyjoy.com)
Printed in the United States of America
10   9   8   7   6   5   4   3   2   1

ROGUE BERSERKER

ROGUE: (1) A deceitful, double-dealing evildoer . . . (4) A fierce elephant or stamodont that has been banished from the herd . . . (10) Having a peculiarly malevolent or unstable nature . . . (11) No longer loyal, affiliated, or recognized, and hence not governable or accountable . . . erring, apostate.

—Galactic Dictionary of the Common Tongue

ONE

The tall thing with four arms came close to catching Harry Silver with its first three-legged rush at him in the dark alley. In frightening silence it burst out at him from the deeper darkness behind a tall stack of crates and boxes. It wasn't really running, but stepping rapidly across the gray resilient pavement on its trio of padded feet. Some inner alarm, a distillation of small clues and experience, clicked a warning in Harry's brain an instant before he actually saw the thing, granting him the essential moment to drop to the ground and roll out of the robot's way. One of its grabbers brushed Harry's right sleeve as its thin legs carried it by.

Dark alleys on unfamiliar planets were good places to avoid; this was the first time in standard years that he'd tried to use one for a shortcut.

The fact that the natural gravity on this world was a bit weaker than Earth-descended normal gave him the ability to move a shade faster than usual. He wasn't moving as swiftly as his opponent, but the disadvantage was not as great as it might have been . . . some part of his mind was still playing the role of spectator, and as he fell and rolled and spun away, he noticed that the alley floor was remarkably clean and smooth. Evidently the people living here on Cascadia prized neatness.

Coming up out of his roll into a crouch, Harry saw that his attacker was ten or fifteen centimeters taller than he was. Of course it would be vastly stronger. That he had managed to dodge it on its first rush meant it was slower than most machines, but no doubt it was fast and capable enough to get its job done, ninety-nine times out of a hundred. By now he'd recognized the type. People who dealt with such devices on a regular basis called them handpads, or more commonly just paddies—a step up from a footpad, an old name for a stealthy strong-arm robber. They were also a long step in the wrong direction, of robots designed to hurt people in some way. Such were thoroughly illegal, on every world that Harry knew about, but right now that fact was of very little help.

Even though a paddy was bad news, the identification brought relief. For just a moment Harry had feared that he was facing something infinitely worse. That fear was already proven baseless, the evidence being that he was still alive.

The robot he was facing would have been built, or rebuilt and illegally modified, in some clandestine shop. Quite possibly it toiled by day, like countless innocent general purpose machines, at some dull routine job. This one was equipped with four padded hands, or grippers—Harry had seen some paddy models that carried five, when you counted a sort of ropelike monkey-tail, which served the same purpose of grabbing and holding on. The monkey-tail had never worked the way it was supposed to, as Harry recalled. The carefully fitted pads were meant to prevent injury to the people they were designed to capture and restrain. The robot's master could hope that this calculated forbearance might offer a chance to avoid draconian punishment, should he or she be caught.

And a human master there would be, somewhere. One certainty was that the machine had not decided to do this all by itself. The robot's fagin would be staying in the background, out of sight, safe from fists and feet and whatever other form of opposition might materialize, waiting until the victim was blindfolded and helpless, before coming on the scene.

The model of paddy currently confronting Harry had no tail. Neither were its grippers divided into fingers—the fagin's all-too-human hands, at this point still remaining safely out of sight, would provide all the fingers necessary. He or she would walk on the scene only after the victim had been rendered helpless, clamped into immobility and probably blindfolded. Paddy's only function would be to hold the victim still while the human operator rifled his or her pockets, or got on with the commission of whatever other offenses against the person that might seem like fun. Robbery, without serious bodily harm, was not punished on the same scale as mayhem or murder. On any world where human law prevailed, as far as Harry knew, the penalties were severe for building, employing, or even just possessing any kind of self-guiding devices intended to actually injure people.

Following the robot's first rush, it had turned, unhurriedly reassessing its target. Now it was methodically stalking Harry. What little the man could see of his dark opponent in the dim light suggested that its head and body and arms were made of some composite material. If he punched any part of that surface with all his strength, he was probably going to break his hand.

To turn his back on it and run would only make the damned thing's job a little easier; he knew he wasn't going to outspeed those three long springy legs . . .

. . . the robot closed in, and suddenly there was an opening, and before Harry could make a conscious plan his body was doing its best to take advantage of the opportunity. His right leg got home with a thrusting kick on the bulky torso. The impact sounded like a note from a bass drum, and would have caved in the thickest human ribs. The robot was rocked back half a meter or so, but that was all. One of its grabbers, flailing wildly, thrown off its aim by the force of the kick, bruised Harry's extended leg but failed to catch hold.

This was not the kind of machine that people used when they set out to commit murder. There were a lot of simpler ways of killing, less trouble and more reliable. So, even if Paddy caught him it wouldn't kill, which meant he could take a bigger chance . . . he decided to let his left arm be seized.

One gripper had caught Harry by the left wrist, and yanked him almost off his feet, but he would bet his life that that one was pretty quickly going to let go of him again . . .

Now another gripper had Harry by one ankle, so he could no longer kick effectively with either foot. One second later it had seized his right arm . . . but his left arm was no longer being held, and he put the newly available fist to good use, rattling the thing's head with a karate blow that he could hope (not much of a hope, really) was hard enough to jar its senses. He struck again and again with his bladed left hand, satisfied to keep pounding even though he could get nothing like full power from the awkward position in which he was being held.

Ten or a dozen hits like that, and suddenly he was free. The robot was reeling back, legs gone awkward, stumbling to a collapse that left it wedged half under a metal railing, a kind of fence that defended a sunken areaway beside a dark-walled building.

Gasping, picking himself up from where the thing had dropped him, Harry Silver stood unsteadily, a dark-haired man of indeterminate age, average height and wiry build, wearing the lightweight boots and coverall that served almost as a uniform for professional spacers. His chosen color for the coverall was mottled gray, almost a camouflage, aimed at avoiding attention rather than attracting it. Another violent encounter, long years ago, had left his nose pushed sideways, and it had never been entirely straightened. What the dim light revealed of his hands and forearms indicated strength.

Before approaching his fallen opponent, Harry looked around. It appeared that whoever might be Paddy's fagin, its human master and controller, was going to remain out of sight. Screw up one robbery, robot, and you're an orphan. Nobody ever heard of you.

But the orphan was interesting. Probably it was not totally disabled, but it did appear to be stuck in a position where a reasonably careful man ought to be able to take a closer look at it with a minimum of risk.

Cautiously Harry moved forward, trying to get a better look at Paddy the Bad, wishing he had some extra light. Now he could see, with a certain satisfaction, that the parts of the robot's body that had come in close contact with Harry's left hand, beginning with one of the machine's wrists and its attached forearm, had been chewed into a ruin.

There were a couple of deep, narrow holes, each one fringed by a raw edge of composite, where material had been shredded into shagginess with little pieces falling off. The side of the robot's stubby head where Harry's bladed hand had pounded was in similar shape. An empty socket showed where an eye lens had been crudely carved out of its lifeless skull. All in all, Harry's quondam opponent looked like it had lost a fight with a giant sewing machine.

It wasn't his merely human muscles and training that had wrought such havoc. Didn't he wish. He twisted the plain-looking, silvery ring on the little finger of his left hand.

As Harry, still breathing hard, backed away from his late opponent, a slight noise made him turn.

A well-dressed man, by his appearance most likely a tourist, was standing some ten meters away, in the mouth of the alley, bending forward a little, watching Harry warily. When Harry looked around, the man straightened and said, almost defensively: "I've called the police."

"That shows good citizenship," Harry grunted. This was one of the rare occasions when he wasn't going to mind having a conversation with the cops. Still keeping a wary eye on Paddy—the well-dressed good citizen had disappeared—Harry moved to a handy curb and let himself sit down.

About five minutes later, a uniformed policeman had stepped out of his vehicle, taken his first look at the robot, and was remarking: "First time I've seen anyone get away from one of these."

Harry was about to retort that he hadn't got away, he was still here, but his better angel reminded him to be nice. Now an ambulance came rolling up, smoothly and silently, to stand beside the police vehicle. Harry grunted, turning his ring round on his finger. He would have to remember to recharge it soon. He was well aware that even with his secret weapon he had not vanquished the robot so much as caused it to recompute the situation and decide to call off its attack.

"Did it look like this when it first came after you?" the cop asked blandly. "I mean, was it all chopped up? Or maybe you had some kind of help."

"Maybe I did."

Approached by the human medic from the ambulance, Harry firmly declined a ride to a hospital, then compromised by submitting to on-the-spot first-aid treatment for his own trivial injuries. These consisted of a few scrapes, and a bruised calf where the grabber had failed to grab.

While this was going on, he gave the officer a good look at his ring, and began an explanation—he had no reason to believe that he was currently being recorded. Any of several combinations of commands and conditions triggered the action of a forceblade concealed in the ring, a nonmaterial cutter somewhat sharper than a microknife and a little stronger than ordinary steel, that stung and stabbed into anything or anyone whose behavior had triggered the defense.

The Cascadian cop was professionally interested. Harry demonstrated, briefly, on the robot's torso. The operation was almost silent, and the thin blur of concentrated force offered nothing at all to see except a little spray of fragments from its target.

Harry had given his ring's programming some thought. On its first flickering thrust, the blade of force stabbed out only one centimeter. The initial wound inflicted on a human body was hardly likely to be serious, but it would get anyone's notice. After an interval of one and one half seconds, it stabbed again, and one second after that blurred into a frenzy, the rate of repetition going up rapidly, along with the depth of the penetrations, the latter maxing at ten centimeters. Good armor would stop the little stabber cold, of course, but Paddy was neither a military machine nor the horror Harry had feared in his first bad moment.

The cop was shaking his head. "Cute. But you know your gadget's illegal on a lot of planets."

"Not here, I hope."

"Not on my beat, not if it gets a paddy off the streets." The policeman had already determined that Harry had no criminal record, at least none that showed up in this planet's database. Now he took a quick look up and down the alley. "But I wouldn't do any public bragging about it."

"I wouldn't either."

Harry went on answering the investigator's continued questions, mainly by coming up with what seemed appropriate monosyllables. Half his mind was elsewhere. His anger at having been attacked was growing, all the fiercer when he recalled that moment of fear when the mechanical body first confronted him.

The cop's next question brought his attention back. "You know anyone who might think they have some reason to—get back at you for something?"

Harry was nodding. No need to ponder that one. "I might come up with a few names. But none of them sent this."

"How do you know?"

Harry was smiling faintly now. "I doubt they'd be satisfied just to pick my pockets."

The ambulance had gone on its way, and a police team of robotic experts had arrived. The team was headed by a human tech, a woman who gave the impression of being dedicated to her job, in command of a couple of specialized machines. These were sturdy, functional units, slightly larger than most full-grown humans. They had two thick arms and two sturdy legs apiece, and their surfaces of scarred metal armor suggested they were used chiefly in jobs considered notably unsafe for humans. That type of work included the immobilization of any of their fellow robots that might demonstrate a tendency to be dangerous or unpredictable.

The lady was soon briefed on the situation, and quietly issued orders. In a few seconds her two mechanical bodyguards, approaching the stranded paddy one on each side, had strong-armed its massive body out from under the guard fence and were holding it clamped between them. Each bodyguard was twisting one of Paddy's arms, and using one of its own large feet to pin down one of Paddy's three.

Precautions having been taken, the human tech herself, optelectronic probes and other gear in hand, cautiously approached the renegade robot, while the cop and Harry stood back.

The lady applied her probes. Vigilant testing showed that Paddy was still quite capable of movement when commanded, but was now inclined to be completely docile.

In another moment the tech, with deft, experienced moves, had produced a kind of soft, eyeless helmet and fitted it loosely over Paddy's head. Immediately she began to get readings on her handheld showing what was going on inside. It seemed that the doors of communication might be opening a bit, but when the tech attempted a voice interrogation, the subject moved slightly but remained mute.

"I order you to answer me," she commanded in a firm voice.

Still no response.

Leaning forward cautiously, the tech put out a hand and plucked a small, thin object from a kind of utility belt that circled Paddy's generous waist. She studied it a moment, then tossed it to her human colleague. Harry, looking over the shoulder of the male cop, saw that he was now holding a flat, narrow band of some composite designed material, about as long as a human forearm. Some kind of ligature, the kind of thing that might be used to restrain people without causing injury.

The tech commented: "That's a newer model, one I haven't seen before."

The cop, with Harry looking over his shoulder, observed: "Looks a little tougher than the cuffs we use. I bet it would leave some marks."

The lady was holding out her hand, and he gave the specimen back. By way of illustrating its use, she put it round the arm of one of her own compliant robots. The instant the band was in place, it molded itself to the surface, as if it were settling in, getting ready to resist removal.

"Can you pull that loose, Holdy?" she asked the machine. "Give it a try."

A powerful metal hand began to work. Fifteen seconds elapsed before the metal equivalent of a fingernail managed to scrape a purchase under the band, and five more before the composite yielded with a snap.

"Holdy's strong," the lady tech remarked. A fine example of understatement, Harry supposed, considering the line of work for which her robot aide had been designed.

She added: "Human being wouldn't have much chance to get away."

Harry could well believe that, too. There was still no response forthcoming from the robber machine. Shrugging, the tech did not persist in her attempts at interrogation.

"We'll try again when we get this cute little feller

in the lab," she commented. Then she frowned, and flicked a finger at the ruined section of Paddy's right upper forearm. "How'd he get so chewed up?"

"I didn't see it," the beat cop admitted.

"I didn't get a very good look either," Harry acknowledged. There was a note of bewilderment in his voice. "It all happened so fast."

The tech gave him an appraising look. "I bet it did," she observed. But finding out what had happened wasn't her department, and she turned to make a signal to the second tame robot in her crew. It extended a thick arm and retrieved the helmet from Paddy's head. Harry's imagination painted a glum look on Paddy's face, made it the image of a human waiting for his lawyer to show up. But a robot was going to have a long wait before that happened.

"No luck, huh?" the patrolman asked his coworker sympathetically.

The woman shrugged. "When we start taking things apart, we'll probably find all its vocal gear has been taken out. Maybe even its language capability. And all identifying marks and numbers will have been removed. Who this belongs to will take some digging to find out—if we ever do."

She looked at Harry one more time. "Consider yourself lucky, mister."

"I always try to do that. Sometimes it works."

TWO

I've had a fagin tell me, with a straight face, that his paddy is a lifesaver," the sympathetic cop was telling Harry. "It's only a safety device, just intended to keep people from getting hurt." His voice became a whine: "'Why, if I didn't use Paddy here, I'd have to bang up some of my customers severely. Or use a gun. Is that what you cops want?'"

Harry offered what seemed to him an appropriate comment. The cop was giving him a ride in a police car, taking him back to his hotel beside the Cascadian spaceport. As a rule Harry didn't talk much, but there were times when once he got started he tended to go on at some length. Tonight he found himself, by his own standards, almost babbling. Discussing your troubles with someone you didn't know was easier than complaining to a friend—not that Harry was exactly surrounded by a roster of interested friends all clamoring to hear what had him down.

He explained to the cop that he had come to this world in search of financing for a new ship. The lease was about to expire on the ship he had been using. He had driven it to Cascadia, with whatever cargo he had been able to scrounge up, because he had heard that a certain company doing business here was making deals with small, independent ship owners and operators. But that hadn't worked out. Even getting another cargo here was proving difficult.

The police car was running on autodriver while the cop just leaned back in the driver's seat and looked at Harry and listened. He seemed to be one of those good cops who could deal with most problems by sympathetic talk. Harry would bet that the total amount of good he had done in the world was never going to show up in his official record.

When Harry paused, the good cop observed: "I suppose owning your own ship is the way to go. If you're in the piloting business."

"Yeah, just about the only way. I actually had my own ship, until about five standard years ago." Soon Harry found himself explaining how the last craft he had owned, the *Witch of Endor*, had been lost in action against a berserker.

"That would entitle you to compensation, right? From one government or another?"

"Sure, in this case maybe from more than one. But their idea of what it'll cost to replace the *Witch* doesn't quite match with mine."

"What kind of ship are you in the market for?" the investigator sounded genuinely curious.

"A nice one." Harry didn't feel like going into details. And he didn't bother to mention that he had a name all picked out: *Sonovawitch*. He wasn't sure this officer was the type to appreciate it.

Over the last few months, in the course of seeking private financing, Harry had made the same explanation a number of times, to a variety of different people, none of whom had seemed overwhelmingly impressed. He had grown tired of repeating that the amounts the various governmental bodies were willing to compensate him did not add up to what he needed for a real replacement for the *Witch*, the kind of ship he was determined to have. People responding to his presentation tended to leave unspoken comments hanging in the air, things like *This is an arrogant so-and-so. Entitled to some special consideration, is he? Who does he think he is?*

Well, Harry knew who he was. Others might entertain different ideas about him, but self-image was not his problem—at least he had never given it any serious consideration. So when, a few weeks ago, Harry had been handed the invitation from Winston Cheng, delivered in a form that suggested it had been sent a good many light-years by special superluminal courier, Harry suspected it was a joke, and his first thought was: *Who would be the most likely perpetrator?*

The Winston Cheng whose apparent signature sat like a foundation stone at the bottom of the message was one of the wealthiest humans in the known Galaxy. Cheng Enterprises was widely believed to be quite capable of organizing a private army or even a small fleet of spaceships if the need arose. It was a name

Harry would never have considered when drawing up his list of possible angels to whom a small fish like Harry Silver might reasonably go looking for an honest loan.

The invitation was as simple and direct as it was mysterious:

Mister Harry Silver—
Please come see me in person at once, regarding an arrangement in which I will buy you the ship you want.
Winston Cheng

Well, it didn't seem at all impossible that Winston Cheng knew that Harry was looking for a good ship. That was hardly a secret—Harry had been bitching and moaning his way across one Galactic sector after another, traversing so much of the inhabited territory that probably half the human population could be aware of his complaints. Harry had gripped the paper—yes, real, simple, single-use paper—in both fists, muttering. "Come see him, huh? Just like that. How the hell am I supposed to afford just getting there? Take a vacation in my leased ship? If he thinks . . ."

Such irreverence seemed to make the human courier, the one who had brought Harry the message, uncomfortable. Not that the courier knew the message content, or the reason it had been sent.

He could, however, clarify one point. Whatever the great man wanted with Harry, it was very serious business and he was in a hell of a hurry. Yes, he could assure Harry that Winston Cheng had really gone to the length of *sending a ship* for him, a full-sized courier with a human crew. Most magnates with half of Winston Cheng's wealth would have expected to be able to buy and sell several Harry Silvers for a fraction of the cost of doing that.

The possibility, even a probability, that the offer might be perfectly serious was beginning to sink in. "Who do I have to kill?" Harry had wondered aloud.

The courier captain, still waiting deferentially for Harry's reply, evidently thought that Harry was trying to be funny, and showed polite amusement. "It's not a joke, Mister Silver. A genuine invitation, I assure you."

Mister Silver waved the document, jabbed a pointing finger at it. "Even the part about his buying me a ship? Under what conditions does that hold?" Harry was making a fuss, but already in his own mind there was no doubt at all that he was going to see the man.

The captain was determined to be as opaque as he was courteous. "Sir, I've told you everything that I know. Details will have to come from the boss himself."

Port clearance and liftoff were routine. After about two days of ride in the fast courier—two restless days of doing little or nothing—Harry arrived at an outpost of Winston Cheng Enterprises, in the middle of a sizable city on a world that was very largely owned by the gentleman himself, where he was ushered with what seemed amazing speed into the great man's presence.

The visitor wasn't sure whether this room at the top of a high-rise building ought to be called an office or a study, but it was appropriately long, high, and magnificent. Long, long, red drapes half concealed windows of crystal that seemed alive with light, their clear depths suggesting rather than displaying vistas of impossible landscaping.

Actually, *presence chamber* was the label that sprang to Harry's mind. But, after all, he had seen breathtaking walls before, with rich patterns scrolling over them. He had seen heavenly furnishings. The truly most impressive thing about the welcome was that he hadn't been made to wait.

A tall, attractive woman of uncertain age, her slender body sheathed in a long, black flow of rich fabric, came to greet Harry once the courier captain had seen him in past the first, preliminary receptionist.

Ignoring the courier captain as he bowed himself away, she introduced herself as the Lady Masaharu, in crisp tones that seemed to want to waste no time. Her smile seemed brittle in a chiseled face, her pale eyes bored into Harry. Evidently what she saw was acceptable, because in another moment she was escorting him into another, smaller and less exotically decorated chamber two rooms away. The private office of Winston Cheng? No, Harry thought not. It was probably the lady's. Or that of the third deputy assistant to the third assistant deputy.

Gesturing Harry to a chair, and seating herself behind a dominating desk, she continued to be pleasant and welcoming, in a businesslike way. All emotions were as firmly controlled as her tightly coiffured hair.

Her voice was soft, in contrast to her appearance. "How was your journey, Mister Silver?"

"Mysterious."

The smile that had gone away came back, faintly.

"I hope we'll soon be able to clear up any essential questions. Mister Cheng wants to do that in person. Were there any other problems?"

"No. Otherwise very comfortable."

Giving the impression of responding to some signal that Harry could not detect, the Lady Masaharu was suddenly on her feet. "Come this way, please."

In another moment she was ushering him into the next room, which outdid the original reception room in splendor. As Harry entered, the space before him, practically big enough for a game of volleyball, was dominated by an impressive though silent holostage display. Obviously it was meant for him to see, and there was no need to point it out.

The two human figures in the silent holo were a vaguely blond, young-looking woman with a face and figure that would pass unnoticed in a crowd, and a delicate-looking boy of about eight who somewhat resembled her. Both were lightly dressed, in sporting togs of richly understated elegance. In the huge room the two life-sized images, faintly transparent, had more space than they needed to move about. They were relaxed, enjoying their leisure, casually playing some kind of game, tossing back and forth the image of a small ball that now and then demonstrated some purpose of its own. Hints of the game's real background, an open space of grass and sunlight, showed through here and there in the recording. The two were laughing as they played, but no sound of any kind reached Harry's ears.

A new voice said something, from behind Harry.

He turned to confront an elderly man who could only be Mister Winston Cheng himself. The tycoon was readily recognizable from public images but looking older in the flesh, a slight figure, almost as plainly dressed as Harry himself.

Cheng gestured toward the vaguely ghostly figures. He looked frail, in the same sense that a sculpture of delicate metal wire might deserve that name.

"There they are, Mister Silver—may I call you Harry?" Winston Cheng's face was a version, grown and aged, of the small boy's in the video. His hair was gray and wispy, and his hands seemed too large and young to match the rest of him. Only the dark, impressive eyes seemed likely to belong to one of the Galaxy's richest humans.

"Suit yourself."

The Lady Masaharu had silently withdrawn into the background, but Harry noted that she did not leave the room. A resource in place, for the master of the house to draw on if he chose. She did not move or blink an eye when the recorded image of the young woman, silently laughing, ran almost through her.

The old man repeated: "There they are, Harry. My granddaughter and her son. Her only child. My only living descendant of that generation. Please, have a seat."

Harry nodded agreeably. "Handsome people." He tried out a chair of interesting appearance, one that received his weight with a slight quiver, as if it might be nervous. Or maybe it was just impressed by the importance of any visitor eminent enough to be invited to sit down in these rooms. "Your message said plainly that you might buy me a ship."

"Indeed it did." Cheng clasped his large hands in front of him. "Let me explain what I would expect from you in return."

"Fire away."

One of the old man's arms moved out, perhaps involuntarily, as if to catch a laughing barefoot child just darting past. But Cheng's extended hand went right through the speeding figure, as if the boy's body were only smoke.

"Winnie," Winston Cheng murmured sorrowfully. "Henrik Winston Cheng, my great-grandson."

"Yes."

"Less than a standard month ago, Winnie and his mother were as you see them in this recording." The fingers of the extended hand closed tightly, the arm fell slowly back to the old man's side. "Today I do not know if either of them are still alive. If they still breathe, it may be in a situation where they pray for death."

"Sorry to hear that, Mister Cheng."

For a moment the tycoon seemed to be drifting. Then he went on. "Mister Silver—Harry—time and life had worn me into an old man before I began to realize the importance of certain traditional elements of human existence. And the triviality of other things, indeed of most of what we strive and suffer for."

He paused again, as if considering the speech he had just made. "Harry, I speak now in clichés and truisms. You are not a young man either, though certainly you are not as old . . . tell me, is the most important thing in your life today the same as it was ten years ago?"

Harry bit back a smart-assed answer, thinking as he did so: *Becky would be proud of me.* Instead he said: "No, it sure as hell isn't. But however that may be, my purpose in coming here was to look for some way of getting my hands on a good ship." Harry fidgeted a bit; the chair was still moving slightly under him, pressing here and there at his bottom and his legs, as if were determined to discover the position that would provide him with the absolutely greatest comfort. Or something. "I'm truly sorry about your relatives, whatever happened to them. What can I do for you?"

Lady Masaharu was still standing silent, back against a richly paneled wall, one arm extended, a long fingernail elegantly tapping something on a shelf. She was watching the men, and seemed to be listening with intense concentration.

Bluntly and efficiently, the old man revealed the stark facts of his problem. His granddaughter, Claudia, and her only child, little Winnie, were missing. All evidence pointed to a remarkable event: they had been kidnapped in a berserker attack on one of Winston Cheng's space yachts.

In the background, the Lady Masaharu was doing something that banished the images of idyllic playtime. A broad conventional holostage rose from the center of the large room's floor, and on the stage a new scene began to play.

It was the lady who provided commentary: "This recording was made by a surviving eyewitness. From another ship that happened to be only a short distance from the yacht."

Several witnesses had been watching from that ship, through magnification. Two sets of testimony came from human, and two more from impartial automated systems.

Harry sat forward in his strange chair, trying to

catch every detail. He could tell that a good deal of time and effort had been invested, setting computers to work to enhance and enlarge the images.

A spacegoing device had suddenly appeared in normal space nearby.

Cheng's voice had taken over the commentary. "The defenses in that system have needed upgrading for some time. They were flat-out fooled by the intruder, for almost a full minute. Logged it in as a small civilian ship. Took them entirely too long to realize that it wasn't a ship at all."

The intruder had seemed to know from the first microsecond what it was after. Only seconds after materializing in normal space, it had literally pounced on the yacht, before the victim could start to move.

An explosion of moderate size had torn open the yacht's main airlock. Out of the intruder had poured a small squad of what looked like berserker boarding machines, the largest no bigger than the paddy Harry had fought only a few days back. They had crossed a very modest interval of space, and plunged into the victim. In what seemed an incredibly short time, the boarding machines were back in sight, dragging living people garbed in helmets and spacesuits.

Berserkers were superbly efficient, fully automated war machines, of ancient lineage, though some were as modern as the latest battlecraft produced by the shipyards of Earth-descended humanity. The prototypes and archetypes of the berserker line had been artifacts of an interstellar war, a gigantic conflict fought across some uncertain, distant region of the Galaxy. That had happened at about the same time that humanity on Earth was discovering the use of fire, and beginning to wonder who had made the star-sparks in the sky, and how far away they were.

Cheng's voice was weary. "Of course I have watched this scene a thousand times. And it has been analyzed in great detail, by a battery of experts."

One side in that ancient war, a shadowy race known to modern humanity only as the Builders, had built the first berserkers, intending them as ultimate weapons, and launched them in the territory of the rival Red Race. Whatever precisely had been the original programming of those machines, the result had been a brood of prodigious inanimate metal killers, driven by a built-in compulsion to destroy all life wherever they could track it down. It seemed obvious that the Builders must have intended to equip their monstrous weapons with effective safeguards, to protect themselves and their own worlds. It was equally obvious that whatever effort they might have made along that line had failed catastrophically.

The berserkers' assault had quickly driven the Red Race into oblivion, where they were followed shortly by the Builders themselves. After them the populations of uncounted other planets had been wiped out. So far, in the known Galaxy, only the Earth-descended variant of humanity had been able—sometimes—to match the unliving enemy of all life in intelligence, ferocity, and strength, combined into overall destructive power.

Either Cheng or the lady had done something to pause the recording.

Watching the capture and pillaging of the yacht, the removal of live people clad in space suits, Harry had ceased to be aware of whatever the furniture might be trying to do to him, or for him. Now, leaning back in a relaxed chair, he shook his head. "That's grim, all right. Not only grim, but almost unheard of. I'm surprised it wasn't on the news."

Cheng nodded slowly. "As yet there has been no account in the media—is that still true as of this morning, Laura?" The lady in the background nodded, and he went on: "I've made a strong attempt to delay any public announcement. You can imagine why. When the news does get out, as inevitably it soon will, my staff and I will certainly face distraction in several forms. There will be fraudulent ransom demands. We will be subject to a heavy volume of lunatic advice, crazy threats of further harm, and offers of psychic assistance, some of the latter guaranteed to be from sympathetic Carmpan."

Harry and the lady were both nodding. The race of Carmpan, a non-ED branch of Galactic humanity, did have certain proven psychic powers. But they used them only rarely to help the race of Earth-descended humans, and never on demand.

The old man's gaze had taken on a burning intensity. "I must not forget to mention the promises I will receive of miraculous intervention by one divine power or another—if only I say the appropriate prayer, and/or make the proper contribution. Nor will I even be spared insane accusations. I, or some of my other relatives, will actually be charged with engineering the abduction of Winnie and Claudia."

The tycoon and his lady were both looking at Harry now, and he needed to come up with something to say. "Then you do have other relatives," he offered.

"A few." Winston Cheng was staring absently into the distance. The fire had gone out of his eyes and voice. "Claudia's husband, Winnie's father, is dead. But I care nothing for any of them who are still alive, nor they for me. You may take my word for it, Harry, they do not enter into this."

"If you say so." The holostage had sunk back into the floor, and the blithely frolicking images of woman and boy were back. Harry was ignoring them, giving the old man his whole attention. He cleared his throat. "The way you phrased it was, your two people are 'missing,' and 'kidnapped.' So you don't believe that this berserker has killed them?"

"You saw the recording, Harry. Killing them on the spot would have been simple and easy. It wanted prisoners."

"Yeah. But—"

"You are about to repeat what all those who know the facts of the abduction have already told me—that Claudia and Winnie are certainly dead by now." The old man's stare challenged Harry to agree with that statement. Harry was silent. For the enemy of all life to choose taking prisoners over simple killing was rare indeed. But he could testify that it was not absolutely unheard of.

"Those who compose that chorus are not trying to wound me, but the reverse. They seek to soften the harsh reality," the measured voice went on. "What they really mean is that my granddaughter and her child may or may not be dead, but if not dead, they are currently being used as experimental subjects in some robotic berserker laboratory, in ways that do not bear thinking about. But refusing to think about the situation does not change it. You must understand from the beginning, Harry, that I cannot let matters rest in this state."

For a moment or two the old man seemed on the very edge of breaking down. "Bear with me, please. Those two young people are truly all I have left. The only things in this damned, literally godforsaken world that I can begin to care about."

"I see," said Harry.

When he had recovered himself somewhat, Cheng went on.

"Let me be thorough, take things in their proper order. There is a little more evidence that you should see."

Ten minutes later, Harry had to agree that if the witnesses and recordings were to be believed, any kind of superpaddy operation could be ruled out. Unless the show he had just seen was a total fake, there could be little doubt that a genuine, indisputable Type-A berserker vehicle had grappled with one of Winston Cheng's armed yachts, on the fringe of a certain solar system, had boarded it with man-sized fighting machines, and killed or removed every human being who had been aboard.

Winston Cheng at last concluded his presentation, and leaned back, awaiting Harry's response.

Stretching forward from his chair, which was still behaving itself, Harry helped himself to a chewing pod from a beautiful display dish on a table crafted from some kind of exotic matter. He expected something of superior quality and got it, a marvelous flavor, not quite like anything he had ever tasted before. After savoring it for a moment—and still wishing he had a drink of scotch instead—he asked: "What else have you been able to find out?"

Winston Cheng began going into technical details, of which he seemed to have an enormous number at his mental fingertips. The fact that the berserker had carried away his people instead of killing them on the spot, as it had killed several of the crew members, gave him reason to believe (or so he had convinced himself) that Claudia and Winnie were still alive. He spoke as if on the assumption that granddaughter and great-grandson must be prisoners in some berserker establishment.

Finally Harry ventured to break in. "Look, Mister Cheng. Given the situation you describe, the chance that your people are still alive seems to me . . ." He made a gesture of futility.

"Small," the old man prompted drily.

"Yes. Actually, calling it 'small' is something of an understatement."

"I understand. But you concede it is *possible* that they are still alive. Even possible that they have not suffered irreversible physical harm."

Harry let out a slow puff of breath. He had shifted position and was resting his folded arms on the back of a second chair, and his chin on his folded arms. "I'm disinclined to say that anything's impossible where berserkers are involved. But—"

"Mister Silver—Harry—my advisers agree there are few citizens of the Galaxy, living or dead, who have seen as many of the bad machines as you have. That is one of the reasons why you are here today."

"I figured that." Mentally reviewing the evidence he had just seen and heard, he could spot nothing to suggest that the attackers had been anything but real berserkers. Nothing, that is, but the starkly puzzling fact that in the recording they had not killed everyone in sight.

Testimony of witnesses offered what Cheng chose to regard as good reason to hope, reporting that his relatives had been handled with great care by the bad machines. For some reason the enemy had clearly taken a special interest in them.

Winston Cheng paused, evidently expecting Harry to come up with some further response. After all, he had invested a lot of money and time in bringing Harry here.

Harry had helped himself to a couple of additional chewing pods, and put the first one of them in his pocket for later. Between chomps on the second one, he said carefully: "Offhand I can think of three or four possible explanations for the odd situation you've described. I warn you, so far I haven't had any ideas that could be called comforting."

"Sir, if you are to provide me with any comfort, I think it will not be by means of soothing words. Go ahead."

"All right. First, leaving aside for the moment the question of whether these attackers were real berserkers or not—looking at the recording here, I see no reason to doubt that—do you think they recognized Claudia and Winnie as members of your family?"

"It would seem almost inevitable that the yacht should be recognized as mine. Beyond that, I have no means of judging. It was no secret that Claudia and Winnie were likely to be aboard the vessel at that time. Through the years there has been a fair amount of publicity about my family, though I don't encourage it."

Harry was anything but a gossip-hound, but without even trying he could recall a fair amount of that publicity. The extended family of Winston Cheng had long been noted for other things besides its wealth: exotic sexual behavior, tempestuous marriages, assorted scandals, divorces, more marriages and more scandals, as well as heroic feats of spending, losing, borrowing, swindling, sometimes giving away, gaining and investing money and other forms of material wealth. If the old man was ready to disinherit almost the entire clan, it would hardly be surprising. Harry could remember no crimes of violence directly associated with them, but then he hadn't been trying to keep track.

"All right." He squinted and thoughtfully pulled at an earlobe. "It appears that the kidnappers, whatever or whoever they were, didn't try to actually hijack the yacht? Make off with it?"

"Correct, although some have suggested that might have been their original intention. The vessel was more seriously damaged in the boarding process than is plain from the recording, and they might have assumed it no longer spaceworthy. It's gone into the dock for repairs."

Harry pondered again. "Did they take any *things*, besides the people?"

"I don't believe so. Why?"

Harry shook his head. "Well, if they did it would be an oddity. Real berserkers don't loot. But to me the really big oddity in what you're telling me is that you haven't mentioned receiving any ransom demands."

"I haven't mentioned it because there have been none. Nothing along that line at all."

"All right. Of course money in itself means no more to a berserker than it does to a stove or a duplicating machine. But over the years the bad machines have learned a lot about human society and how it works. They're well aware that having wealth means having power, influence in the human world."

"I understand that." The old man was being patient.

"Yeah." Harry shook his head. "Well, I guess it doesn't make any sense for Harry Silver to be lecturing Winston Cheng about money. My point is, berserkers and their goodlife friends have been known to practice blackmail, in an effort to gain the only kind of coin they do have any interest in—more lives to terminate. Especially human lives."

THREE

Winston Cheng, big hands casually out of sight in the side pockets of his jacket, was watching him stoically. Harry went on: "It looks like the bad machines have got your people, and it would be foolish to assume they don't know who they've got. If your Winnie and Claudia have been kept alive, it's for a reason. You'd know better than I do what kind of help you're in a position to give berserkers."

Before Harry had finished, Cheng was shaking his head slightly, expressing disagreement. "Once the fact of the kidnapping becomes generally known, as it must sooner or later, every ED human in the Galaxy will be watching me to see what happens. If berserkers tried to blackmail me into playing goodlife tricks, they would soon discover that my possibilities of action were severely limited." *Goodlife* was the universal term, coined by the berserkers themselves, applied to people who, for whatever reason, cooperated with them.

Harry was thinking steadily. "We should discuss the alternative."

"Which one?"

"You mentioned it earlier, but we haven't really talked about it. I mean the possibility that, despite the good witnesses and the fortuitous recording, some kind of trickery has been worked on you."

"Yes?"

"Maybe, despite what the recording shows, it *wasn't* really a berserker that snatched your people. Instead, human kidnappers used a disguised ship, devised some kind of superpaddies, and for all I know bribed witnesses—"

Cheng's head-shaking had become emphatic. "You've just seen some pretty good visual evidence to the contrary. But of course the possibility of trickery has been in my mind from the start. The trouble is, that hypothesis simply won't fly."

"Why not?"

"I've already indicated that. Human kidnappers would have the strongest reasons to present their demands, whatever they might be, as soon as possible. To keep me from immediately calling in the Templars or the Force. If they hope to collect ransom, they must first tell me what it is to be. Also they must give me some hope of getting my people back alive."

Harry was thinking that if the kidnapper was truly a berserker trying to extort some favor, Winston Cheng might not be out of the woods yet. There could have been unforeseen delays in the process of formulating demands and making them. The tycoon could soon be getting a delayed message, passed along some circuitous route through several intermediaries, living or unliving, telling him what sort of favor the bad machines required of him to keep his loved ones from being sent back to him one little piece at a time.

Centuries of berserker war had provided ample proof that the enemy was not intrinsically sadistic. The killer machines cared nothing one way or the other about the suffering of any kind of life, any more than they cared for wealth. The berserkers' objective was universal death, not pain. But they had taught themselves to be virtuoso torturers when such behavior seemed likely to advance their cause.

After studying his host for a while, Harry said: "I think it's possible, Mister Cheng, that you've got that message already."

"No. I haven't." Winston Cheng leaned forward. "Look, Silver, we must understand each other. It would be absolutely crazy for me to make the effort I'm making to obtain your help, and the help of others in this horrible situation—while all the time I was secretly negotiating a deal with the enemy.

"Would I give in to blackmail, extortion, by either humans or machines, if I eventually received the message you describe? Yes I would, like a shot—*if* I could somehow be convinced that the enemy would keep their part of the bargain, and I would get my people back unharmed.

"No. The only reason you're here is that there's been no ransom demand. No attempt at a deal, no bargain. Nothing, not even gloating, which would surely happen if this were from a purely human motive, like revenge. When I say I have received no communication of any kind from any kidnappers, animate or inanimate, I am telling you the simple truth."

There was silence for a while. Harry began to wish that the woman in the background would say something, but that didn't happen. A kidnapping for ransom would at least have offered some kind of hope, but apparently that hadn't happened either. The obvious alternative was the bad one: Berserkers had some kind of experiment going for which they needed living subjects.

Harry didn't see any way to avoid discussing it. "It's probably the last thing you want to hear, but you mentioned it yourself earlier. And it is well established that they do that kind of thing. Sorry, but you asked, and I think it's a real possibility."

"I did indeed ask, and I want you to tell me what you really think. Go on."

Harry couldn't find much more to say. From the corner of his vision he could see that the Lady Masaharu had moved forward a couple of steps, as if she could lend support to the man she worked for.

When she finally spoke her voice had become sharp and direct. "Have you no further comments, Mister Silver?"

He got slowly to his feet. "I don't suppose I saw anything in the recording that you people missed, not if you've watched it fifty times. The berserkers look perfectly genuine." Still, he had to admit to himself that the situation had its oddities. "You said there was some attempt at pursuit."

"Yes. Quite unsuccessful. But it did succeed in establishing that Mister Cheng's people were not carried off in the direction of any known or suspected berserker base."

"Oh? Where, then?"

"There were convincing indications that the strange abductor had set its course for a certain peculiar solar system, part of this extended stellar neighborhood. That system is informally called the Gravel Pit, not previously known to be a haunt of berserkers."

A sheaf of technical data appeared, and Harry studied what it told him about the Gravel Pit—it appeared to be one of the vast number of solar systems that were absolutely devoid of life. If life had ever established a foothold there, it had doubtless been obliterated early on.

"It is, as you can see, somewhat overpopulated with planets and planetoids."

That was an understatement; the system looked like a shooting gallery of flying rocks, a great spinning centrifuge of innumerable collisions. There the kidnapper seemed to have deliberately lost itself and its haul of freshly acquired prisoners in the system's bizarre mechanics of swarming multiple planets and planetoids.

So far Cheng hadn't specified exactly what he wanted Harry to do, but it wasn't hard to see where this presentation must be headed. Mentally, Harry was already shaking his head: *No. No sir, no thanks, too bad you brought me all this way for nothing. No new ship for Harry Silver.* The results of this hour of uncomfortable talk would be strictly limited: for the visitor a small handful of superb chewing pods—and for the grieving old man only a flat turndown.

The great man's voice had settled into a monotone. It sounded more implacable than grieving. "Harry, you must know what I'm about to ask of you. But let me state it plainly. Whatever the nature of the power that took my granddaughter and her son, I'm going after it—or them. I would do it if the villains were humans, and I'm going to do it if they're machines. If rescuing Winnie and Claudia alive proves to be impossible, I will do the next thing that needs to be done, and make their killers pay. I'm putting a maximum effort into this."

With a firm gesture, signaling the concealed projector, Winston Cheng swept away the ghosts of his two missing people, still cheerfully playing.

Again the silent woman had moved a little closer. The Lady Laura was standing with arms gracefully folded and chin raised, regarding Harry as if he were a doubtful real estate investment she had committed herself to make.

Meanwhile Cheng was doing something that brought the big holostage up out of the floor again. In a moment he began to show clear detailed images of two armed yachts that he told Harry would soon be available for the punitive expedition.

"Two yachts." Harry said distantly. He had sat down again, and now leaned back, rocking slightly in his chair. "Both of them really tough, I suppose. Even tougher than the one that already got grabbed and turned inside out?"

"Yes, actually. Both of them are bigger and faster vessels than the one that was so inexcusably taken by surprise in that attack. Yes, and these are tougher too. Harry, trust me, what I can show you at this moment is only the beginning. More force is on the way. And there's something else. I am neither deluded nor bluffing when I speak of a secret weapon."

"Secret weapon."

"Yes. But I can't go into any details on that subject until you're definitely signed on."

Harry had no comment. He waited, in silent patience. He thought he owed this man the courtesy of hearing him out, getting the full presentation.

Winston Cheng drew a deep breath. He paced the room. He went on: "I assure you, the expedition I intend to send into the Gravel Pit will have a much better chance of success than would seem likely on first consideration. I'm putting together a fine team of people—the Lady Masaharu is the chief coordinator"—Harry glanced in her direction, and she lowered her eyelids briefly in acknowledgment—"who are, as you can imagine, all very capable, dedicated, and experienced.

"Harry, I intend to have you as a member of that team. In fact, you may be its key component."

"No, thanks."

His prompt refusal made very little impression. "I haven't finished. What I could discover of your official record is impressive, and your reputation, among those who know about such things, even more so."

"I would have thought that certain parts of my official record might disqualify me."

"Not from this job."

The impossibly luxurious chair seemed finally to have decided just what support Harry's body needed. At least it had stopped violating his personal privacy in subtly suggestive ways. He was turning the plain-looking ring round on his little finger. When he spoke, there was still no enthusiasm in his voice. It was as if he were simply going down a required checklist. "I take it you've already called the Space Force."

"That, naturally, is the first place I turned. I spoke to a general who told me, in effect, that the chance of any berserker captives being recovered alive, especially after the lapse of so many days, was simply much too small to justify the expenditure of time and wealth in such an enterprise, not to mention the severe risk to people and ships. Though the Force of course sympathizes with my loss, they have their own methods and timetables for fighting berserkers, et cetera, et cetera."

Harry was still waiting. The Lady Masaharu, now primly seated in what appeared to be a perfectly ordinary chair, was listening patiently, her face revealing nothing.

Winston Cheng drew a deep breath. "I'll anticipate your next question, Harry, and tell you I've also communicated with the Templars, at a very high level in their chain of command. Of course they too gave me their sympathy—though I thought they were just a little chilly—and expressed a hope that in the future something might be done about this particular enemy. They saw no possibility of dispatching any expedition to the Gravel Pit in the near future, because they assume the two missing people must have been killed—or effectively turned into something less than human—many days ago.

"They also tell me that Templar resources are already stretched too thin. To be fair, I must admit they're probably telling the truth in that regard."

Harry was silently trying to remember certain rumors

that he had heard, to the effect that Winston Cheng and Templars had a long-standing feud in progress. On the question of what exactly had brought the feud about, the rumors disagreed. He saw no point in bringing up that subject now.

He sat still, having reached a kind of truce with his chair. The old man was physically closing in on him, walking slowly toward him, eyes fixed in an unwavering stare.

"Now I'm coming to you, Harry. To you and a few others, as I said—all carefully chosen men and women, some of whom you may know. I realize it's taking time, precious time, to do things this way, but we must make our very best effort if we are to have any chance of success at all.

"I said before that we're going to have a better chance than people realize. When you're signed on, you'll see who the rest of my crew are, and I think you'll be impressed.

"In my offer to you, I mean just what I said in my message. Give me an honest, all-out effort, and I'll buy you the ship you want—or, if you prefer, and are willing to wait, have it built to your specs. On top of that, if our effort succeeds—by that I mean if we can get at least one of my people out alive—I'll throw in a good bonus. Let me emphasize, a *good* one.

"It would be foolish to try to minimize the danger of this expedition, but if you're killed, I, or my estate, will send that bonus to your heirs. Of course we can put this all in writing, if you like."

There was silence for three or four breaths. Harry could feel sympathy with Templars or anyone else who felt themselves stretched thin.

Winston Cheng was silent too, having stopped his steady advance. He was skillfully not pushing Harry, not trying to hurry him, but waiting. He had even turned his head away. The romping, gentle game his two heirs played had started up again, and it was as if he drew some kind of nourishment from watching their bright insubstantial images.

At last Harry said: "I repeat, Mister Cheng, I'm sorry about your loss. I really am. And I'd give a lot to have the kind of ship you're offering. But the neatest, sharpest vessel in the Galaxy won't do me a bit of good if I'm dead."

The Lady Masaharu got to her feet and turned her back to Harry. Behind her back, the long-nailed fingers of her clasped hands made a knot.

Winston Cheng did not even blink, much less turn away. He seemed neither surprised nor angered. He was facing Harry again, hands casually in the side pockets of his jacket, listening calmly, waiting to hear more.

Harry went on. "What it comes down to is, you're planning a private-enterprise kind of raid on a berserker base."

"That's exactly what I'm planning, yes."

"Let's consider that for a minute. No one has ever seen this supposed berserker installation, no robot scouts have taken pictures of it."

"That's quite true. Unfortunately."

"We don't have any idea of its size or strength, or where it might be, maybe within a billion kilometers, inside this Gravel Pit system. We don't even know for sure that it's there at all. The berserker could have started out on a course directly toward that system and later changed directions."

"An accurate appraisal of the situation, as far as it goes—proceed, Harry."

"All right. Suppose it is there. Berserker ground installations come in a variety of sizes and configurations. Whether they're big or small, I assure you nobody's ever yet run into one that's weak. Launching an expedition against a base of unknown size and strength is a job for a major task force, including several battleships—not a couple of armed yachts and maybe a secret weapon. And you say the only two organizations in the Galaxy who could put a real task force together have already told you that in this case they don't want to try."

"And so—?"

"So. My answer has to be the same as theirs. I'm just not sorry enough for your troubles, or hungry enough for a ship, to throw my life away, signing on for the kind of thing you're talking about." To himself Harry thought: *My wife would kill me if I did.*

Aloud, he rephrased the silent thought: "I've got a family too, who are kind of depending on me."

Winston Cheng was still not astonished—or even much surprised, it would appear—by the flat rejection. It was hard to tell if Harry's announcement of a family of his own was something the old man had expected or not. His voice had softened somewhat. "Is that so? Where are they?"

"On Esmerelda. We've lived there a few years now." Then Harry shook his head. "Hell, that's not quite right. *They've* lived there. I drop in from time to time, when I'm not out on a job."

The woman, poker-faced again, had turned back to face the boss and his visitor.

Winston Cheng was nodding thoughtfully. Some of

the intensity had faded from his voice. He seemed not so much discouraged as philosophical, almost as if he had expected Harry to refuse. Not that he gave any impression of giving up. He said: "Esmerelda's a pretty place. I've been there." And after a moment the old man asked: "Got a picture, Harry?"

"Matter of fact, I do." Harry reached into a pocket, drew out a small cube, and squeezed its sides. Beside his chair, two glowing images popped into existence, solid-looking, life-sized and standing upright.

Not nearly as elaborate a display as Winston Cheng's, whose two lost souls were once more moving gracefully in the background. But Harry's show was not bad either. A slender, young-looking woman with blond hair, dressed in a silvery but simple gown, sat in a plain chair holding hands with a five-year-old boy who stood beside her, wearing only shorts.

The two of them were gazing at each other as if they shared a happy secret. The boy's hair matched his mother's in curliness if not in color, and he had a lot of Harry's face, though fortunately not the broken nose. Every time Harry looked at his family it bothered him a little that Becky had subtly enhanced her image. She was trying to improve, as she thought, her appearance—but she didn't need to do that.

Winston Cheng was silent, gazing at the display. He stood regarding it somewhat longer than Harry had expected.

"My congratulations," the old man said at last, convincingly.

"Thanks."

Winston Cheng sighed. "How about a drink? You look like a drinking man to me."

"Don't mind if I do. Scotch, if you've got it."

"I think we might manage that."

It was the woman and not a robot who poured the drinks in an adjoining room, a smaller chamber that reeked less of power. The Lady Masaharu performed the task efficiently, silently declining to take even a symbolic few drops for herself. When she sat down it was again at a little distance from the men, as if once more determined to stay apart from their confrontation but remain available if needed.

Winston Cheng, sitting on a plain chair, nursing his own glass of fine amber liquid, made it plain he had not yet given up on Harry. He resumed the campaign by drawing Harry out on the subject of what details he would like in the next ship that he owned. Then he made sure Harry understood that the very vessel he was describing now lay within his grasp.

Cheng was too shrewd a salesman to belabor this particular prospect with talk of money, money, money. He had not got to where he was by so seriously misjudging the people he was trying to persuade. Instead, he expanded on how well his two yachts were going to be armed—intriguingly avoided even mentioning the secret weapon again—and offered to clear up any other misunderstandings that might help to change Harry's mind.

When these efforts failed to sell the customer, he perceptively abstained from what would certainly have been an unproductive effort at the hard sell, and graciously offered Harry a ride to anywhere in the charted portion of the Galaxy he would like to go.

Winston Cheng's expression had changed into a

faint, sad smile. "Having practically kidnapped you to get you here, I figure I owe you that much. What'll it be—Esmerelda?"

That was tempting. Really tempting—but no. Harry would accept a return ride back to Cascadia, where the Cheng courier had picked him up, but he didn't want to be under any obligations.

In this room he had gratefully chosen a plain chair too. "Thanks anyway, Mister Cheng. Just take me back to where you found me, I've got some unfinished business there regarding a leased ship."

"There'll be a little something for you when you get on the courier."

Harry raised his voice a little. "Thanks, Mister Cheng, but I can't—"

"No, no. Nothing like that. My parting gift consists of nothing more than a prepaid courier message capsule. Just in case you change your mind."

"I won't. But thanks."

And a liveried, blank-eyed robot servant came to show Harry out. The last impression he took with him of the magnificent apartment and its occupants was the woman's face, her pale eyes regarding him with an absolutely unreadable expression.

FOUR

Several weeks had passed since his grim and unproductive visit with Winston Cheng, and three days since his encounter with Paddy. Harry was up early in yet another cheap hotel room, greeting a late, modestly spectacular sunrise on yet another world. This planet was more thickly populated than Cascadia and, according to the latest crime statistics, less marred by strong-arm robbery. At least he thought the local sunrise modestly spectacular, because it had hues and shadings, and a way of seeming to stick to the horizon, that he found unfamiliar.

The billions of stars in the ten percent or so of the Galaxy so far more or less explored by Earth-descended humans were known to support hundreds of very Earth-like planets, with new ones frequently turning up. The philosophers among Harry's restless ED race, as well as those from branches of Galactic humanity less devoted to physical exploration, endlessly debated the reason for this profusion of comfortable places. Some thought it was due to sheer blind luck, the vagaries of quantum fluctuation from which the Universe had been born, while others saw commendable foresight on the part of the universal Designer. Either way, one consequence of such a respectable number of very similar worlds was that Earth-descended human travelers sometimes tended to lose track of just where they were.

Having redeemed a somewhat restless night with a reasonably good breakfast, Earth-descended Harry this morning was pondering whether he should try to make one more run with his leased ship, carrying a partial cargo that at best could be only marginally profitable, and might actually lose money—or if it would be better to formally terminate the lease and just leave the vessel sitting where she sat.

He was practically certain that he could get some kind of a piloting job before too long—and also pretty sure that it would not be the kind of job that he enjoyed. Nor would it allow him to get home anytime in the near future.

Thinking back to his meeting with Cheng, he was reflecting on his own state of mind, then and now. Harry wanted to find out if he was really tempted, on any level, to change his mind and accept the old man's offer. Of course it might already be too late to do that. But the sheer, out-and-out craziness of the plan made it dangerously attractive to some part of Harry's nature. If only . . .

But no. Forget it, he warned himself sternly. Let him sign up for any such scheme, and Becky would certainly kill him, if somehow the Gravel Pit's berserkers—if any were lurking there—and its chaotic flying rocks failed to do a thorough job.

Harry hated to admit it to himself, but there were moments when it seemed to him that what he needed was not really a ship at all but just a ticket home. If a powerful genie were to appear at such a moment, offering to grant him just one wish, he might burn that wish—or three wishes, if they came in package deals—simply to get back to Becky and Ethan.

He sighed. None of this was getting him anywhere with his immediate problem, which was what to do about the leased ship. Trying to make up his mind on that boring subject, he walked half a kilometer to the spaceport. On arrival he stood on the ramp, regarding from a little distance the undistinguished and unprofitable mass of metal, basically a blunt cone, as big as several houses, standing on its base. Nothing wrong with it, really, as a means of transportation. It was good enough to haul people and modest loads of freight from here to there among the stars. But that was about it.

Actually Harry was glad this pile of mediocre technology didn't belong to him. It was somewhat bigger than his old *Witch*, but nowhere near in the same class for performance—or for comfort, either.

. . . someone was calling his name.

Turning, he looked a hundred meters or so across the flat and level ramp, to see a couple of men approaching steadily on foot. One of them was wearing spacefarer's garb, the other some kind of local uniform. The spaceman, to Harry's surprise, soon came into focus as Hank Aragon, an old friend and former Space Force officer. Aragon was raising an arm in salute, hailing Harry.

Harry grinned and waved in answer. The grin faded slowly when he saw the look on his friend's face as he drew near. Both Aragon and the uniformed stranger, who did not appear to be a cop, looked seriously grim. The stranger was wiping sweat from his face, though the morning was brisk.

The first thing that Hank Aragon said was: "We've been trying to find you for a while. This fellow's with the Port Authority."

"Hello." By now Harry's smile had faded entirely, and he could feel the beginning of an inward chill. "What is it?"

The two men, taking turns, were explaining that they had traced Harry's whereabouts through the police record of his fight with the robot.

So?

"Harry." Aragon's voice was that of a man who didn't know how to say what he had to say, but was compelled to make a stab at it anyway. Finally the words came out. "It's your family."

"What?" *No. Anything else but that.*

"It came in the official courier, coded, but thoroughly verified, I hate like hell to say. Someone's trying to keep it quiet at the other end, and the newsorgs don't seem to have it yet, but there's no doubt . . . your wife and son . . . they've been caught, taken. By berserkers."

Harry had been trying to brace himself, to take the bad news of some kind of accident, but not this. This was simply crazy. He felt an impulse to lash out, to knock some of the big white ugly teeth right out of Hank Aragon's mouth, because the man must have gone insane, trying to make up a joke on such a subject. But at the same time, Harry knew he wasn't going to hit anyone.

Now they were telling him irrelevancies. The bad news had been transmitted through the local Space Force office. The story sounded to Harry like some crazy kind of demonic echo. Harry's own wife and child had joined the small roster of berserker captives, the only other members being Winston Cheng's two relatives. But nobody now was mentioning Claudia Cheng and her son. Evidently the news of that kidnapping was still being suppressed, despite the fact that leaders of both the Force and the Templars had been told early on about Cheng's loss.

Harry had to hear the story of his own disaster a few more times, the impossible truth phrased in a couple of different ways, before it truly started to sink in. Then it was as if he'd had an arm or leg suddenly hacked off, the deadly shock that drained your life before the true pain started. His core vitality seemed suddenly to have been exhausted.

Now Harry's informants were telling him, as if it mattered, as if anything could matter, how the people at Space Force sector headquarters had been unable to come up with more than a few isolated records of anything like these bizarre captures happening before, to anyone, anywhere in the Galaxy. Berserkers killed—that was what they did, the task the damned machines had been created to perform. They had no craving to kidnap victims, and they never did—except on very rare occasions and to serve some special purpose.

Some portion of Harry's mind still functioned, in a way. At least a few people at Space Force headquarters, he realized, must now be aware of both kidnappings. There were some shrewd folks there, and they would undoubtedly be trying to discover some kind of link—and some kind of link there had to be.

As far as Harry could see, his meeting with Winston Cheng, their brief consultation on the subject of Kidnapping One, formed the sole connection between himself and the tycoon. It was also the only link between their two families. But why should a simple meeting have provoked a copycat crime? There must be some hidden depth to the series of events, some links in the chain that Harry could not yet see . . .

For a moment he literally couldn't see anything at all, because the world was turning gray in front of him, and it seemed that he was likely to pass out. He tried to tell himself that it was all a bad dream, and soon he would come out of it.

While he was waiting to wake up, Harry stumbled and stuttered: "How could that have happened? They were home on Esmerelda . . ." Of course no world was ever totally safe; but everyone liked to think that their own chosen sanctuary might be the glorious exception.

"They weren't snatched there," his friend's reluctant voice was telling him.

"Then where? What . . . ?"

Patiently, Aragon repeated the few sketchy details that he'd been handed. The local authorities at the site of the kidnapping had managed to reconstruct a partial record of Becky's actions over the preceding few days. People she had talked to on the trip said she spoke of having suddenly, unexpectedly, come into a substantial sum of money. No one could remember her saying anything about just where this inheritance had come from. But Harry was nodding vaguely; this part of the story did not astonish him. He was aware that his wife had a couple of elderly grandparents, and Becky had given the impression that the old folks could be well off.

Hank and his companion were shoving several printouts under Harry's nose.

"Harry. This is what we got. This is all we know."

He read it, trying to make sense. According to the report, or the message, she and the boy had taken ship to come to see Harry, planning to surprise Daddy with the good news that suddenly they had lots of money! And wasn't that wonderful!? Knowing Becky, Harry thought she had probably used up half the windfall, whatever the amount, just in celebration and travel. It was just the kind of impulsive thing she was likely to do. And what made her think she could be sure of finding him, when his business kept him on the move . . .

Somewhere in the course of their travels, changing ships at a system that served as a minor transport hub, she and Ethan had boarded a small shuttle. Just a simple ordinary vessel, one that would have seemed no more dangerous than any of a thousand others . . . but before the simple journey was half over, something, some damned *thing*, darting from the outer darkness of deep space had pounced on it . . .

Harry could remember vividly the recordings shown him by the old man, Cheng, driven into a controlled craziness by his own grief. Harry wasn't sure at what moment he had decided to sit down on the ramp, or exactly why it had seemed like the thing to do. But here he was, his bottom on the ground. The people who had come to inform him of the end of the world were standing over him awkwardly, looking down at him across a gulf. Some kind of shadowy world might still be going on, up there where these other people lived. But the universe that Harry inhabited had come to a crashing halt.

The two men standing over him talked at him for a while longer without his really hearing anything they said. Then Hank Aragon had him by one arm, and was tugging. "Harry. Come on, old man. On your feet. I'm sorry, God, how sorry. You've got to walk a bit."

Why there should be any need for him, or anyone, to walk was beyond Harry's understanding. But then, if someone wanted him to stand up, why not? Getting to his feet again was a difficult process, the details hard to work out; and when he had accomplished the move he found it didn't make a bit of difference. Emptiness, light-years deep, still stretched out from him in every direction . . .

He was walking, and there were people at his elbows, guiding him. Now and then the men who were with him spoke, but the words just went by Harry, leaving no impression. At last he did hear someone say they were going to the spaceport's operations building. Harry couldn't imagine why, but he went along because it made no difference.

It turned out there was some kind of a medic on duty in operations, a nurse. After the people with

Harry had talked to her, and she had tried to talk to him, she bared his arm and gave him a shot of something . . .

As soon as Harry could move and think again, and even talk a little, he had no problem in deciding what action he ought to take. His only remaining goal in life was to find out exactly what had happened to his wife and son, recover them if possible or die in the attempt.

The shot in the arm had brought him out of it a little, enough to realize that hours had passed since he was hit with the shock of the bad news. He was wondering dully why none of the news vultures had yet managed to track him down, when he received another message, this one bearing all the remembered earmarks of a note from Winston Cheng.

The nightmare was going on. Another echo from the recent past. Like something coming true that had been predicted in a dream. He had never known while he was dreaming it just how bad a nightmare, and how endlessly long, it was going to turn out to be . . .

Hank Aragon had been spending the whole day hovering near, and now he closely watched Harry's face as Harry pulled the little capsule open. "Not more bad news? Is it?"

"No." Harry's voice was clear and firm. He could answer that question with flat confidence, even before he'd read the message. The truth was that nothing that could happen anywhere, in the Galaxy or beyond, nothing imaginable, was going to register as bad news with Harry Silver. Because Harry Silver had already been destroyed.

It took him a couple of readings before the meaning of this latest note came through. In a sense, one strange little sense, the news was even good. It was about as good as anything could be to a dead man, because it fell right in with what Harry had already decided he was going to have to do.

> Harry—
> Have just learned of your tragedy. The courier bringing this message is at your disposal. Can we talk again?
>
> Winston Cheng

Harry still had the prepaid reply form that Cheng had given him, and without even waiting for the relative numbness brought on by the medic's shot to start to wear off, he took advantage of it. The words seemed to form themselves, while Harry only had to watch his hand do the writing.

> Personal to Winston Cheng—
> If offer still open, I accept.
>
> Silver

Then he crumpled the form and threw it away. No sense in sending a message when he was going to be on the courier himself.

Just before boarding one of Winston Cheng's ships for the third time, Harry, meaning to study en route whatever data he could obtain, called up a standard news source to show him all available information about recent kidnappings in this sector, in which robots of any kind had played some part, while screening out the common types of paddy robbery. Only a few such crimes fit the narrowed classification, and in none of them was there any suggestion of berserker action. He tried a second newsorg, and then a third, all with the same result.

Before even leaving the operations building, Harry had hastily requested and signed forms disposing of his leased ship, and had received and read an urgent letter from one of Becky's elderly grandparents, who, still very much alive, had learned that something bad had happened to her grandchild, but had not been able to discover exactly what. It was a polite message, with overtones of desperation, and Harry answered that he was investigating and would talk to them later.

Then, following a kind of instinct to see that loose ends were tied up, he dispatched a message to a caretaking agency on Esmerelda regarding his small property there. That last communication went much more slowly and inexpensively. Now there was no one and nothing that he had to worry about.

None of the civilian crew of the half familiar courier ship were people Harry had met before, but they were all respectful, and attentive to his wishes. Without surprise he noted that he seemed to be the only passenger.

As soon as the courier was under way, Harry retired to the elegant, small suite assigned as his cabin. There he began to study such evidence as was so far available, from the Space Force and the sources connected to Winston Cheng, regarding what had happened to his family.

The available facts were meager, but they were

enough. A brief study left Harry with no room for reasonable doubt: Becky and Ethan, joyfully proclaiming that they were on their way to join Daddy, had been among a group of half a dozen people, all passengers on the same small shuttle, who had been mysteriously carried off. Harry could recognize that, according to witnesses, the technique of abduction was practically identical with that earlier employed to snatch Winston Cheng's people. Again, a Type-A berserker, coming seemingly out of nowhere, had struck, and got away.

There was one notable variation, this time. The nearby ship that had recorded the incident was lightly armed, and had succeeded in getting one turret into action and potting one of the enemy boarding machines before return fire shut the turret down. Semi-intact wreckage had been retrieved from nearby space, and identified as true berserker technology, providing convincing proof that the odd incident had not been faked.

Again, none of the local authorities as much as mentioned the similar tragedy that had so recently befallen the Cheng family. Harry took this as a sure sign that the first crime was still being kept under wraps.

Again, as in the earlier kidnapping, no ransom demand had been made on any of the victims' relatives. In this case there seemed no reason to think that any of them were spectacularly wealthy.

The list of witnesses to the latest outrage included one combat veteran who gave every indication of being a shrewd observer. He and all the others were unanimously convinced that they had seen a genuine berserker in action.

❖   ❖   ❖

This time the indications were even somewhat clearer that the escaping kidnapper's destination had been the peculiar solar system called the Gravel Pit.

Harry kept staring at the words before him, trying to force them into making sense. So, Becky and Ethan had been carried off to the same crazy place that had already swallowed up Winston Cheng's granddaughter and great-grandson. The Gravel Pit, the solar system considered by most travelers as too dangerous to enter, where neither Space Force nor Templars thought it worth their while to risk lives and expend precious resources in a hopeless search for a berserker base that might or might not exist—where one of the wealthiest humans in the Galaxy was already planning a secret attempt to rescue people who, if they were lucky, had already been dead for many days.

FIVE

The courier, a good solid ship with nothing spectacular about it, went clipping along in flightspace, bypassing all the monstrous magnitudes of normal space and time, the domain of Einstein where relativity was still in charge. For some reason the statglass ports in the control room had been left fully cleared, as if neither of the two humans aboard, both space veterans, would admit for a moment the possibility of being turned queasy by an occasional deep look into nothingness. In ordinary circumstances the sight might have bothered Harry enough to make him turn the glass opaque. But in his current mental state it was going to take something much worse than the sight of raw flightspace to have any effect on him at all.

Since coming aboard, Harry had been wandering the confined spaces of the ship, not knowing what he was looking for or why. On entering the control room, he had let himself down into the copilot's chair, but only because it had seemed the handiest seat available. He wasn't doing anything, not even thinking clearly, just waiting for this ride to be over.

The captain-pilot wasn't quite sure yet how to deal with this special passenger, who had to be important in some way the captain had evidently not figured out. He touched a pilot's helmet hanging on its umbilical. "Care to take the helm for a while, Mister Silver?"

Harry roused himself from a dark place. "No, thanks."

The captain cleared his throat. "Sir, now we're securely spaceborne, it's time I leveled with you. We're not really going to the destination listed on our flight plan."

That awoke some interest. "Oh?"

Deferentially, the courier's captain explained that the planet name in Winston Cheng's latest message had actually been a code word. Their true destination this time was not one of Cheng's palaces, or corporate headquarters. Instead, they were traveling directly to an operational base of some kind that Cheng Enterprises had established within a couple of hours' flight time from the Gravel Pit.

"It seems like there's something pretty hush-hush going on around there," the captain offered, then paused, looking closely at his passenger.

Harry shook his head and puffed out breath. He had signed on for a technical operation, and it was time he began to get a grasp of practical details. "What solar system?" he wanted to know.

"None. We're headed for a wanderworld. The address is WW 207GST." The captain went on to give Galactic coordinates.

The term "wanderworld" was generally applied to rocky masses that were large enough to be in some way interesting and attractive to humanity, but were currently free of gravitational attachment to any solar system, though some of these Galactic vagrants showed signs of having spent long periods of their early history, sometimes hundreds of millions of standard years, as members of systemic families. Like other bodies of its type, WW 207GST could be thought of as a citizen of the Galaxy. Many were of suitable dimensions for suited ED humans to walk on them in natural gravity and reasonable safety, though the lack of solar heating generally kept any atmosphere that might be present in a firmly frozen state.

Harry reflected that with the sprawling empire of interstellar real estate that Winston Cheng had at his disposal, it wasn't surprising that the old man had been able to come up with a handy rock on which to establish a secret operational base of his own, from which to launch the secret effort that he liked to call a rescue expedition. Of course secrecy would be important; let the Space Force catch wind of his plan, and they would certainly try to close it down.

The onboard data bank revealed that wanderworld WW 207GST was currently plowing through space at a modest few score kilometers per second relative to the nearest stars, in the general direction of the Gravel Pit. In another thousand standard years or so it might even be in a position to apply for membership in that chaotic system. Meanwhile, it was tens of light-years distant from any of Cheng's major business operations, or any of the worlds on which he maintained a publicly acknowledged residence.

❖   ❖   ❖

The courier captain, no doubt in the belief that he was being subtle, warily refrained from trying to pump Harry for information on the mysterious happenings on WW 207GST. But it was obvious that the captain knew the big boss was planning something very much out of the ordinary there, and he was curious about it.

After a while he asked Harry: "Have you met the Lady Masaharu?"

Harry was taking a break in his restless, compulsive wandering. They were sitting in the courier's little galley, and the captain had a mug of something hot in front of him.

"Once," Harry admitted.

"Then you probably know she's Winston Cheng's chief personal assistant."

Harry didn't answer.

"She's on 207GST right now. And he depends a whole lot on the lady."

Harry, whose attention had already started to drift away again, looked up, faintly curious. There were certain things it would be good to know about Cheng, as they got ready for what was to come. "I take it they're not married."

"To each other?" The courier captain seemed to find that amusing. He confirmed that she was Winston Cheng's most trusted associate, and had been with him for some great but uncertain number of years. "Lady Laura's never married anyone, as far as I know." As for the old man himself, it was more or less common knowledge that the last of his succession of wives had enjoyed an amicable separation and settlement some years ago.

The captain went on, providing Harry with what he evidently considered juicy inside information, obviously in hopes of getting similar material in return. Maybe, thought Harry, the man was spying for some rival corporation.

"The only people old Cheng seems to care much about are his granddaughter and her kid. They spend a fair amount of time with him. Oh, Masaharu's usually at his side—except when he's in bed. Sleeping is one thing they don't seem to do together."

Harry was getting tired of it. "So where are you watching all this from—under the bed?" That earned him a lengthy period of silence.

The silence had hardly started to erode before the courier in its preliminary approach to the clandestine base made contact with an early warning system. Looking at the display as it came through on instruments, Harry could see it was a very simple and primitive one.

He slightly adjusted the fit of the copilot's helmet on his head. The perception was vaguely perturbing. "That's all the eyes they have?" he asked the world in general. Not that he really gave a good damn about defense anymore, but where there was one deficiency there were likely to be others; and he wanted the mission being planned to be technically first rate.

The captain had regained his voice, if not his cheerfully confiding manner. He remarked stiffly: "Whoever's in charge on this rock isn't putting much time and effort into defense. Probably no bad machines expected in this zone. Maybe they found some exotic matter on the wanderworld. Wish I knew what it's all about."

"If you don't know what it's all about, you ought to keep your mouth shut."

The next period of silence was satisfyingly long.

Certainly none of the occupiers of WW 207GST, past or present, had made much effort at serious fortification; faint scars on the rock suggested there had once been some tentative beginnings along that line, which had later been removed, probably when the first ED human visitors decided to abandon the place—perhaps a hundred standard years ago. Harry supposed that even then old Cheng might well have qualified as old.

One result of that previous cycle of activity on WW 207GST had been, the courier captain said, the creation of somewhat spartan living quarters for more than a hundred people, along with docking facilities capable of handling several small ships.

What natural warmth the mass of rock enjoyed—and that was very little, in terms of human needs—was generated only by the long-burning fires of its own deep radioactivity. Uncounted millions of bodies similar to this one, the debris of ancient cosmic accidents, drifted in the depths of interstellar space.

As the courier on its final approach pulled within a kilometer of the wanderworld, Harry, looking out through a cleared port, could see plain docking facilities, all open to space, next to a sprawling building. There was room for perhaps half a dozen ships, but only one, another courier, was visible at the dock.

Crowding up beside it were the smaller shapes of about half a dozen superluminal robotic couriers, no more than elaborate message capsules, ready to be loaded with information and fired off at a moment's notice. Until now the space traffic at 207CST had never been heavy enough to require a landing field; a second reason for the absence was the weak natural gravity, so feeble that parked ships would be unstable, subject to accidental tipping. No star was close enough to be called this world's sun, but the Gravel Pit's primary came closest.

Harry could see no sign of the two armed yachts that Winston Cheng had spoken of with restrained enthusiasm. Evidently those ships were not yet ready. Or they might be engaged in some test flight or scouting mission. There was no sign of anything that might qualify as a secret weapon. Well, Harry had not a whole lot of faith in secret weapons anyway.

Harry found the minimal signs of activity, this lack of martial hardware, disturbing. How many days had already passed since Cheng's two family members had been lost? He realized he had lost count. How much longer was the business going to be dragged out—or might old Cheng have lost his fiery urge to battle? Somehow Harry doubted that.

At some level of his mind, he had been vaguely, unrealistically, looking forward to being able to step out of this courier right into a fight against berserkers. But of course organizing a rescue attempt, or even a suicide attack, wasn't going to be that simple. Few things ever were.

In his mind Harry hadn't yet made the faintest attempt at detailed planning. Maybe it was better that he shouldn't. Every hour that passed must reduce the chances of any of the four kidnap victims being still alive—but if, as hard reality insisted, those chances had been microscopic to begin with, perhaps the loss of time was not important. Now, belatedly, Harry started to attempt a mental calculation of just what the odds might be on prisoner survival, but could get nowhere. On this subject his mind was still flatly refusing to grapple with practical details.

And now the wanderworld was right in front of them, so for all the eye could tell they were about to land on the nightside of a real planet, barren and forbidding. A minute later they were on the dock, where inhuman-looking robots waited to secure the ship, and the building was extruding an air-filled passenger tube/gangway to let two fragile humans walk from ship to shore without bothering with spacesuits. They went walking and not drifting; artificial gravity generators had been built in, to fit the place for long-term occupation.

Harry disembarked from the courier with the captain at his side. On emerging from the gangway the two of them found the tall figure of the Lady Masaharu waiting, her pale eyes fixed on Harry, glowing with what might have been enthusiasm. The captain murmured something respectful, enacted a slight bow, and promptly retreated to his ship.

The lady hardly seemed aware that the officer had come and gone. Her body looked even thinner than before, perhaps because she was dressed quite differently, in spacer's gray coverall and boots. But the impeccable hairdo was still in place.

Almost her first words to Harry were: "Mister Cheng is here. And he is anxious to see you."

Harry nodded. There was something else he wanted to do first. "Be right with you."

Turning his back on the building's main entrance that hulked nearby, Harry moved to stand looking out through a statglass port. The port had been placed to give observers a direct view of the brightest single star in the dark sky, the sun of the Gravel Pit system. It was a bigger and more elaborate installation than anything on shipboard. There wasn't any doubt of which star he ought to look at. A couple of globular clusters hovering relatively close were near enough, at only a few hundred light-years, to furnish useful light, and if you squinted at them they took on the aspect of fuzzy suns.

Ignoring the nearby rocky surface of the wanderworld, he dialed the port to high magnification, giving him the best look possible at the place to which Becky and Ethan had been taken, and where he was going to follow them.

The wanderworld possessed no atmosphere worth mentioning, but it definitely looked to him as if that star, the central sun of the Gravel Pit, was twinkling.

"The irregular variation in intensity is not intrinsic," a voice from some nearby machinery assured him. "The cause of twinkling is the intermittent passage of ponderous masses of opaque material across its tiny disk."

Becky and Ethan. If they were anywhere, they were there.

Apparently the lady's schedule was not able to accommodate more than about ten seconds of stargazing. Her voice was even sharper than usual. "Mister Cheng has a number of urgent things to do."

"So do I," said Harry over his shoulder. Ten more

seconds passed before he turned away from the port and in silence followed her stiff back to a chamber much different than the site of their previous meeting.

Some of the rooms in the refurbished installation were big enough to have contained a hundred people or more in reasonable comfort. Some of these chambers had not yet been reopened, but there was already plenty of volume available for the current staff to live and work in. Parts of the complex had been constructed on the surface of 207GST, while other parts were housed in cavities blasted or melted into solid rock.

The rocky fabric of 207GST, like the great majority of wanderworlds of its general size and type, contained no fossils to show that there had ever been native life. It seemed to Harry the kind of world that berserkers ought to heartily approve.

As Harry entered the small room, Winston Cheng looked up from where he sat in front of his virtual desktop, a flat surface before him on which strings of pictures, graphs, and symbols came and went. He said: "You're looking well, Harry. How are you bearing up?"

"I'm not. But here I am."

The lady had conducted him on foot along one passage and another, catching sight of a few other people in the distance, to a fairly small interior room, with only one door that was soon snugly closed behind them. Primitive ventilation whispered audibly, and the lighting seemed barely adequate.

"No one can hear us now, Harry." Rising from a simple chair and extending a hand in greeting, the old man seemed confident of the fact, and Harry was inclined to believe him.

"Fine with me," said Harry. It didn't seem worth-while to wonder aloud why it should matter whether anyone heard them or not. He got right to the point. "Coming in to land, I didn't see any weapons."

This time all three of them were sitting in very ordinary chairs, there were no exotic chewing pods in sight, and no semi-intelligent furniture. The holographic ghosts of Cheng's dear departed had also been left behind.

Cheng was looking vaguely military, in a tailored kind of spaceman's coverall in ordinary fabric. An odd-looking robot, anything but anthropomorphic, stood, or rather crouched, at the tycoon's elbow. Eyeing the machine, Harry decided it was probably a communications specialist, present for the sole purpose of making sure that no one and nothing else could overhear.

In fact the old man himself did not appear to be bearing up all that well. "Good for you. Together you and I, with the help of some good friends"—with a stately inclination of his head he included the lady—"are going to achieve—all that is left in this world for men in our position to accomplish."

Harry said: "I don't suppose this robot is your secret weapon."

Cheng looked tired, and the lady answered. "No. It is only here to assure security. It has a short-term memory of only thirty seconds for new information, and a long-term memory that holds nothing but its wired-in instructions. As for the weapon you speak of, arrangements have been made, and delivery is expected to be on schedule."

"So that's not what you want to talk about."

No, it wasn't. It came as no surprise to Harry to learn that their investigation into the kidnappings had reached the same conclusion he had come to himself: there had to be some connection between the two events. But they had made little progress beyond that point.

Cheng was saying in a fatalistic voice: "We have no real evidence regarding the possible nature of this tie. We still have no more than shadowy suspicions."

"Isn't that about where we started?"

The lady inclined her head in a grave bow. "I regret that is correct."

Harry was looking steadily at him. "I don't believe the point actually came up last time we talked, but it seems distinctly possible that there's a traitor somewhere in your organization. Someone who told the bad machines just when and where to snatch your people, and then told them of our meeting. Someone who has turned goodlife."

Cheng sighed. "Of course, and we are looking into it. The investigation advances very slowly. You will surely understand that it is complicated by the fact that I must take no steps that might jeopardize our mission here." He paused for another sigh. "I must ask you, Harry: Have you ever talked about our previous meeting, mentioned it to anyone at all—?"

"No."

"I hadn't expected that you would." After a pause the old man added: "It kills me, Harry, to think there's someone in my organization who could do such a thing, sell out to the enemy in such vile, cruel fashion. But I find it hard to come up with any other explanation."

The lady said: "In any organization the size of Cheng Enterprises, there will always be a few who hate the one on top."

That wasn't news to Cheng; he only nodded gently.

Harry went on: "If we're right, the really strange thing is that there's one of your people who not only hates you but hates me too. Enough to . . ." Somehow he couldn't finish.

Cheng glanced at the lady, perhaps signaling that it was time for her to enter the conversation again. She said: "Mister Silver, there is one person in the organization, in fact now present on this base, with whom you have had dealings, and in fact notable disagreement, in the past. His name is Del Satranji."

It took a moment for the name to click. Harry got up from his chair, took a few paces, and sat down again. "Yeah, I know him . . . knew him. Only slightly. 'Notable disagreement'? I wouldn't call it that."

Both people were still looking at him, and he went on. "I haven't thought of him for years. As you've discovered, we were in a certain military thing together, a long time ago."

When Harry thought about it, he supposed it wasn't really strange that Satranji should be here now, on the wanderworld. People who might be considered expert at the job of fighting berserkers made up only a very small segment of the vast Galactic population.

"What was the nature of the trouble between you?" The lady's question was professional; just gathering the facts.

"It was . . . something to do with our job." Harry frowned. "Damned if I can even remember the details now. An argument about piloting techniques, as I recall . . . at least that's how it started.

"Satranji and I just rubbed each other the wrong way, I guess. He liked to challenge people. Everything had to be a competition. Certainly we weren't friends. But all that was years ago. I wouldn't describe him as an enemy." Harry shook his head. "It's hard to picture him coming up with any devilish plot."

"Was there a woman involved, in the difficulty between you?"

"A woman." Harry was about to deny that, but then something elusive caught at his memory, and he couldn't be sure. He shook his head, doubtfully.

"In the days ahead it will sometimes be necessary for the two of you to work closely together."

"I don't see any serious problem with that."

"That is good. He has given me the same answer to the same question."

Winston Cheng sighed. It was a delicate, snakelike sound. "I employ many human workers. Perhaps the malefactor who works to arrange kidnappings is one of my other people, who hates you for some reason we have not yet discovered. Or perhaps one of my machines has been subverted. There are several extremely intricate corporate information systems. Of course an artificial intelligence cannot hate. But . . ."

"But it can be programmed to give a bloody good imitation of hatred," Harry finished. The point needed no elaboration, not with the perfect example of the berserkers themselves in constant view.

He went on: "Anyway, that's about as far as I've been able to get, just trying to think about it. I say 'trying' because there are only certain days when I can even try. There has to be a connection between one crime and the other, between your people being snatched and mine. I haven't been able to take it any further. But I don't have an army of people to put to work finding out what the connection is. I've been assuming that you do."

Cheng was nodding, slowly, gently. "Naturally I have already taken steps, and the effort you suggest is well under way. Of course it is not the type of problem where the literal employment of an army would be of material help. Rather the issue has been placed in the hands of a chosen few. So far, I regret to say, without any very useful result."

SIX

Certain things Cheng had said had made Harry suspect the old man might be intending to appoint him field commander of the planned expedition. Harry was prepared to argue against that if he had to; leadership skills were not his strong point. But as matters turned out, he might have saved himself the trouble of worrying. There was no suggestion that he might be put in any command position higher than chief of scouts. Instead, he now found himself working with a motley crew of people, each of whom brought some special talent or knowledge to the enterprise.

Moments after leaving the confidential meeting with Cheng and the lady, Harry saw the figure of a shapely woman he did not recognize approaching him from the far end of a long corridor. The first thing that struck him was the way she was dressed, suggesting that her job might be to provide an evening's entertainment before people took off on their last mission. The second thing was that she wasn't a woman at all, but an anthropomorphic robot, about the last thing he would have expected to meet on this or any other combat base. The resemblance to humanity was strong enough that for a moment he had been taken in.

The figure approached, smiling, and stopped close in front of him. "Mister Silver, I am Dorijen." The machine's voice was softly feminine, and so was its form, done at least as realistically as that of any other robot Harry could remember seeing.

"Pleased to meet you, Dorijen. Do they call you Dorry?"

"Yes sir, people often do."

The more Harry studied the machine, the more certain he was that whatever Dorijen's current job might be, she had started her career as a provider of sex. There were humans who for one reason or another preferred to get their satisfaction that way. The machine's clothes were only subtly seductive, and also in tune with the recent styles, a sharp contrast from the simple uniform usually worn by anthropomorphic robot servants.

Most people would have been somewhat disturbed, some truly offended, by the fact that the configuration of the robot body beneath the clothing appeared to be shamefully close to the current conception of an ideal human form. The shame lay not in the fact that sexual characteristics were emphasized—that was only to be expected in any sex provider. Rather it was in the lack of gross exaggeration, the very verisimilitude of the creation. Machines that even roughly resembled humanity made some people edgy; one that came as close as this was certain to stir controversy anywhere.

Centuries ago, before the settled portion of the Galaxy had been ravaged by the berserker plague, such realistic robots had been fairly common, even though officially discouraged in most polite societies. But the onslaught of the death machines had ignited a fear that berserkers would someday, somehow, learn to imitate the human form with intolerable accuracy. That had never happened, and some basic quirk in berserker programming seemed to guarantee that it never would. Still, the idea of any robots too closely imitating the appearance of humanity had become in itself intolerable.

Robots in general minded being stared at no more than kitchen tables would, and Dorry was no exception. It asked: "Mister Silver, what luggage would you like conveyed to your room?"

Belatedly Harry realized that he had packed nothing for this trip. It must have been in the back of his mind that Winston Cheng could be counted on to provide essentials, and beyond the essentials Harry did not care. He said: "I have no luggage."

Dorijen accepted that without comment. "I have been instructed to bid you welcome to the base. I am also instructed to ask you a few more questions."

"Go ahead."

"There is the matter of your pay."

"Pay?" It suddenly occurred to Harry that he had never bothered to find out if he was being paid for this adventure or not. But from what he knew of Cheng, he had no doubt that something had been arranged.

Dorijen named a figure. The scale turned out to be roughly twice as much as a good pilot would expect to get for ordinary work. Harry stood considering, unable to extract any further meaning from the numbers.

After allowing him a few moments to think it over, the robot added: "Cash if you like, of course, sir. But cash will be of limited usefulness here on the base, unless you enjoy gambling. Alternatively, where would you like the money deposited?"

This discussion seemed hellishly irrelevant. Just like the rest of Harry Silver's own prolonged existence. Who in the Galaxy would he want to leave his money to? Harry said to the robot: "Just hang on to it for the time being. I'll let you know."

"Very good, sir. With your permission, I will establish an account in your name with Cheng Enterprises, on which you may draw at any time."

"That'll be fine."

Dorry had turned and seemed about to lead the way, but before they had actually got moving, a young- ish woman of unquestionable humanity had appeared and began to introduce herself.

"Mister Silver—"

"What?"

"I am Louise Newari, and I assist the Lady Masa- haru." Newari was dark-skinned and fine-boned, dressed in a simple utilitarian fashion that contrasted with the robot's clothes.

"Pleased to meet you, Louise."

"I understand you have suffered a loss very similar to that of Mister Winston Cheng."

Harry only nodded.

The young woman nodded in sympathy, while she

continued to watch him carefully. "Then all our sympathies must be with you as well."

"Thanks."

She had turned to the robot. "It's all right, Dorry, I'll show Mister Silver to his room." And back to Harry. "Are you carrying any baggage?"

As Harry watched the robot bow and turn away, it occurred to Harry, who had been vaguely expecting to go immediately to work, that yes, he was going to need a room. From time to time it would be necessary to sleep. He looked at his empty hands.

He said: "Actually, I didn't bring anything. I came away in something of a hurry."

Louise Newari seemed to accept this without surprise. "Let me, or any of the support staff, know your needs."

Following his guide deeper into the base, through a corridor carved from rock by smoothly precise machines, he looked around him at simple living quarters that bore few traces of the luxury prevailing at the site of his first meeting with Winston Cheng. The hard rock walls were generally bare of any decoration. There were recyclers of respectable quality for food and air and water. The chilled rocks of the wanderworld contained substantial deposits of water ice, from which hydrogen, and therefore power, could be extracted in abundance.

He grunted something, and followed his guide down the short corridor, until she stopped to open a door.

"Satisfactory, Mister Silver? If not, other accommodations can readily be made available. We really have much more room here than we need."

Harry glanced inside, saw a narrow bed, single chair, small table, and in the far wall another half-open door with indications of standard plumbing beyond. Clearly the lights and air were working. Standard communications terminals stood waiting. He nodded. "It'll do."

His escort began to tell him something about meal arrangements and schedules. She seemed on the point of saying something nice about the robot chef, when she suddenly stopped. "Or are you not a gourmet?"

The idea of food, and certain faint smells wafting down the corridor, reminded Harry that in recent days he had eaten very little. "You know . . . I think I used to be."

"Then shall we go to lunch?"

"There's a lot of hardware I'm going to have to look at, stuff I need to learn—but yeah, now's as good a time as any."

Lunch turned out to be totally devoid of the gourmet decadence that obtained at headquarters, but Harry's stomach welcomed the first full meal he could recall having had in days. As soon as it was over, he informed Louise Newari that he was ready to get to work, and five minutes later was sitting in the base's newly established operations room, being introduced to several more new colleagues, all of them looking at a composite telescopic image of the Gravel Pit's inner system.

Studying the image, Harry found it impossible to see anything that might help the newly established force accomplish their mission. The image was a smoothed-out blend of data from several observation posts, and it had been left deliberately indistinct in all the areas where information was still scanty. There was an uncomfortable amount of blurring in the image.

"They're somewhere in there," he mused aloud.

A gaunt, balding man of indeterminate age had appeared at Harry's side, and offered a comment. "It seems they must be. If all of our suppositions can hold water. You'd be Harry Silver. Sorry about your loss. Call me Doc, I'm on your assault team too."

The first order of business for the expedition's planners was to discover exactly where within the Gravel Pit system, if anywhere, the berserker had established itself. Until such base or installation could be discovered, the expedition could have no goal.

Harry settled in and started to familiarize himself with the equipment available, and with the latest recon reports, having to do with the crazy swarms of orbiting rocks, dust, and fragments that had given the system its informal name. The astrophysicists had not yet agreed on a single explanation of how such a seemingly ordinary sun had acquired such a large and unruly family.

As dinner time approached, Harry was introduced to a few more people—one of them a Space Force veteran, another a Templar dropout—who had been detached from other duties in the service of Cheng Enterprises and brought in as pilots. There would be a lot of scouting to be done, as the berserker base had not yet been located.

One of the junior pilots had heard of Harry by reputation, and appeared seriously impressed to discover that he was going to be working for him.

Presently Harry came to the conclusion that he

had now been introduced to most of the other active participants in the expedition, only a minority of them actually combat specialists of one kind or another. It seemed there would be only eight people actually landing on the enemy base, assuming they could survive long enough to reach it: Cheng himself, of course, and the Lady Masaharu who was not going to be separated from him. Harry and Satranji made four, and Doc five—exactly what Doc's function was supposed to be, Harry had not yet discovered. Most of the people now inhabiting 207GST were only support workers, who would be evacuated on the last courier to leave before the attack was launched.

Altogether there were fewer live humans on 207GST than Harry had somehow expected, no more than a couple of dozen in all. But certainly that number was great enough that the secrecy Winston Cheng was trying to maintain could not be expected to last much longer.

Communication with the outside world was not forbidden, or even actively discouraged. But in practice it was restricted, and Harry suspected that not a bit of information actually left the base on any of Cheng's ships without passing through informal but careful censorship.

Had he not been forewarned, Harry thought he might have had some trouble recognizing Del Satranji, when the two of them arrived in the common room for dinner at approximately the same time. As it was, neither of them had any difficulty.

The years did not seem to have mellowed Del Satranji; in fact Harry could not remember him looking as taut and tense as this. He gave an impression of tightly controlled energy, of danger just below the surface. At the sound of Harry's voice, his eyes flicked up, registering no surprise. He turned away from the buffet where he had been standing, and came to confront Harry.

"Haven't seen you for a while, Silver." The raspy voice was vaguely familiar too, now that Harry heard it again.

"Likewise."

Satranji was somehow smaller than Harry remembered him. Not physically large at all, in fact somewhat below the average in height and weight. Nor was he extravagantly muscled, but as Harry now recalled, he owned some kind of advanced belt in martial arts, with a skilled and vicious and energetic look about him.

With the living man before him, Harry could remember hearing somewhere that Satranji was an unfrocked Templar, who had been expelled from the order for unspecified reasons, probably having to do with his ruthless treatment of suspected goodlife.

The robot Dorijen appeared somewhere in the dining room, dressed now in a different gown, but maintaining the same cool elegance.

The Lady Masaharu had turned her head to watch, and was observing the robot's entrance with icy, silent disapproval.

Now the robot had come to stand at Satranji's side. Softly, possessively, it placed one hand on the man's arm.

Satranji was smiling faintly. Jerking his head slightly in Dorry's direction, he said to Harry: "My wife tells me that the two of you have already met."

Harry looked from the man's dark eyes, to the cool blue eyes of the machine, and back again. "Your wife."

"That's what I said." Satranji's voice was very soft and very certain. His eyes bored into Harry's. With this man, everything had to be a challenge.

Other people in the hallway and the common room were watching. It was as if each of them wanted to be wrapped in a cloak of noninvolvement. Harry thought for a moment. Suddenly he felt very tired. He said: "I don't remember you well enough to be able to tell when you're joking and when you're not."

"So you don't remember me." Still the same soft, deadly voice. "Have I said anything that sounded like a joke?"

"That's what I can't tell. You don't see me laughing."

Satranji nodded slowly. "That's good. Believe me, Silver, from now on you'll remember me just fine." He turned to give his wife Dorry a sharp glance, which the robot was evidently well trained enough to interpret correctly. It followed him closely when he went to take his seat at the table.

Harry moved on with the routine of getting his own tableware. No doubt about it now. Satranji's little lady, his better half, the machine called Dorijen, was joining the assembled members of the team—those who could manage an hour away from their work—for dinner.

Harry helped himself to the nearest available place. There was obviously going to be no formality about this gathering. Harry's meal was gently interrupted by another casual introduction or two. People came in and sat down and started eating, some in a hurry and others ready to take their time, while machines brought additional food and drink. On Harry's visit to Cheng's headquarters he had seen several human servants, but here on the wanderworld the generality of household and maintenance workers were as robotic as the bride. Harry had seen no other that was anything like as human as Dorry in appearance.

During the dinner hour the inanimate staff serenely ignored the presence of their mechanical colleague sitting at table, in front of a full place setting. Humans, including her husband, and machines seemed to be agreed that Dorijen was served nothing in the way of food or drink, and being a robot she naturally did not mind.

There was one exception to this lack of service, in the form of a single glass of red wine, poured at the start of the meal as if by prearrangement. This the robot sipped and drank with delicate grace, while her husband contented himself with water.

Someone sitting next to Satranji, evidently just making conversation, asked him if he wasn't having any wine.

"Got to keep the mind perfectly clear for just a little while yet. I'll have mine later. Actually, I'll have the same wine later, after Dory's warmed it up a bit for me." He licked his lips and leered.

No human or robotic voice had any comment on that. Meanwhile Dorijen had been occasionally taking part in the human conversation, as blandly as a visiting politician, and listening to others with far more courtesy than many humans Harry had encountered. From time to time Dory's pale, graceful hand toyed with a utensil or touched a cup, so that a casual observer might never have noticed that the figure in that chair was ingesting nothing but the wine.

The dress Dorijen had put on for dinner was elegant, but still there was, of course, something wrong about the robot's personal appearance. To the best of Harry's knowledge, no one had ever crafted an imitation human that would stand the test of a full minute's scrutiny, while moving and speaking in a good light. But the machine called Dorijen came about as close as any that Harry had ever seen. Its smooth skin, looking warm and fine as that of a live baby, stretched with the appearance of nature over other components neatly imitating the body parts of a young female human. Beneath the convincing skin there were imitations of muscle and bone, of veins and tendons, and a healthily thin layer of something standing in for subcutaneous fat.

When, half an hour later, Satranji rose from the table with a stretch and a yawn, and announced that he had had a full day and was going to bed, the machine rose and went with him. Halfway across the room, it began to sway into a closer approximation of a seductive human walk.

Harry and a few others were close enough to overhear what the Lady Masaharu said to Cheng in a low voice. "Mister Cheng, that fellow should be replaced. I do not, of course, say that solely because of the robot. I understand that you consider Satranji's cleverness and skill, his knowledge of the Gravel Pit, of great importance to the expedition. But I no longer have faith in his reliability."

Cheng's eyes were far away, but he was listening. He nodded gently. "I will soon have an announcement to make regarding Mister Satranji."

The Lady Masaharu bowed her head in silent acquiescence. It was plain that other people in the group had been really offended by Satranji's behavior. Harry heard a quiet murmur: "But he's living with this robot. Sleeping with it."

And another: "It shares his living quarters, and perhaps his bed."

A snort. "No 'perhaps' about it. He brags about the fact."

People, some of them mindful of the earlier near-confrontation, were looking at Harry

Cheng was looking at him too. "Have you an opinion on the matter, Harry?"

Harry shrugged. "What I've seen so far means nothing to me. He can sleep with a garbage disposal if he wants." At the best of times, Harry was not inclined to be diplomatic. And these were not the best of times.

SEVEN

Early next morning, base time, after Harry's first dinner aboard the base, he found himself working closely with Satranji in one of the small hangar bays, going over a robot scout to see why the robot crew chief repeatedly redlined it when it was due to go out on a mission.

The scout was a wingless pod the size of a small aircraft, now made somewhat larger by the fact of several panels having been swung open in its smooth surface. At the moment no other human was in the workshop. Nor had Harry seen Dorijen this morning; maybe, he thought, she was sleeping late after a long night of debauchery.

Satranji broke a silence in his abrupt way: "Why d'you fight 'em, Silver? The bad machines."

Harry came to a stop, straddling the scout's metal

fuselage at one of its thinner points, a test probe idle in his hand. He seemed to remember that earlier Satranji had been well aware of his loss. "You're asking me that?"

The compact man pulled his head out of a metal cavity. "All right, sure, now one of 'em has eaten up your people. That makes it personal. I can see that. But even before your wife and kid had the bad luck, you'd already spent a good part of your life shooting it out with berserkers. How many years was it, anyway?"

Harry didn't answer.

Satranji just wasn't going to let it rest. He seemed determined to provoke some kind of violent response. "So, tell me—why? There are a lot of good pilots, better pilots than you, who never get into that."

Mentally Harry stepped back for a moment to consider piloting. It was crazy to claim that there were a lot of people better than he was. Possibly one or two. But what difference did any of that make to anybody now?

At last he only said, distantly: "You're here, Satranji, ready to get your stupid head shot off in a fight. Must be some reason for that, besides the fact that the pay is good." He resumed the process of running the instrument he was holding through a nearby cavity in the scout's metal hull. So far it had told him nothing very useful.

Satranji liked that answer, it kept the steam of his pointless anger going. "Oh, my pay *is* good, depend on it. Better than yours. And we were talking about you." Satranji was still smiling, but with a new intensity. He was acting like a man who for some mysterious reason had set his mind and heart on having a knock-down brawl.

As was the case with almost everything these days, Harry discovered that he didn't much care, one way or the other, whether he and Satranji had a fight or not. But their brawling wasn't going to kill any ber-serkers. He shrugged, and reviewed the last several readings that his test probe had given him. So far he had been able to find no reason for the crew chief's rejection of this bird.

"How much are you getting paid, Silver?"

Harry sighed a private sigh. Evidently this had to be settled, somehow, before they could get anything done. Harry gave the question as much attention as it seemed to deserve—a little more, in fact—and remembered he had been told. But somehow he had forgotten what the numbers were. "I don't know."

"You're a liar."

"Then you're kind of stupid to keep asking me questions."

"When I heard you were coming to work for Cheng," Satranji said, "I hit the old man up for a raise. I made a point of insisting that I get more than you do."

Harry grunted.

Time passed. Satranji seemed to feel that the ball was still in his own court, and it bothered him. "Want to know, really, why I'm here, on this motherless chunk of rock?"

"No, I don't give a damn why. Or how much you get paid, or anything about you."

That had not been a soothing answer. Well, so be it. Something deeper than casual bravado was stirring in the eyes of the smaller man—something like deep rage. His voice was choked into a lower volume. "I can handle you, Silver, you're supposed to be so famously motherless tough."

"All the famous motherless tough guys I ever knew have one thing in common—they're all dead."

But it didn't matter what Harry said, Satranji wasn't listening any longer. "I can handle any human being that tries to stand up to me—"

"Yippee for you." Harry shifted the probe into his left hand. He recalled now that he had never got around to recharging his fighting ring. But he didn't think it would be needed.

"—but maybe somewhere there's a fighting machine, a berserker, that'll give me a real challenge, when I'm in a suit and in the pilot's chair!"

A door to an adjoining corridor was easing open. Dorijen appeared, face bland as usual, shapely body clad today in modest coveralls.

Harry said: "Your lovely wife is here. You can ask her about my pay."

Later in the morning, Louise Newari, talking to Harry alone, told him that Satranji had been working for Cheng Enterprises for several years, and had been brought in on the expedition because he was the best available expert on the Gravel Pit system, as well as a fine pilot and combat veteran. He was currently supposed to be engaged in planning the tactics of the raid—but so far no one had been able to do much in the way of planning, because there was still a total lack of any solid data about the objective they were going to attack.

Evidently having heard something of the near-collision

in the hangar bay—could Dorijen have been gossiping?—Louise concluded by putting a hand on Harry's arm. She said: "I'm glad you didn't fight him, Harry. I'm glad you walked around him."

"Same way I'd walk around a pile of doggy-do on the sidewalk."

He hadn't really been trying to think back to the days of his first encounters with Satranji. Still, there came every once in a while a faint flash or two of intuition, of a suspicion that at one time he and this man had nearly been friends. But then their relationship had started to go sour, for some reason Harry could not remember now. It was just one of the many things in his life that he had never bothered to figure out.

Satranji had one other claim to distinction, much more interesting from Harry's point of view. He was the only person that either Cheng or the lady had mentioned as a suspect in Cheng's investigation. But so far the investigation had not produced a molecule of evidence to link the angry man to either crime. And obviously both Cheng and his coordinator considered him of great value to the expedition.

Lady Masaharu, and Cheng himself, in conference with Satranji and Harry, agreed that more data was required on the numbers and positions of several hundred of the larger orbiting rocks before a serious attempt could be made to reach the inner system. Of course it would be hopeless, even with the aid of robot scouts and computers, to try to track individually the millions of chaotic fragments. The best that could be done was to try to select a representative sample. The only useful calculations lay in the realm of statistics and probability.

The Lady Masaharu made a firm announcement: "Whatever tactics we decide to adopt, we must take adequate time to prepare. Otherwise we will simply be killing ourselves uselessly, before we even get near the enemy."

Doc and Harry immediately got along, and when Harry allowed himself time off, he spent much of it playing variations of computer chess with Doc, sometimes discussing certain aspects of the universe. Now and then another subject came up, for example the expedition's prospects for success.

Another example was Satranji and his claimed wife. Doc speculated that an attempt might have been made to download a real woman's personality into the machine called Dorijen. There was always some human experimenter, somewhere in the Galaxy, making new efforts along that line. People had claimed success, with various degrees of credibility. But Doc, something of an expert in the field, doubted very much that Dorijen's mind grew out of anything but hardware.

Doc seemed more interested in the questions involved than in the individuals. "Is the urge to have sex with machinery an illness? If so, would Satranji be any better off if he were cured? Or is it that imitation flesh is safer, more reliable, than the real thing?"

"I think sex is secondary to him, and I don't know if he really screws his doll or not. His real compulsion is to offend as many people as he can."

Doc was among other things a physician/surgeon,

expert in healing and restoring human bodies, especially brains and nervous systems, that had become badly embedded in or entangled with advanced optelectronics systems—berserkers in the past had tried to incorporate into their own devices some of the strengths and flexibilities possessed by living systems.

No one liked to discuss the bottom-line reason why Doc's specialized expertise was thought likely to be needed on this job, and why the coordinator had assigned him to the landing party instead of someone skilled in combat trauma. The truth was that his skills and expertise in rescuing and restoring human cells, organs, and in some cases practically recreating entire bodies could be of great use if the prisoners, when they could finally be pried loose from the berserker's grip, had already been disassembled in some horrible way.

Doc's work with cultured embryos paralleled, in some ways almost duplicated, certain research projects in which the berserker enemy was thought to be also engaged.

From time to time he dropped hints suggesting that he also felt he owed Winston Cheng a great debt of some kind—Harry assumed he might be trying to repay it.

It had long been established that berserkers at times used live humans as research subjects, trying to learn more about the most serious opposition that they faced in their effort to sterilize the Galaxy. Harry had heard speculation that the bad machines were trying to create their own version of an ultimate weapon, in an all-out attempt to win the war with life.

One intriguing theory was that high berserker

command had come up with some projection indicating that otherwise the great effort to exterminate all life could fail. Or, if ultimate failure was not an option that a berserker could allow itself to consider, at least it could be drawn out endlessly.

Harry said: "Any forecast like that would be mighty cheerful from the human point of view. I'd like to see it."

There were times in the absorption of piloting or game-playing when Harry could feel the nightmare that had trapped him lifting momentarily, giving him a sign that eventually some return to full life might be possible—and he wasn't sure that he welcomed the development. Grief at his loss was easing, just enough to allow anger to rise toward the surface, seeking an outlet.

The customary gathering space for the whole crew was in the common room—wardroom, or refectory. During the previous occupation of the base, this space had served researchers and miners as a real mess hall, accommodating three or four times the small number of people who used it now. It tended to make the current occupants uneasy by suggesting that their numbers were too few, their force inadequate.

One wall was enlivened by graphic promotional materials for Cheng Enterprises, encouraging everyone present to make use of the corporation's products and services. No one seemed to pay them any particular attention.

At the moment all recon ships were either inaccessible to communication, somewhere out amid the flying rocks, or else were grounded for maintenance.

Harry stood, painfully idle, leaning his back against a wall of smooth, raw, lifeless stone, almost blankly watching Doc play against the computer.

The other, somehow aware of being watched, looked over his shoulder. "Care for a game?"

"Sure." The board and pieces offered a way to occupy the mind, keeping a space cleared in the middle of the darkness.

It seemed plain that the chess set hadn't come with the territory. The board was an ancient artifact of genuine inlaid wood, in the thickness of which the required optelectronic circuits had long ago been skillfully and invisibly buried by some talented microengineer. The men were no less authentic, a fine antique set. Harry had been curious enough to ask a robot, and had learned that the black army had been carved, long ago, of some dark and heavy horn, and the white of true stamodont ivory. For the purposes of modern play, the machine had tagged each man, and each square of the board, with a tiny dot that let it keep track of all the pieces—also marked individually and invisibly—and physically move them when required. It seemed to Harry very likely that the whole set was extremely valuable—probably just another of Winston Cheng's generous contributions to the cause.

The most favored variant of this game was a half-computerized version of the ancient struggle, in which two or more humans each moved a separate team of pieces, fighting as allies to bring down the machine. There was a piece called the herald, who blew a tiny horn to signal an attack. The game had been crafted in such a way as to allow each of the two basic kinds of intelligence to benefit from its own innate advantages.

Some players favored a version in which pieces could be captured and then ransomed and released.

Doc lost, in less than thirty moves. Then, while the pieces rearranged themselves for a new game, Doc studied him, elbow propped on table, head in hand. At last he said: "You're tougher than I thought you'd be."

"Everybody's got their own estimate of how tough I am—what the hell, it was just luck."

"Luck, in this game? Come on. I suppose when you made that move with the herald you just chose a piece at random, and then just closed your eyes and put it anywhere. Nothing but pure chance. Yeah, sure."

"Do you know anything about chance, Doc?" Harry's voice had suddenly gone slow and quiet, as if he might be talking in his sleep. "I mean, really know anything? What is it? What can it do?"

Doc looked round, almost furtively, though it seemed doubtful that anyone would be bothering to spy on their conversation. Probably it was just out of habit. He said: "Talking metaphysics over a drink or a chessboard is one thing. Living with it day to day is something else."

Harry squinted at him. "I don't—"

"What I'm saying, Harry, is that in the real world, if any strange happening seems too unlikely to be the result of pure chance—then you had better believe that it is not."

"Doc. Do you know something I ought to know?"

"I've got no secret knowledge about kidnappings. All I mean, all I know, is what I said."

"So you don't believe in coincidence. But sometimes it has to happen."

Doc was shaking his head. "Not on the level of the

two kidnappings, it doesn't. Not in the world where you and I are trying to make a living."

"But you forget, Doc. That's not what we're trying to do. Not on this rock. Not any longer."

In moments when Harry allowed himself to ponder the reality of what he was doing, he realized that it really made little sense to claim to be preparing for a rescue operation. What had really brought him here was the chance to get some satisfaction out of hitting back. He was on 207GST because he wanted to fight berserkers until they killed him, and he just wanted to get the business over with. Why Satranji had to complicate it all, he couldn't say. Soon enough there was going to be more fighting than any of them could stand.

Doc was somewhat bolder than anyone else in expressing his doubts about the usefulness, or even the sanity, of trying to organize a rescue expedition for long-term berserker prisoners—though he allowed himself to voice his reservations only after he had got to know Harry a little better.

"I think you understand as well as I do, Harry— maybe better than I do—that what we're preparing for is not really a rescue attempt. We all keep telling ourselves so, but that's just delusional."

"What is it, then?"

"We're going on a punitive expedition, organized against machines."

"Is that what you think? Or is Winston Cheng organizing it to punish himself?"

"Punish himself for what?"

"Haven't you ever wondered? Why didn't Cheng

have the two young people with him, if they were so all-important in his life?"

Both of Harry's hotshot young pilots, having had time to get a good look at the situation, were having second thoughts about the exciting adventure for which they had signed up, and casting about for ways to get out of the contracts they had most recently signed with Cheng.

The one who had been so honored by getting to work with Harry was grumbling now: "I didn't sign on for no motherless armed excursion into hell."

Harry grunted. He himself was already about seven circles down in the place of hot damnation, and the only visible way out was the road on which old Winston Cheng was leading the way. That path would carry Cheng and his crew right straight through the middle of the pit, right in among hell's devils, close enough to shoot back at them.

A couple of times Cheng had quietly let it be known that anyone who got a serious case of cold feet, even up to the last hour before launch, could be excused from taking part. But the last courier would already have left the wanderworld by then, and late dropouts would be compelled by circumstances to remain there until another ship showed up. And by then the job would have been concluded, one way or another.

Harry had grunted. Satranji had made a tough little speech expressing his great contempt for any suggestion of backing out.

Doc proclaimed, cautiously at first, that he had never met anyone who had been a prisoner of berserkers and lived to tell the tale.

Satranji looked up from something he had been reading. "What's the matter, Doc? Can it be you're losing faith in our mission?"

Doc looked at the smaller man thoughtfully for several seconds. "Seems to me human lives are kind of important."

"If you're so anxious to go on living, Doc, I don't know what you're doing on this project."

"Same thing you are, I guess. As you say, the pay is great. And if I don't live to collect mine, no one's going to miss me."

So why *was* he, Doc, here, risking his life? Harry heard pieces of the story, with variations, from different people. Doc had run here to escape authorities who were trying to arrest him. He was a physician (that much was confirmed) who'd got into legal trouble on a distant world by having "something to do with abortions."

Not performing them, no, that was legal there—his supposed crime had been described as an attempt to rescue or preserve certain human embryonic entities, organisms created and destined to serve as production facilities for certain types of cells that were in great demand for research purposes. Doc's ambition had been to acquire a number of artificial wombs, and use them to grow the pilfered embryos up to full-term fetuses, establishing them on the path that led through birth to normal life.

The one time he'd talked to Harry about it, he had concluded tersely: "Corporation that owned the embryos wasn't too happy about all that."

Harry grunted. "I guess they wouldn't be. What happened, finally?"

Doc shrugged. "I'm here, where most of the law in the Galaxy will have a hard time getting at me."

A lot of specialized medical gear had been assembled, including some of Doc's machines that he had used to rescue embryos. The devices were upsized, of course, to be able to handle larger fragments of humanity. A carefully chosen selection of them was going to be packed on the ship that led the assault.

Some members of the assault group were having a hard time controlling their impatience. "If things keep going at this pace, standard months will have passed between the first kidnapping, and the time when we actually reach the place where we think the victims might be held—if we ever get that far. Do any of us seriously believe that a berserker's prisoners are going to last that long?"

Harry knew from experience that it damn sure didn't happen often, captives of a berserker getting out alive; but he could testify that it had happened.

Harry had not been surprised by the prolonged delay in the arrival of the secret weapon that Winston Cheng had hyped at their first meeting—or even by the fact that Cheng had never mentioned it again. In Harry's experience, secret weapons tended to have only tentative existence, sometimes evaporating completely. But Cheng wouldn't be simply bluffing. Harry's guess was that it had to be some kind of specially outfitted ship. What did worry Harry were what he took to be certain indications that the whole project was in danger of collapsing into hopeless farce.

The Lady Masaharu did mention the weapon once, quite calmly. She said that no more information could be given out just yet, but that it was real and would play a key role in their attack.

By this time other members of the crew were catching Harry's concern.

One of the more practical members of the group observed: "What worries me is, where's this secret-weapon bomb or ship or whatever it's supposed to be? All we've seen so far are yachts, and they're not going to come close to getting the job done."

In Harry's opinion, the whole operation looked like it was on the verge of falling apart.

"Or are we just going to keep postponing and postponing, until we talk ourselves out of the project altogether?"

"That's not going to happen." For once Satranji seemed to be in firm agreement.

The Lady Masaharu stayed very much in control and did not seem to be perturbed. She had serene confidence that Winston Cheng would accomplish exactly what he said. "The boss says that's all being taken care of."

In her capacity as field commander of the expedition, she made scouting a priority. Recon efforts, crewed and uncrewed, were necessary to locate the enemy, and help the newly installed supercomputer find a survivable pathway to the inner system. Little else could be done until that had been accomplished.

To that end, Harry also might be called on to put in long hours as a pilot—driving a military scoutship that Cheng Enterprises had somehow obtained as Space Force surplus. The small vessel had been stripped of its insignia and armament before being sold for civilian use, and no attempt had been made to reinstall the weapons, though the scout had drive power and maneuverability to burn. There were reasons why any moderately heavy armament that became available would instead be installed aboard the yachts, with the best of it going to Cheng's favorite *Ship of Dreams*.

As far as Harry was concerned, there was no bloody use in weighing yourself down with armament on a scouting mission, if your objective was to discover the location of a berserker base without being detected.

"If some berserker sees me first, a couple of little shootin' irons aren't going to do me any good."

And the lady was in agreement. "Of course—if you're trying to sneak up on the game, the last thing you want to look like is a hunter."

However many organic assistants Harry had left, he kept them busy, driving small unarmed scouts around the system. It was important that the living supervisors should get closer to the whirling rock slide, so they could better manage the horde of flying robots that were sent plunging right in, sending back packets of data, on missions that often were suicidal.

Just getting close, into the zone where Harry and his living helpers went, was risky business. But no one objected. They were a couple of young men, recruited from other projects that Winston Cheng had going on, drawn by the prospect of adventure, not to mention the excellent pay.

Cheng put in another of his frequent appearances at the advanced base.

He told Harry: "At the time of the first kidnapping Satranji was engaged in a routine mapping mission for Cheng Enterprises. A solo flight into the Gravel

Pit—of course we were not, at that time, looking for berserkers. According to the log of the ship Satranji was using, he could not have been anywhere near the scene of the kidnapping at the hour when Winnie and Claudia were lost.

"At the time when your Becky and Ethan were taken, as confirmed by another ship's log, he was working in the Gravel Pit again. By that time, of course, we had begun scouting missions looking for the berserker base."

Despite Lady Laura's objections to the robot wife, Cheng appeared totally indifferent to the sex lives of his team members. Harry thought the old man wouldn't care much if one member of his crew had tried to murder another, as long as the problem had now been solved or somehow put aside. The only thing that Winston Cheng really seemed to find appalling was the danger that something would delay their getting on with the project as quickly and efficiently as possible.

The point was emphasized, that the old man was ready to sacrifice the lives of others, and to take great risks himself, to bring closer the realization of his own goal.

Now and then, on average maybe two or three times in a standard day, robotic couriers came and went from the little base, conveying business messages to and from various other destinations in Winston Cheng's empire.

It remained possible for team members to send and receive personal mail by the same means, though they were increasingly encouraged to keep such traffic to a minimum, just enough to keep friends and relatives from growing too worried or too curious. Communication with the outside world was still not overtly censored—but Harry felt sure that someone, probably the Lady Masaharu, was secretly reading all the messages before they actually went out. All members of the group were frequently reminded of the need for secrecy.

None of this was of much concern to Harry, who felt that he had already been violently separated from the world. Once or twice a day now, probing messages arrived at the wanderworld, from news organizations that were trying overtly or covertly to locate Harry Silver. People out in the great Galactic world were finally starting to catch on to the strange dual kidnappings. So far, Lady Masaharu was putting the questioners off with bland misdirection, for which Harry was grateful.

Shortly after the arrival of a certain robotic message courier, Winston Cheng's appointed coordinator, in the absence of Cheng himself, announced that the secret negotiations for the ship they were going to use had just been completed.

The Lady Masaharu instructed Harry to drive one of the available couriers to a certain Templar base, only a relatively few light-years away, where the ship that was going to be their main attack vessel had now at last become available.

"I don't suppose this is the secret weapon, finally?"

"That is the implication."

Harry was surprised. "The weapon is a ship that we're borrowing from the Templars?"

"I think you may assume that we're buying it and not borrowing. Currently this particular vessel is not the property of the order, it just happens to be berthed at one of their bases."

Harry was squinting. "I don't get it."

"There's no great mystery. They had first crack at buying the ship in question themselves, but decided to pass. Which is fortunate for us."

"Then who is the current owner?"

"The designer, builder, and only owner to date is Aristotle Gianopolous. Perhaps you've met him?"

No, Harry had never laid eyes on the fellow. But he knew the name, as did much of the rest of the inhabited Galaxy, in particular the minority of people with a professional interest in advanced ship design and military hardware. Harry's personal opinion was that the man was probably part genius and part fraud, the exact proportions hard to determine; but Harry hadn't made a study of the matter and wasn't going to be dogmatic about it. Thinking it over, he decided that with the expedition's chances being what they were, the truth about the secret weapon probably didn't really matter a whole lot, as long as they could get the show on the road.

"What do I do with the ship I'm driving, when I get to the Templar base?"

The Lady Masaharu told Harry that he should program the courier he had driven there to make its way back uncrewed, on autopilot, to 207GST.

The next part of Harry's job, and an important one, would be to inspect the newly acquired vessel.

"As soon as you have satisfied yourself as to its general spaceworthiness, you will drive it back here,

to 207GST, using the time en route to familiarize
yourself as thoroughly as possible with its capabilities
and controls. You will be the pilot when we attack."

"All right.

"Lady Masaharu, one question."

"Of course."

"You have several other pilots here, and I can't be the
highest rated in diplomacy. Why are you sending me?"

"I understand you're well acquainted with the base
commander there, Colonel-Abbot Darchan."

"Oh." Light dawned. "Yeah, but I didn't know he was
there. Emil and I know each other pretty well. Or we
did, I haven't seen the good abbot for a few years."

"You're definitely on friendly terms, then?"

Harry nodded.

"Good, we were hoping we could bank on that.
Personal acquaintance should smooth things out a
bit. I'm not sure most Templars would be eager to
cooperate in a project, once they knew it was being
funded by Winston Cheng."

Harry recalled the rumors of ill-feeling. "You may
have a point there."

"There will be one more part to your mission, Harry.
It's a fairly important part. If it is at all possible, you
will bring the inventor back here with you. Mister
Cheng intends to offer him a job as a consultant."

"A consultant. Not to go on the assault?"

"I should hope not."

"And if he doesn't want to come?"

The lady smiled faintly. "Well, we don't expect you
to use force. Actually I suspect that you may find him
rather eager, when he learns the offer's source."

"Oh?"

"Of course, if he should be reluctant, do your best to persuade him. Mister Cheng and I both feel he could be very useful as a consultant in the final stages of this project."

"His ship is that tricky to operate?"

"He claims the very opposite, that any qualified pilot should have an easy time. But the truth is we're not sure yet."

"Great." Harry's tone reversed the meaning of the word. "And I get to drive. What inducement can I offer him?"

"As far as the price we are offering for the ship goes, just tell him you don't think he'll be disappointed."

"I can do that."

"I would strongly advise that you not reveal the exact nature of our project to Professor Gianopolous, until you are both on your way here in his ship."

"I can see that. Well, I'm not the smoothest salesman you could find."

"You underrate yourself, Harry. Sincerity counts for a lot. If you can't sign up the inventor—well, we'll manage without him. But be sure you bring the ship."

"I understand."

He was on his way out when the lady called after him: "I think you'll find it an interesting experience."

Harry grunted. Then when he was halfway through the doorway he stopped and turned to ask: "Are you talking about the ship or the designer?"

The Lady Masaharu showed him one of her rare smiles. "I doubt that you'll be bored by either one."

EIGHT

Winston Cheng's visits to the wanderworld were never more than two days apart, and there was at least one standard day when he dropped in twice. Harry didn't see much of the old man during most of these appearances, but thought that Cheng was starting to look grimly, quietly frantic. Not that Harry was paying much attention to the behavior of other people; he had enough trouble trying to organize his own.

On some of his drop-in visits Cheng got no farther than the dock, or the enclosed platform just inboard from there, an air-filled space where everyone could take helmets off and converse in relative comfort. There the tycoon stood or sat talking to the Lady Masaharu, never penetrating any farther into the base, before he jumped back on the ship that had brought him, or another that was standing by, and hurried away again. Doubtless there were business matters that needed his personal attention, even more than usual when he was forced to marshal extra resources to prepare and supply his striking force. Once he told Harry that he wanted to give, as much as possible, the impression of maintaining his regular activities. At other times Cheng walked through very nearly the whole base, looked at everything there was to be seen, talked to everyone, and prolonged his visit for several hours.

Mostly the old man arrived in one or another of his fast business couriers, but there came a day when Cheng arrived aboard his favorite armed yacht, *Ship of Dreams*, and abruptly ordered Del Satranji to drop everything else that he was doing to take over as his personal pilot.

As Harry heard the story later, Satranji seemed almost stunned. He immediately protested that he wanted to be involved directly in the fighting.

Cheng assured him that he would be. "I can assure you, my friend, that by staying close to me you will see all the action anyone could possibly want."

The pilot had tried further argument, everything short of threatening to quit. But Satranji's toughness, in a matter like this, had to crumble when it ran into the old man's. Cheng closed the discussion by saying Satranji could follow orders, or he could pack his things and leave, and an immediate decision was required.

There was one slight hitch involving the robot Dorijen. Be it wife, chattel, or assigned to some other category, Cheng would not have it on his yacht, and Satranji was forced to put his robot into storage on the base.

❖   ❖   ❖

Now, at last, the nature of the secret weapon could be revealed to the whole assault team and their support people.

Cheng said to the assembled crew, or as many as could be gathered at one place at one time: "The secret weapon I have been talking about is, as you will see in a few days, indeed a ship. Not a very large vessel, or especially heavily armed. But it has, from our point of view, one outstanding attribute: it can disguise itself as a Type-B berserker."

That made an impression on Harry, and the vast majority of his other listeners, and drew a murmur.

The old man went on: "The disguise is not only visual, but extends to identification codes and signals. It can carry a combat crew of six humans, and has a cargo bay that can hold several tons of machinery, such as small assault vehicles. If all goes well, it will enable us to reach the enemy base before the enemy knows we're anywhere around."

Harry raised his eyes abruptly, to give Cheng a searching stare. It was Lady Laura who met Harry's gaze, and her lips silently formed the one word: *later*.

Winston Cheng continued briefing his team. He was convinced that the mission's chance of success depended very heavily on deception, on being able to fool the defenses of the enemy base. To trick casual human observers ought to be comparatively easy—but to deceive the real thing, with all its IFF capabilities, over a span of approach time that might equal a full minute or even more, would pose a tremendous challenge.

❖   ❖   ❖

Minutes after the meeting broke up, Lady Laura told Harry privately: "Naturally, Mister Silver, it will have occurred to you that this vehicle, or something like it, could have been used in one or both of the abductions. That the identifiable berserker hardware recovered in one case might have been deliberately seeded in nearby space in an attempt at deception."

"Naturally. Except I still don't know why anyone would want to do it."

Cheng stepped in. "I assure you, we have considered the possibility, however faint. But we have solid evidence that the ship we are about to purchase was in dock on the day I lost the people dear to me; and very recently I have learned that the Templars were testing the same ship when your family was taken. To the best of our knowledge, no similar craft exists anywhere."

Cheng's investigation had still not been able to discover any connection existing between their families before the kidnappings, nor could Harry remember anything that might have formed one. Whatever association existed must have been forged during the few days that had passed between crimes. The only alternative seemed to be that the second set of kidnapping victims had been chosen purely at random, a coincidence so monstrous as to be a practical impossibility. (Harry remembered the caution about coincidence that he had recently received from Doc.)

No matter what explanation was tried, puzzling questions remained. The fact of the first meeting between Cheng and Harry, even if berserkers had learned of it as soon as it took place, would seem to give them no reason to go out of their way to pick on Harry's family. Human tycoons and pilots were holding meetings all the time, a habit they shared with much of the rest of their restless race.

Endless speculation was possible, but no certainty, except for this: something—or someone—had deliberately selected Becky and Ethan as targets, in the process effectively destroying Harry's life.

Again and again, Harry found himself calling up a mental image of Satranji, who was no longer on the base, but spending all his time aboard the *Ship of Dreams* . . .

Harry was scanning that mental image again when another, very different possibility drifted into Harry's consciousness. The thought was an ugly one indeed, and Harry didn't quite know what to do with it. Did he find himself here on this forsaken wandering rock, preparing for death in a berserker fight, because he had been deliberately set up, his life ruined, by Winston Cheng himself?

But no. That seemed insane. Imagine the old man as ruthless as a forceblade, still he would not collaborate for a moment with the very berserkers he had dedicated himself to destroy. Cheng's sincerity was very convincing—no, that was too mild a word. Say instead maniacal. Would Captain Ahab work out a deal with Moby Dick, feed the great white whale fresh victims, just to get a certain harpooner signed on for a voyage? And would Moby Dick be likely to cooperate?

Crazy as it seemed to suspect Cheng, were the alternatives really all that much better? Once more, what were the odds that the enemy had selected the two sets of kidnap victims purely at random?

Harry could hear himself making small sounds of anguish in his throat. Every once in a while it all started to come over him like this. He had to squeeze his eyes shut, and bring up his hands to his head, as if to hold his brain together. Never mind the logic, never mind the reasoned search for answers. What had happened to Becky and to Ethan was still beyond the limit, outside the domain of things that he could think rationally about.

Winston Cheng, convening in the common room a meeting of all the humans who could be gathered at short notice, told them that he and his coordinator had decided to make an all-out effort to recruit Professor Aristotle Gianopolous, designer and builder of the fake berserker Winston Cheng wanted to use in his raid, as a consultant.

A quarter of an hour after getting his instructions, Harry was alone in one of Cheng's standard couriers, driving the ship toward the Templar base where he would collect the secret weapon.

Obeying a sudden impulse, Harry programmed in an unscheduled stop en route, allowing his machinery to pick the exact point in normal space, specifying little more than that it must be light-years away from anything and anyone. After days of the constant pressure of people in a small space, he needed time, a little time at least, just to be alone.

Following his inner prompting further, he even put on a spacesuit, something that he almost never did except when absolutely necessary, and went out briefly through the courier's airlock. Why was he doing this, just for the nonexistent fun of it? Just to enjoy the feeling of being so extravagantly isolated from other human beings, from every form of Galactic life?

And from life's remorseless enemy as well.

He stared for a few moments at the naked Universe, then, as usual, had to turn away from it, sheltering his gaze against his ship, a curve of mostly metal only a couple of meters from his face. Looking at his dim reflection in the faint brightness of a protective forcefield, clinging to the smooth ship's metal flank. Harry caught a glimpse of his own reflected face, mildly distorted.

His nose looked even worse than usual.

The two of them had been lying in bed somewhere when Becky asked, seemingly out of nowhere: "Why didn't you ever get your nose fixed, Harry?"

"What's wrong with my nose?"

"What's wrong with it? It's bent around until it's pointing at your ear."

"Come on. That is a slight exaggeration. Anyway, I like my face the way it is."

"Why, for God's sake?"

"I need it to remind me of a couple of things." He shifted his position.

Becky knew the signs of when a line of questioning ought to be abandoned. She had moved closer and kissed her Harry on the arguable nose. "If you like it that way, then I do too."

"Feels straighter already."

If you started to cry inside your helmet it could create a minor problem. But actually he wasn't going to start. Not even close. He had already gone way beyond anything that tears might do to him or for him.

❖   ❖   ❖

The Templar base commanded by Emil Darchan was perhaps the most important one the order had established in this sector of the Galaxy, and for it, for reasons doubtless similar to Cheng's, the Templars too had chosen a wanderworld, free of gravitational or political allegiance to any solar system.

WW 132CAB was reasonably located, fairly readily accessible to convenient nodes of flightspace travel. Outside the boundaries of any solar system, the Order was free to run its own shop in its own way, not having to contend with the laws or sensitivities of any planetary or system government.

The capabilities of base defense here were very serious, in sharp contrast with those on WW 207GST. Harry, though he was more or less expected, needed a quarter of an hour to negotiate his way in on approach. In the meantime he was free to look around, and his ship's scopes showed him interesting things.

The base as a whole was a sprawling installation, covering several square kilometers of airless rock. Harry could see another huge domed structure that he assumed would be the Trophy Room, a research facility where all the Templars fighting and working in this sector of the Galaxy conveyed any items of berserker hardware that they were able to find, steal, or collect in the aftermath of combat. This particular Trophy Room was generally acknowledged to be one of the best maintained by any organization in the known Galaxy. Members of the Order were justly proud of this establishment, claiming that neither the Space Force nor any local authority could boast its equal. Information gleaned by the work in its laboratory and on its proving ground was distributed freely, not only to other Templar forces, but to the Space Force and any local government that wanted to be in the loop.

Material for the Trophy Room scientists and engineers to work on was hard to come by. Harry had heard it estimated that, during the centuries of their bitter war against ED humanity, something like a thousand berserkers had been destroyed for every one captured with any of its vital systems still intact.

Harry brought his ship in for a landing, heading as directed for the main hangar, which hospitably opened the doors of a vast forcefield airlock in the surface of its enormous dome.

Harry had announced his arrival from half an hour out, and the abbot, his tall figure arrayed in the full robes of office, was waiting on the dock to welcome him.

"Harry! You're looking great!"

Harry, being shaken in a double grip, then pounded on the shoulder, doubted that. The smile on his own face felt strange, but it was there. "Hello, Emil."

The abbot looked pretty much unchanged since Harry had seen him last. Generally energetic, and somewhat excitable. Perhaps the flowing white hair was just a little longer, and the bright pink face, despite its owner's apparently robust health, a little closer to looking apoplectic.

"Welcome to our base."

"It's looking great too."

It was the first time Harry had seen the place, though at their last meeting, six or seven standard years ago, the abbot, then newly appointed, had invited Harry to pay him a visit at any time. The buildings and fixtures were a mixture of old and new design. Some of the equipment had a venerable look, while some was absolutely state-of-the-art.

Harry's old friend promised him a tour of the entire base before he left.

"That would be great. We'll see if there's time."

When the initial greetings and comments had been got out of the way, the abbot proclaimed: "Harry, you come at a most opportune time!" The abbot's voice was pleasant to listen to, though it was not the vocal equipment you'd want to have if you were inclined to sing. "You must see what we have, at this minute, in the Trophy Room! Beyond a doubt, one of the most important projects ever undertaken at this base! Or, quite possibly, at any other."

The man's enthusiasm was contagious. Almost against his will, Harry found a corner of the dark cloud lifting from his mind, himself getting interested. "Then I can't wait to see it. What's going on?"

"A berserker courier, my friend! What do you think of that? An *entire courier!*" The two words came out in a dramatic whisper. "Some of our enthusiastic young people have recently captured one with its data storage practically intact."

The abbot's mood dimmed for a moment. "It is true that we lost one scoutship, and three members of our boarding party were killed, may the First Cause bless them, in disabling the destructor system."

"A full-sized courier?" Harry stared. Even snaring smaller messengers intact was considered something of an achievement.

"I promise you. One of a precise type I have not seen before, almost the equivalent of a new species."

"That *is* impressive."

"One of our very skillful young officers commanded the interception team, and everything worked beautifully. It happened just—well, I shouldn't tell even you precisely where. Highly classified, you know."

"I understand."

"But all in good time. Before we go to the Trophy Room we must have a talk. Come, come along to my cell! Have you eaten recently?"

"Yeah. I'm okay."

The abbot frowned conspiratorially, and lowered his voice a notch. "Then how about a little nip of something to warm the blood?"

"Well. You know me. I'm not likely to say no to that."

A visit from an old friend was a social occasion, offering a good excuse to break out a private and semiofficial bottle of brandy.

With Abbot Darchan talking almost steadily, and now and then gripping Harry by the arm again, they walked past meeting rooms and storerooms and what looked like schoolrooms, some empty and some occupied with busy classes. Harry saw, with no great surprise, that what the inhabitants of this abbey called a cell was actually—at least in the head man's case—a suite of rooms, small in number and size but running somewhat to luxury.

He could see no evidence that anyone was cohabiting with Darchan, though in this branch of the Order long-term, monogamous sexual relationships—between real people, of course—were quite acceptable. The religious symbols on the walls, forming quite an eclectic collection, all looked to Harry like valuable works of art. But all this was still remote, making only a slight impression; other matters still dominated Harry's mind, and the memory of Winston Cheng's palace was still reasonably fresh.

So it was with the brandy. The taste was everything it should have been, but in Harry's current mental state it afforded no real enjoyment. The Templars had so far failed spectacularly in their centuries-old mission, to rid the Galaxy of berserkers—but on the other hand they had done a lot to keep the bad machines from succeeding in their own effort. And in other ways the Order had done humanity some favors. The grapes pressed to yield the wine distilled to make this drink had doubtless been grown at Templar vineyards, maybe in some cavern on this wanderworld, or on another, most likely beneath a finely tuned spectrum of artificial light. As Harry recalled, it had not been alcohol that was Emil's weakness in his unhallowed secular civilian days. It was probably a good thing for the abbot's career that he had never met Dorijen.

Harry stared into his glass, swirling the contents around. He was thinking that this was the first real drink he could remember having since he had sampled Winston Cheng's scotch during their first never-to-be-forgotten meeting. Thinking that Becky had never been much of a drinker, though she would have one now and then . . .

Abbot Darchan had put his sandaled feet up on an antique hassock, and was letting out a sigh of contentment. "By Karlsen's mustache, Harry, it must be—what? Eight standard years? Ten?—since we've had a chance to talk."

"Yeah. It's been way too long."

"It has indeed." Here the abbot began to reminisce about some battle in which both of them had taken part. Presently he was making an effort to date events by that standard.

"I seem to make it seven years," Harry announced. He had been computing silently, by the use of other landmarks in his life, that the battle must have taken place a year before he and Becky had finally tied the knot, almost two years before Ethan was born. Even the calendar now seemed to revolve around the key dates of his demolished life.

". . . probably you are correct," the abbot was saying. "But good to see you, in any case, however long it may have been. By the way, that's a classy little ship you're driving. Yours?"

"No, just borrowed for the trip."

"You have no other crew, no passengers?"

Harry grunted something. The courier he had just docked was no more than a fairly representative sample of Cheng's extensive fleet, and probably not recognizable as belonging to the tycoon. "If all goes according to plan, I'll be sending that one back where it belongs on autopilot, and driving a different one away from here." He pushed aside his empty glass, and with a shake of his head declined a refill.

"Oh?"

"You sound surprised. I came here with the idea that my employer was buying a ship from Professor Gianopolous, and the professor was here already, more or less expecting me."

"Oh, the great man, the famous inventor. Aristotle." The abbot's tone gave the name more than a touch of irony. "Yes, he's here, all right. He's been waiting, though I wasn't sure just who or what he was expecting. As you probably know, we've been holding talks regarding this ship he boasts of as his invention. But you, Harry? You're going to work for him?" The abbot seemed to think that a dubious, unlikely proposition.

"Not *for* him, exactly. There's a kind of joint project being planned. I know, it looks like one of us is scraping the bottom of the barrel."

The abbot took a moment to consider. "Well, *he's* certainly not scraping the bottom of anything, not if he came up with you. I suppose your joint project is somehow going to employ his experimental ship . . . he brought the vessel here to offer us a demonstration, wanting us either to buy it, or invest in his ongoing work. Or both."

Harry sipped brandy. "You've tested the ship?"

"Yes."

"That was a nice short answer. Fairly extensive testing?"

"Yes, over a period of several days. But under a pledge of confidentiality. I'm afraid I can't discuss any of the results with you."

"All right. But you decided not to buy it."

"That is correct. The professor failed to be entirely convincing in his presentation . . . but I suppose I shouldn't discuss that either." Darchan waved a hand in a vague gesture. "Well, I won't pry into the nature of what seems a rather confidential project. Whatever the reason you're here, I'm glad to see you."

"Same here."

The abbot had paused as a new thought struck him. "And not just for old times' sake." He slapped his forehead theatrically with an open hand. "Great spirits of space, how could such a thing have slipped my mind? We had a bulletin come in—it wasn't that many days ago—from the Superior General's office. Your name was on a list and it caught my eye."

"Oh?" Harry was thinking that it was probably some old criminal charge. Right now he simply didn't care, except to be wary of the possibility that legal entanglement could loom up interfering with the way he planned to spend the next few days. He fully expected them to be the last days of his life.

The abbot had swiveled his comfortable chair to face the workstation in the corner of the room, and was rummaging optelectronically through reams of data, ghostly images of things and people flickering on a battery of small screens and stages, most of them evaporating again as fast as they appeared. Harry got up and moved to stand looking over one robed shoulder.

"Hah! Here we are."

Now Emil was getting a printout, while he went on talking. What he was saying and what Harry saw on the printout had nothing to do with criminal charges after all.

Abbot Darchan leaned back in his chair, and spoke in a voice that might have put across a sermon. "The Lifeless Ones, the servants of death, have thought up a new trick. They're custom-building assassin machines, each one dedicated to seeking out and killing a particular human being. The focus is on people they describe in a code that translates out as 'superbadlife.' There are about a hundred names on the list that someone in our order managed to intercept. Yours is prominent among them."

"I'm impressed," said Harry slowly. "I'm honored." He really was. In fact the news brought him about as close to enthusiasm as anything could have done these days. No human authority had ever awarded him a medal, and he doubted that any ever would, but this was better—insofar as anything, these days, could be truly better than anything else.

In the next moment, bleak realization was setting in. Of course this listing might easily have been the worst thing that had ever happened to him. It might have been the fact that killed his family, providing the enemy with a special reason to target them. That could mean that looking for any human goodlife traitors in the game was only wasted effort. There was no need for any malign intelligence, human or artificial, to be discovered lurking in the systems of Cheng Enterprises.

Harry had to force his attention back to the abbot, who was still nodding. " . . . yes, you should be impressed. Unfortunately, the machine we've got strung out on the trophy rack now has nothing directly to do with your designated assassin. We've dissected out the brain of a courier, as I said before, along with a few attached support devices. One that happened to be carrying a few scraps of useful information."

"Mind if I take a more thorough look at the list?"

"Of course not! I'm sorry, here."

Harry sat down with the printout in hand—suddenly his hand was slightly unsteady—and scanned it slowly, taking time to focus briefly on each name. He recognized one or two.

The name of Winston Cheng was indeed there, and so was that of Del Satranji, who wanted so badly to find a berserker that could offer him a real challenge. That he would succeed in that quest now seemed a good bet. Missing, however, were all the other members of the rescue expedition. Nor was Abbot Darchan himself among those who had been granted special status by the enemy; in fact Harry could not be sure that any of the people here marked for destruction were Templars. He thought in passing that that must irritate the Order.

Of course there was no way to be sure that this list was comprehensive. It might be only one installment of some kind of periodic bulletin. Prime targets for this standard month. Machines, fulfill your quotas.

Harry pondered for a few moments. Then he asked: "These dedicated assassin machines—do they go after their target's family members?"

The Templar looked thoughtful. "Good question. I haven't had any information on that point yet, but I shouldn't think so. The bad machines are very practical, as you know. The purpose here is to eliminate a dangerous life-unit, not to inspire him or her to seek revenge—but you don't have any family, as I recall."

There was a slight pause. It seemed that the news of the second kidnapping, at least, was still being effectively suppressed. "Right, I don't." Harry continued staring at the list. "One thing I don't have to worry about."

Escorting Harry on their way to visit the Trophy Room, the abbot detoured a few steps to the base library, saying there was another visitor who also wanted to observe the courier's interrogation. The additional visitor turned out to be the person Harry had actually come to this Templar base to see.

The abbot told Harry that before his arrival on base, Professor Aristotle Gianopolous had rather huffily declined the abbot's first invitation to visit the Trophy Room.

"I'm surprised."

"So was I. The implication seemed to be that we Templars and our investigations couldn't possibly tell him anything about berserkers that he didn't already know. Well, I'll try a little gracious coaxing."

Why bother? thought Harry. But then, no one was ever going to make him the abbot of anything.

Professor Gianopolous was a maverick scientist, an inventor working outside the regular military and industrial organizations, one who had developed a controversial theory of how berserkers might be deceived, and claimed he had constructed a spaceship that would do the job.

Harry had heard no details of the theory, but that was hardly surprising since Gianopolous was supposedly keeping his great ideas secret while trying to arrange some kind of profitable deal. But certain rumors, that had been passed in a whisper to Harry by the abbot, said that it involved a coding system of fathomless complexity, and required receiving and transmitting a lot of optelectronic signals.

The cavernous series of rooms was fairly well populated by a selection of Templars of both sexes and the full range of human age, from adolescence upward.

Entering the library, they had to probe deeply through the traditional hushed silence, into archaic-looking stacks and alcoves, to find the man they sought. He was dressed with a kind of muted flamboyance, a confusing effect exaggerated by the old-fashioned eyeglasses hanging on a cord around his neck. The twist of his thin lips suggested that he might have just bitten into a sour chewing pod. Behind him were what looked like the reserved shelves, containing, in considerable number, old books with permanent printing on their paper. In the foreground were the shelves of modern cybercodex.

Harry was briefly distracted, and came near being interested, impressed, at the sight of the old books. Volumes of ancient paper, even predating the era of space travel, with each page shimmering in its distinct modern forcefield binding.

Professor Gianopolous had a large table to himself, on which he had evidently been comparing two such fragile folios side by side. He looked up as if startled when the abbot and Harry approached, and rose to extend his hand when the abbot began to perform introductions. Harry was faintly surprised at the strength of the grip that met his own.

The professor's look seemed hopeful. "I have heard, sir, that you are an excellent pilot. That gives me hope that you will appreciate my ship."

"I've heard that you are an excellent designer and builder. I intend to give it a real try."

NINE

While on his landing approach to the Templar base, Harry had noted a domed structure that was by far the biggest component of the Templar complex except for the main hangar. He had assumed that the huge dome must contain the Trophy Room. Observing the same structure from the ground, he could see that it was separated by fifty meters of covered tunnel from the rest of the installation. The only means of entry from inside the base was through this single interior corridor.

Statglass ports had been set at intervals into the right wall of the corridor, giving passerbys a view of part of the local proving ground. The view was largely uninformative, because that was the zone where certain tests and experiments deemed too energetic and dangerous for any indoor venue were carried out. As

Harry had also noted on his approach, it was an airless wilderness of black sky, almost empty space and grayish rock thousands of cubic kilometers in extent, running along one slab-sided flank of this angular wanderworld. All its borders were clearly marked by navigational aids that stood out boldly on the holostages of ships entering the system.

Striding down an internal corridor between the professor and their host, going to see the show, Harry could see certain indications of high security in place, and he could feel, as always when he was getting close to a Trophy Room, tension in the air. As usual, his own heartbeat quickened.

He had visited some similar establishments where full-body armor was required on everyone who entered. The rules here were not quite that strict. But as the three men approached the end of the covered corridor, Harry observed a pair of heavily armed young Templars standing guard, at parade rest in full combat armor, helmets closed. They were standing with their backs to the approaching people, facing the doorway leading to the inner lab, focussing their attention in that direction. That door was colored red and surrounded by serious warning signs. Guarding against external attack was not the prime concern of people pulling this assignment. Instead, they were intent on seeing that the dangerous entities being housed and investigated in the lab remained securely inside it. Sentry duty at a Trophy Room was not a job to be performed casually or haphazardly, though the captive bad guys had of course been stripped of all hardware that might qualify as efficient weaponry, and deprived of power beyond the amount required for testing. Testing here was focused on the capabilities of berserker brains; the auxiliary hardware, once definitely separated from anything like an optelectronic brain or control system, was generally looked at elsewhere.

Briskly returning the guards' salute, the abbot led Harry and the professor on through the red door and into the domed space, big enough to have housed a village, as privileged guests. Harry looked around in appreciation; he had never before been in a Trophy Room this big. Here and there were details confirming that this structure must once have been a spaceship hangar.

Darchan was pointing to the far wall of the cavernous room, where the outer hull of the captured courier was displayed—they had gone to the trouble of skinning it like a trophy snake. The length was fifty or sixty meters of scorched and battered metal, the unrolled partial diameter at least half that much. Glowing symbols, laser-painted, outlined the spots from which certain components had been removed.

Avoiding the lift that would have carried them to the statglass-windowed observation gallery on an upper level, the abbot led his two favored guests to a forcefield platform that gently lowered the three of them right down into the pit. The center of the dome was sunken several meters below the level of the rocky ground outside. The whole dome glowed with gentle light, making the arena ideal for human observation.

The broad floor was surfaced with some flaky-looking composite material, but Harry had the irrational feeling that it ought to be sand or sawdust, as if in some primitive barroom, or, more likely, a gladiatorial arena. He supposed that the actual flakes, as of some kind of cleaning compound, could serve the same end of easy cleanup and disposal.

The suggestion was that those in charge expected things to get messy here. Then the cleaning machines would have an easy job of it, simply removing the whole top layer.

A couple of human techs, or more likely engineers, fitted in protective suits and gloves, their faces protected by clear shields, small tools in their hands, were busily at work on today's guest of honor. Harry and the other visitors put on shields and gloves before approaching.

Here, the abbot and his two honored visitors were able to stand almost within arm's length of the rack on which the most important components of the captured enemy were pinioned. The rack itself was but little bigger than any ordinary dining table, and had been constructed partly of what looked like simple, natural wood. Some of the enemy's intimate parts exposed on it were crystalline, and some metallic, while yet another category consisted of mere blurry little globs of force, flickering in and out of existence somewhat faster than the human eye and mind could follow.

This was a much smaller selection of key components, in volume probably not enough to make an adult human body. The collection included no type of hardware that Harry had not seen before, yet he could hardly take his eyes off it. The whole made a brightly lighted display, spread out over a space not more than a couple of meters square.

In midair, just a couple of meters above the rack,

there glowed a full-sized schematic image, showing what had been discovered so far. The inner workings looked infernally complicated. Some components were dark and some were bright, some looked almost familiar in terms of ED human technology, and some did not.

The colonel-abbot felt constrained to apologize once more to his guests for being unable to give them any details as to how this particular enemy unit had been captured—all that was highly classified. He spoke to Harry in an apologetic tone. "I have promised, under oath, you see."

Harry once more assured his host that he understood how such things were managed. Gianopolous merely nodded, as if amused at the abbot's taking such rules and restrictions so very seriously.

But the civilian Gianopolous felt free to wax enthusiastic regarding the latest interrogation methods.

Harry groaned inwardly; the inventor was turning out to be one of those people who had to be an expert on everything. They were as wearing as tough guys, though usually easier to shut up.

Abbot Darchan was going on: "Since the beginning of human history, the interrogation of prisoners has always been considered something of an art. And we are carrying the art to new heights."

Gianopolous was reverting to arrogance. "Ah, excuse me, but hasn't the interrogation of prisoners always come down to threats and punishment?"

Harry put in: "Not in this game we're playing now. Nobody's yet figured out a way to torture a berserker."

Gianopolous raised an eyebrow and looked smug; *maybe I have*, he seemed to be implying. *No doubt that I could if I really tried. Anyone want to give me a contract?*

Abbot Darchan was answering the inventor in his own way. "Relying on such crude methods is a mistake. Of course, by those means it is almost always possible to induce any human prisoner to tell you what he believes you want to hear. But the value of information obtained in such a way is rather limited. And of course, as Harry says, threats and punishment are as meaningless to a berserker as to any other machine."

"What method do you use here, then? Argument?" The last word bore a load of sarcasm.

But the abbot accepted the question at face value. "That would hardly do. No, the optelectronic brain is much less subtle, much more vulnerable to direct investigation than the organic brain, which is a thousand times more complicated. The methods we use here come down to basic techniques, carefully applied. The measurement of voltages and other optelectronic qualities, a deciphering of the code of information."

Harry was still looking around. "You've made this place into a real arena," he observed.

"Precisely what it is." A new aspect of the abbot's character was coming into view, he seemed to be quietly expressing some real hatred. "Here the dark forces are momentarily given free rein, the chance to be very active. We must know our enemy if we are ultimately going to defeat it—and we must do that, or it will wipe us out. No third outcome is ultimately possible.

"If you deprive one of these obscenities of its functions gradually, weaken it a little at a time, the hope is that it will never fully realize what's going on, and it will never employ what powers it can still exert to destroy its own memory, or scramble all the information. Because doing so would deprive it of useful tools when next it had the chance to kill."

There was a stirring of movement visible in the upper gallery, a section elevated behind a statglass wall. Harry looked up to see that a class of ten or twelve Templar officer acolytes, people the Space Force would have called cadets, clad in the simple robes/uniforms of Templar novices, with first-year tabs on their uniform collars, had been brought in to stand looking down into the pit from behind a thick statglass barrier. Almost certainly this would be the first time that any of them had been able to get a direct look at the enemy they had sworn to fight.

Some kind of communication channel was evidently open, because a murmur of restrained conversation came drifting faintly down to the lower level of the broad arena floor where the techs and visitors were standing.

Great care had already been taken that at this point, the berserker's circuits had been extensively disconnected, shorted out, disrupted to the point where the remaining central intelligence was stone deaf and blind. Soon that would be remedied.

Either the instructor above or the abbot below, the latter probably with the thought of monitoring how well his teacher taught, did something that brought the instructor's voice down from the sealed gallery into the pit.

" . . . basically three ways a berserker can react when it realizes that it's been captured—or is about to be. Who can tell me what they are? Yes?"

Harry was watching and listening now. The class, who all appeared to be nearly the same age, looked back, showing the usual assortment of student reactions, from smug to bewildered to absent. Male and female wore their hair in the same simple style. For the males, facial hair was under current rules forbidden.

The first hand raised was that of a fresh-faced girl. "It can blow itself up."

The instructor nodded routine approval. "Yes, or melt itself down, if it incorporates a self-destructor device, as the great majority of them do. You must expect any and all of their machines to be equipped with something of that nature. Today's subject had one, but our people were skilled enough, and lucky enough to be able to disable it.

"Self-destruction is possibility number one, and we have to consider it the most likely. But it could be fatal to ignore the other choices an enemy might make." He nodded toward an eager face. "Yes?"

This novice was ready with a different answer. "It might play dead."

"Correct! As you might expect, they can do that very convincingly. A variation on that theme is to attempt an imitation of some innocent machine, one that is perhaps temporarily out of order.

"It's very important to keep that possibility constantly in mind. A berserker having chosen that mode might remain in it for a year, or if necessary for a hundred years, while to a casual examination appearing totally inert. Then, when it detected a substantial life form, preferably a human, within striking range—sudden death."

There was a moment of silence.

"I said there were three basic possibilities." The teacher looked around, but it appeared no one was ready to complete the trio.

"Option number three is what I like to call the mode of just keeping busy. Keeping its hand in, as it were. Microscopic organisms make up the vast majority of the Galaxy's living things—there may be ten to the thirtieth power of them on an average habitable planet. And they are to be found in a great variety of environments. If a death machine has the tools to detect them and kill them—and it very likely does—it may simply keep on with simple killing until it exhausts its remaining power, or has sterilized its environment as far as it can reach, or until some better target, like an ED human who is not fully alert, presents itself."

Harry's attention had shifted back to the actual berserker on the rack. The technicians, murmuring a few words of jargon back and forth between themselves, were well along in the process of detaching the separated modules from the rack and fitting them back together in a more compact form. Harry could see where the courier's brain, or a large part of it, was going to go. Around it a new body was taking shape, vastly smaller and simpler than the massive hardware provided by its original designers. Most of the parts of this new incarnation were of human manufacture, color-coded to show their origin.

Harry watched as the strange, alien form took shape under the techs' careful hands. It vaguely resembled a scooter, as yet lacking wheels, of a convenient size for some ED human to be able to stand on and ride. Now the empty rack, on which the half-dissected enemy had been pinioned like some huge exotic insect, was being raised up out of the testing space, to disappear behind a panel in the dome. Harry knew regret that the damned thing could feel no pain, no terror. But maybe it felt something analogous to sickness. He could at least hope for that.

Something the instructor in the upper gallery was saying caught at Harry's attention, and he looked that way again.

"The bad machines of course operate their own extensive intelligence and counterintelligence systems; unfortunately, there are always people ready to turn goodlife. The berserkers study Earth-descended humanity at least as intensely as we study them. There's no doubt they have rooms analogous to this one, where human prisoners are tested. Where the different layers, the different modes of human memory are searched, probably by methods of gradual disassembly similar to . . ."

"What is it, Harry?" the abbot was asking, sounding faintly concerned, while the instructor's voice droned on.

"Never mind. Nothing." He took a deep breath, and made an effort, and was standing still again.

One of the most recent refinements of interrogation and discovery technique involved keeping the subject device concentrated on an activity down near its most basic level of programming: finding a way to kill something. There were almost always some life forms within reach, though many of them presented a difficult challenge when the berserker had been deprived of all sophisticated weapons.

The students' instructor was trying what was doubtless a standard joke. Smiling at the group, he offered: "Therefore, we need a life form to feed the berserker. Any volunteers?" There was a dutiful titter of laughter.

One of the acolytes observed: "Sir, that thing our people are putting together looks like it can't even move."

"It will move, adequately for our purposes, when they've finished. The technicians are now adding the final touches—there are the wheels—restoring some mobility, of course in a vastly different mode than what the device originally possessed."

Two small wheels had appeared, one mounted straight behind the other, as on a children's scooter. A pair of hardware arms, of a size to fit a human toddler, were also being attached, in the place of steering grips or handlebars. Each arm came equipped with a matching four-fingered hand, also small, reinforcing the impression of a child's robotic toy.

"Where will they put the brain?" one of the acolytes was asking.

"We're on our way to getting the central computer put back together—with just a few small omissions. It'll occupy that box near the top, where the steering handles would sprout out if there was a human rider."

". . . mobility will be restricted to just a little low-speed rolling instead of space travel. We have already stripped away courier functions, and are now reenabling the basic brain to move and act, within the limits imposed by the diminished body. The trick is to allow just enough capability to provide us with the data that we're looking for."

The human engineers who had been working hands-on seemed in need of a bit more room, so the abbot stepped back, motioning his two guests with him. This partial reassembly of the machine would give the restored brain more choices, allow it the possibility of planning. The process was quickly accomplished.

Or was it? The new arms tightly fastened on and so were the small wheels, but it seemed the human engineers were not quite finished after all. One of them was dabbing at the subject with a small stick or brush in one gloved hand, while holding a small flask in the other.

"What's he up to?" Gianopolous wondered aloud, forgetting for the moment his pose of omniscience.

The abbot's answer came in a low whisper. "He's painting it with a bit of fresh animal blood, just enough to give it an appropriate scent."

The professor's jaw dropped slightly. "In the name of all that's chaotic, why?"

"You'll see, in a moment." The abbot looked around. "Now we must get out of here."

Suddenly all the humans were evacuating the lower, arena level, getting up out of the pit. A scattering of flashing red lights appeared, and an audio warning began to hoot. The abbot made a point of being the last to leave the level of the arena floor, making sure that he had shepherded everyone else ahead of him.

In moments they had joined the other watchers in the upper gallery, where students deferentially made way.

Not until the abbot and his guests had ringside seats was the monster released from the rack, and one of its power cells restored to allow it some physical activity, of course at a vastly restricted level of power and energy.

"We must not reduce its capabilities too much, of course. Otherwise it will sense its own absolute weakness, and probably play dead. We will learn little or nothing."

The innocent-looking berserker/scooter swayed upright, a simple gyro mechanism allowing it to balance easily on its two small wheels. Its first controlled movement was a slow turn in place, evidently trying, with partially restored faculties, to take the measure of this new and simplified environment. After that it began to move in a large circle, at a creeping pace. Within half a minute it was slowly making its way around the arena, remaining close to the steady curve of boundary wall, probing the limits of this new world with dimmed-down senses. Only once did it put on a burst of acceleration, evidently testing its capabilities.

Readings from all the onboard telemetry were continually pouring in. "It's still trying to orient itself," the instructor explained. Presumably no sound from the observers' stations could now reach the arena, or at least none that would register on the subject's attenuated senses.

"It will also," the abbot was saying in a low voice, "be attempting to identify the nature of this unfamiliar environment. And also to deduce some reason for the gaps in its recent memory, and compensate for them as well as possible."

The inventor seemed to be growing fascinated despite himself. "Does it realize that it's a prisoner, undergoing interrogation?"

The abbot shook his head. "We can hope not. But at this point we cannot be sure."

Moments passed. The only sound in the large space was that of the machine's small wheels on the crisply flaky arena floor. A faint scrape and a rattle, clearly audible in the waiting silence, where one of the reassembled parts perhaps was slightly loose.

The scooter had completed nearly one full circle of the arena wall, when it abruptly changed course, taking a straight line across the open space, back to the place where it had first recovered its awareness.

"Now it has some grasp of its new surroundings, and a realization of its diminished powers." The instructor's voice had, perhaps unconsciously, fallen to a whisper. "Time for the next step."

The teacher was telling his class: "We must present this berserker with a challenge. Set it a difficult task, one that will cause it to mobilize all its computing capacity to solve the problem. The idea is not to leave it with any surplus capacity for planning trickery."

"Sir, that sounds difficult."

"It is."

A panel about two meters wide that had been invisible at the base of the curving wall now slid open. A faint murmur went up from the acolytes when they saw the shape that moved out of darkness to fill the opening.

The low growl that the animal gave came as no surprise to Harry, but the beast was larger than he had expected.

Fur had been shaved away in a few places, spots

surrounding the brightly colored plugs or probes of composite material, that had been inserted in several sites on its long skull and along its backbone.

One of the acolytes was making a sound of sympathy, pity, almost of physical pain. No words were formed, but what those words would have been was plain enough: *Oh, the poor animal—*

The abbot immediately frowned, as if he had been expecting this particular objection and had his disapproval ready. "What did you expect, young woman? Feeding it a mouse or a snail, or even a deer, would not gain us much information." Harry remembered that there was a Templar doctrine, a dogma, of being ruthless in the defense of life.

Large, hungry cats or similar predators were considered the best distraction, because they posed the crippled berserker a problem, forcing it to concentrate on overcoming a life-unit's resistance.

The beast was about the size of a mountain lion, but leaner, some genetic variant. Harry wondered if it had somehow been specially bred for this task. Another Templar sideline that he had never come upon before.

The comparatively massive predator had begun to stalk the vehicle that so strongly resembled a child's toy.

The cat moved forward as if under irresistible compulsion, as if it might find the scent of fresh blood overpoweringly attractive. The hungry predator snarled and continued its advance.

The berserker did not crave blood, or meat. Its only want was for the fuel to keep it going, and for something less material than that.

The innocent-looking scooter was somewhat shorter than its live antagonist, and doubtless many kilograms lighter. And the brain controlling the machine was working with a certain disadvantage, in that it could not yet be certain of the strength and toughness of this unaccustomed body that was suddenly all it had to work with.

The scooter's two small arms and their child-sized hands, now raised with fingers spread, reminded Harry of the delicate forearms on a T-rex. That would not be the only resemblance, and certainly not the strongest, but it was the single characteristic of the scooter that even suggested fearsomeness. The metal joints, and the composite panels sheathing the thing's flanks had a fragile, rickety look. If it was going to succeed in harvesting the raging, hungry life in front of it, it would have to improvise some weaponry.

Harry was fascinated. For the moment, the constant pressure of his own loss had been lifted from his mind. What would the damned thing do, what could it do, with the meager tools it had been given? Might it discover some way to drain its modest power supply to produce a terrific electric shock—?

Maybe it would, but that was not the only idea it had come up with. Reaching down along its own flank, stretching one small arm to its maximum extent, the rebuilt berserker was prying off one of its own thin side panels, that were only loosely attached to the vertical column.

The animal closed in with a charge. The berserker raised the thin panel in two hands. The movement appeared clumsy, but before Harry could revise his thinking there was a blur of metal under the bright lights, as if a simple steel frame had turned into a sword, and a splash of fresh, hot blood.

The great cat yowled, and in the next instant it was backing away, moving on three legs while the fourth hung maimed. In the first clash it had been forced on the defensive, its raw wound displaying white broken bone.

The cadets were gasping, murmuring, calling out. The scooter, the panel swinging swordlike in the two small hands, reversed the direction of its slow retreat. It advanced steadily, relentlessly. No doubt it was studying the movements of its crippled adversary. Then presently it charged again. The broad arena had no corners, only the vast oval offering unlimited possibilities of retreat, but no place to hide.

The animal sent up a snarling yowl. It might have managed a limping run, attempting escape on only three legs. But its instinct was to fight back.

The pursuit went on, changing directions. The acolytes were watching, a slightly different expression on each of their twelve faces.

The scooter rolled closer, cleaving to a curving path. Then it darted in, as quickly as it could move, and struck again. A small cloud of dust and flaky fragments rose up from the fight. The snarling outcry of the beast became a sound like nothing Harry had ever heard before.

At one point the lion's powerful hind legs, both still intact, kicked the scooter meters away. Sharp, strong claws tore metal fingers from one of its small hands. But the machine spun back to the attack as soon as its wheels had touched the ground.

Harry's original idea about the electric shock might be proven right—if the machine had been allowed the

ability to reconfigure itself internally. But one shock
did not finish the predator. In another moment it
had turned, reduced at last to trying to flee, and was
trying to get away, with the innocent-looking scooter
snarling after it.

The best pace that the cat could manage now was
more like a crawl than a run.

And all the while the fight went on, the Templar
investigators kept mining data from their probes
embedded in the berserker's brain. One of them kept
letting out short bursts of elated murmuring. "Look
at that sigma interaction! Got it . . ."

The mountain lion turned back once more, snarling
bloody froth. Half a minute later it died, twitching
and convulsing, the little sword-panel had been used
until it broke. Then the machine went in to finish the
job with wheels and hands . . . it was a bloody mess,
and two or three of the acolytes were turning away,
struggling not to be sick.

Harry was not at all surprised to see that the little
robot jeweler's hand, even though half of its metal fingers
had been broken, was still powerful enough to dig one
out of the probes that was still half-buried in the newly
lifeless head of the animal. The cat was motionless at
last, but the machine's work was not yet done.

The child-sized digits, displaying surprising strength,
uprooted the thing, producing one more airborne streak
of blood. Then the scooter's body spun, its short arm
flashed, hurling the dislocated probe with great accuracy
at the nearest spot where its dimmed-down senses had
somehow managed to perceive the ultimate horror. The
horror of swarming life, intelligent, defiant . . .

"*Look* out!"

It was fortunate that the warning was unnecessary, because it came a full second too late.

Every human in the observation gallery had instinctively ducked away. A checkerboard pattern of shock-waves sprang into brief existence all across the broad statglass surface. Over the next few seconds the pattern slowly faded, the tiny squares winking in and out of visibility, to reveal the defensive barrier undamaged.

In the room behind the barrier, a murmur of discordant prayers went up. Templars shared a strong tendency to be religious, but were not all of the same creed.

When there seemed to be no more useful data to be derived from the situation, the reactivated berserker was quietly immobilized, by foam sprayed out of nozzles descending from the roof, foam that hardened quickly into a mass that looked as solid as concrete.

An observer just coming on the scene might have doubted that such a precaution was really necessary. The scooter had collapsed into a startlingly small pile of inert hardware immediately after hurling the probe, having seemingly expended the last of its available power in that effort. Were it not for the streaks and spatterings of blood, it would have regained the look of total innocence, a child's toy broken and abandoned. But no one would be taking any chances. The first approach to the new pile of concrete would be made only by tame robots, and they would be very careful.

The cadets were murmuring softly, sobered by the demonstration. That was part of its purpose.

When the three men had moved on out of the Trophy Room, all of them were at first silently thoughtful.

The abbot was looking expectantly at his guests. He seemed a trifle hurt that neither of them were properly enthusiastic. At last he said: "I think it was a good show, if I do say so myself. I can tell you that we obtained a large volume of data to be analyzed."

"It was." Harry nodded. "A good show."

Professor Gianopolous, looking a touch pale, murmured something about the sight of blood affecting him. Then he immediately excused himself to go to his room. If the show had impressed him in any way, beyond making him sick, he was not inclined to reveal the fact.

The other two watched him out of sight, before slowly starting down the other branch of corridor. Abbot Darchan asked: "What was it you wanted to see Gianopolous about, Harry? If it's any of my business."

"Oh, the project?" Harry found he could be casual. He might have been talking about the last days of someone else's life. "More or less routine. I'm just going to do a little driving. That's my usual job. But thanks for the tour, that was quite a demonstration, even if my mind was elsewhere. And thanks for the warning."

"Yes, Harry, let me emphasize the warning. You watch your back, my lad. I know you've got no nerves, but even so. I admit I'm glad my name is missing from the list. I wouldn't sleep too soundly if I knew that one of those damned things was on my trail, never sleeping, never resting, calculating day and night on how to get at me."

Harry managed a smile for the abbot. He had the feeling it was his first smile in a long time. "That's where you and I are different, pal."

TEN

The abbot, pleading many demands upon his time, was not coming to the hangar to see his visitors off. Harry and Professor Gianopolous, unaccompanied except for a single mildly anthropomorphic robot, were walking another enclosed passageway, this one taking them directly into the giant hangar. The inventor's robotic personal assistant, named Perdix (Harry wasn't going to ask where that name had come from) was following its master at three paces' distance, carrying a fairly substantial amount of baggage. Harry had no porter, but then he didn't need one. His material burden was quite light, consisting of only one traveling bag, small enough to be easily forgotten, that he had brought with him on the courier from 207GST. It contained a single change of clothes, as well as the few personal articles he had managed to accumulate since going to work for Cheng.

❖ ❖ ❖

It was not in Harry's nature to be anything but serious about the job of test pilot. He intended to give the *Secret Weapon* a thorough looking over before he tried to drive it. Harry hadn't heard anyone say what the secret ship's name might be, or even if it had one. But in his own mind he had already christened it with that title.

If he was satisfied with what the inspection showed him, according to the not-too-demanding standards that had been conveyed to him by the coordinator, Harry and the inventor would soon be departing the Templar base.

So far, Harry hadn't mentioned the fact that his sponsor was the Galactic power Winston Cheng, and that Cheng wanted to hire the inventor as a consultant for the tycoon's private space force. He figured he would get around to it soon enough, and there did not seem to be any driving hurry. Gianopolous could play it cool as well. So far, he had not even hinted that he might be anxious to know who was financing this latest party.

Fundamentally, Harry had not much hope for the secret weapon. He could not see how disguising any single piece of hardware, no matter how effectively, was going to make any real difference in the outcome of an attempted raid on a berserker base by a tiny squad of hastily organized militia. Trying to startle the bad machines with a secret weapon, or even hitting them with it, wasn't going to throw them into a panic. Nor were berserkers going to be awed by the reputation of the secret weapon's inventor. The name of Aristotle Gianopolous had been missing from the enemy's roster of murders to be accomplished. Certainly they wouldn't be impressed by how much Gianopolous imagined he knew about everything—to them either genius or charlatan would be just one more errant life-unit, badly in need of reprocessing into safe and satisfactory death. Harry hadn't mentioned the list to him, and he found it hard to guess whether the inventor would have been relieved or angered by his omission.

Harry said: "Let's take a look at what you're offering."

They had reached the vessel, resting in one of about a dozen berths at the Templars' bustling dock, constructed entirely inside an enormous hangar, vaster even than the Trophy Room, which had once served as hangar before this one was built.

Harry was thinking that on his arrival in Cheng's little courier he must have docked within a few meters of the secret weapon without suspecting it was there, or even being aware that its particular berth was occupied.

The entire lean length of Gianopolous's ship—looking closely now, Harry could see it must be something like a hundred meters—was covered with a kind of camouflage tarp, which the professor proudly announced was also of his devising. The tarp was made of some intelligent material that deceptively, slowly and continually, changed the appearance of whatever it was covering, and even seemed to change its shape.

Similar cloaking materials were fairly common, but Harry couldn't remember seeing any quite as lightweight and convincing as this.

"Lift it," Gianopolous suggested. When Harry only looked at him, he smiled his superior smile, and made an encouraging gesture. "Go ahead."

Harry tried and promptly succeeded, his one-handed effort meeting amazingly little resistance. When he raised one edge of the lightweight camouflage, his hand briefly turned into a lumpy projection of the composite material of the dock. Looking beneath, he finally got a good look at the secret weapon. Pulling the covering farther away, he gawked some more. The vessel had been specially built and equipped to look externally very much like one of the smaller standard models of berserker spacecraft.

It took a real mental effort for Harry to make himself reach out and touch the hull, while trained-in instinct was clamoring for his body to back away.

Meanwhile, the inventor's assistant, Perdix, had started rolling up the camouflage, bringing the entire small ship into clear view. With robotic neatness Perdix was folding and packing it into a compact bundle. Perdix was vaguely male, nothing nearly as lifelike as Dorijen.

"Yeah, maybe," Harry muttered. "We can hope. Where's the entry hatch?"

Gianopolous smirked. "Bet you can't find it."

"Bet I'm not going to play games."

That got rid of the smirk for the time being. The look of restrained and noble suffering that replaced it was almost as irritating.

The entrance to the main airlock was indeed quite cleverly concealed, in the space between two squat imitation beam-projector turrets. Once admitted to the ship's interior, Harry went through the accessible compartments, looking things over. He maintained a fairly rapid pace, but he was thorough, and in no hurry. All of the weaponry currently installed appeared to be fake, boiler plate and quaker cannons installed to aid the engineering of the overall design. As long as there was no need to use it, this hardware could also provide a convincing imitation of standard berserker gear. But with Winston Cheng's resources, what was lacking ought to be readily suppliable. Again, as always, there was the nagging question of how much time battle preparation was going to take.

Half an hour later, when Harry had finished a preliminary inspection of the entire vessel, he told Gianopolous: "Very convincing. But you must find it a little dangerous to drive around in this thing. Every time you enter an inhabited system, the automated defenses must—"

"Ah, but you see, it doesn't have this appearance, visually or on any observer's holostage, when I, as you put it, drive around. It won't look like this when you and I deliver it to your mysterious patron."

Harry frowned. "What will it look like?"

"Nothing that would interest any ED defense. Come back to the control room, I'll show you." Now Gianopolous's triumphant look was back, that of a master of secret knowledge.

Harry was soon given a brief look at how the special shape-changing equipment worked.

It really was impressive. Very much so. What had looked, and even felt, like solid elements of the hull had now shifted into new shapes and new positions, changing visual size and contour and even the texture of their surfaces. No more a Type-B berserker, but a nondescript, more or less standard model courier or utility boat. The apparent type was now one barely capable of interstellar travel, that would be riskier and slower in that mode than the vessels humans usually employed.

Then, in less than a standard minute, Gianopolous and his well-trained cadre of onboard computers orchestrated the shift back to berserker shape. Inside the control room and the crew quarters, the only visible change was in certain readings on the flight instruments. These assured the humans inside that the transformation was complete. Harry opened a hatch and went out of the ship and stood on the dock to confirm the transformation, which from that viewpoint certainly looked convincing. In the middle distance, a small assortment of Templars had paused in whatever they were supposed to be doing, to watch the show.

Harry went back in through the hatch, to confront the silent, beaming triumph of the man now occupying the pilot's chair.

"The illusion will hold for any kind of radar, for . . . ?"

"Of course. For any test, for any probe the enemy might use, short of actual physical contact."

"You can do the conversion both ways while in flight?"

"Of course." Gianopolous, his spirits fully recovered, was ready once more to sing the praises of his own invention: "Otherwise I have the devil's own time, I can tell you, approaching any Templar base with it. Each time one must go through a slow, painstaking process of convincing the defenses I'm not what I appear to be. Same goes for the Force, of course. All automated defenses insist the shape is that of a berserker, no matter what identifying signals I present."

Harry let himself down slowly on the copilot's couch. The foundation of some of his recent thinking had shifted, leaving him looking at things from a different viewpoint. His mind was suddenly too busy with important things to care whether the inventor smirked or not. "I take it you haven't actually tried sneaking up on any berserkers yet."

Gianopolous was content to answer that with a mysterious smile. But naturally he would have recorded any such encounter, had it taken place—and he would certainly be boasting of it.

Eventually Harry had concluded his preflight check, and the two of them were getting ready to lift off from the Templar base. In the dome overhead, the inner curtain of the enormous forcefield airlock scrolled back.

A minute later, the ship was outside the dome and they were on their way, with Harry in the pilot's seat.

Apart from the familiar pilot's and copilot's chairs, and attached helmets, the control room had an idiosyncratic layout. It also contained a fair amount of equipment that Harry at first glance could not identify.

"That, of course, will be the real test, Harry. The moment of truth. But there are some valid preliminary experiments that could be made."

"Such as what?"

"Not, of course, by approaching any machine that realized it was being held in captivity—like the little drama we just witnessed in the Templar temple. That would undercut the validity of any results that might be achieved."

The inventor paused briefly, sighing. "Until very recently, Harry, I had nursed hopes of persuading the

Templars to graciously provide me with a fully active berserker for such a test."

Harry was staring at him. Then he shook his head. "Don't hold your breath until that happens. If I know Templars, Darchan and his people are never going to risk turning any active berserker loose, letting it get out of their control. No. But just possibly, if you had asked for some crippled, disabled unit, something like what we saw today . . ."

"No. Out of the question. It would be utterly useless for my purposes."

Not only was Harry by nature disinclined to salesmanship, but he realized it would be difficult to do any recruiting without letting the subject know what kind of operation he would be consulting for. Harry decided that if a reasonable chance came up during the drive to 207GST, he would put in a good word for Cheng as an employer. If not, he would leave the salesmanship to those back on the base who were psychologically better equipped to handle that kind of thing.

Gianopolous was showing signs of optimism for a change. He seemed glad, perhaps even a touch eager, to give Harry a tour of his special ship. Emil Darchan was a skilled pilot in his own right. And Harry was interested in finding out why the abbot, after making a series of inspections and flight tests, all presumably aided by a crew of Templar experts, had decided not to grab the secret weapon for his own organization.

Maybe, Harry thought, despite Emil's protests of secrecy, he should have tried to pump his old friend for more information.

But at the moment he had to deal with the inventor. Harry never cared for trying to find things out by dropping subtle hints. "Why didn't the Templars want this ship?" he asked bluntly.

Professor Gianopolous was unperturbed. "Oh, I wouldn't say they didn't want it."

"Well, they didn't take it."

Gianopolous was silent.

Harry found it irritating to be ignored. "Did they ever make you an offer? Or maybe they thought you were asking too much?"

Now the inventor turned on him with a haughty look. "Harry, look—are you empowered by your employer to conclude a deal, including the financial terms?"

"No, not at all. I'm just a test pilot."

Gianopolous smiled his superior smile. "Then, with all due respect, I prefer to reserve my discussion of money matters until I can talk to the people who make decisions.

"As for the Templars, let's just say there were were certain difficulties, or the Templar bureaucrats believed there were. In the end, we could not agree on terms. Who can fathom the ways of a bureaucracy?"

Harry let it go at that. He was thankful that negotiation was not his job. The man seemed disinclined to talk about anything except how great his ship was, and how great he was to have invented it. How much of all the spouting had any relation to the truth would not be easy to determine.

Gianopolous was proud of his creation—as well he might be, Harry thought. "What you see is actually the easy part of the transformation—it's in the communication codes, the identification of friend or foe, where I have surpassed all previous human efforts."

Harry grunted. If someone could really fake a Type-B berserker as effectively as this—then he didn't see why it should be impossible for someone to imitate a Type-A as well. Maybe, with a somewhat greater effort and investment, to convincingly fake an entire berserker attack.

"Anything wrong, Silver?"

"I'm not sure . . ." Then Harry asked suddenly: "This ship won't imitate a Type-A, will it?"

Gianopolous drew himself up, as if Harry had asked whether all this noble hardware could make popcorn. The inventor sounded vaguely injured. "As a matter of fact it can—I was planning to demonstrate that later."

"Sorry if I forced your hand," Harry muttered, staring at the bulkhead in front of him.

"What is it, Silver?"

"Nothing. Never mind. Just let me think for a minute." Now looming foremost in his thoughts was a small pile of scrap parts, fragments retrieved near the place where Becky and Ethan had been grabbed. Even if this ship could somehow have been fitted with real weapons, used to imitate a real berserker for the purpose of his family's kidnapping, whoever worked the scheme must also have been able, somehow, to commandeer a squad of genuine berserker boarding machines, or impeccable imitations, to do the actual kidnapping.

It was maddening. Here and there, now and then, a couple of pieces of the puzzle looked like they might fit together. But still none of it really made sense.

Harry swept his gaze around the modest interior space of the control room. If a squad of such near-anthropomorphic killers had ever been aboard this vessel they were certainly gone now. Well, he was going to be conducting a thorough inspection of the ship, as a purchaser's test pilot had every right to do. He wasn't going to find a berserker, but there might be . . . something.

He had the sensation of edging close to some kind of revelation. It stirred unsettling hopes, even while the nature of what that epiphany might be remained obscure.

He pressed Gianopolous: "And this is your only model? I mean, you don't have another working prototype anywhere? Like a berserker boarding machine, for instance?"

The inventor seemed remotely hurt by the suggestion. "No, sir, I do not. If you had any conception of the amount of time, effort, and expense that have gone into the creation of this ship, you would not ask."

"And no one else is building anything like this—doing this kind of thing."

"That no one else is imitating berserkers successfully seems a safe bet, my friend. No one else in this sector of the Galaxy, certainly, or in either of those adjoining." Gianopolous paused. "Your patron will not be able to buy this more cheaply from anyone else. Indeed, I think he will not get even a poor imitation elsewhere at any price."

Harry grunted. Saving his patron money had been about the furthest idea from his thoughts.

Gianopolous seemed to enjoy the idea of getting acquainted with Harry, who in his own offbeat way was also something of a minor celebrity, and he seemed to want to adopt Harry as an ally. The inventor was also glad to have a more or less sympathetic ear into which he could pour his disappointment and outrage over the cool reception that all the major organizations had so far given him and his ideas. Harry had finally revealed the identity of their sponsor, though not the specific nature of the planned project, and the revelation had boosted his passenger's self-esteem to a new level. A deal with Winston Cheng, when it could be publicly announced, would serve as powerful vindication for the scorned inventor.

"Hah. I have been assured so often that what I have already done is quite impossible, that anyone else would have been discouraged."

Everyone who knew Harry knew that he, too, tended to fit the model of the eccentric outsider. And such was his reputation.

Perhaps they had been traveling for an hour or so when Harry, nagged by a sense of duty unperformed, finally came out with his sales pitch—if his half-hearted effort could be called that. He had already revealed his sponsor's name—the coordinator had assumed he would have to do that, once matters had progressed this far.

"I can tell you this much. It's likely that Winston Cheng is going to try to talk you into taking a job with him. As some kind of a consultant."

"Ah." Though Gianopolous tried to conceal it, he gave the impression of being pleased at being invited to play in such a big league. Or maybe it was just the vision of vast amounts of money about to come his way. He asked: "You've heard this from the great man himself?"

"That's right. Matter of fact I've talked to him several times in the last few days." That certainly made an impression, though Gianopolous was struggling not to show it. Harry didn't bother to explain that talking to the great man was no marvelous sign of favor. Cheng might have some reputation as a recluse, but in this emergency he talked freely to everyone who might be of help. Nodding, he assured the professor: "Your name came up more than once."

The inventor announced, as if he were gracefully granting some concession, that he was glad to have Harry traveling with him aboard his ship, that he felt confident they could reach an agreement on the final details regarding sale of his ship, and that he might be willing to accept the rather mysterious job offer from Harry's employer.

Harry was a superb pilot, and perhaps even Gianopolous was content to have Harry drive his special ship rather than preferring to settle the pilot's helmet on his own head.

"You know, Silver, I think the maneuverability is actually improved with you at the controls." Gianopolous sounded faintly surprised. But for someone in whose importance he was gradually beginning to believe, like Harry, he was willing to condescend to be gracious.

Harry made a sound indicating insincere surprise. "People tell me I sometimes have that effect. Well, it's not hard to drive. It's a good ship."

The inventor offered what he probably intended to be a winning smile, but his face wasn't quite designed for that. "The truth is, though I do well enough at the controls when I put my mind to it, I don't really enjoy the job. Often I prefer to just turn on the autopilot, tell my ship where I want to go, and sit back to take a nap or think about something else."

Harry mumbled something. He often preferred to use that method himself. It would almost always get you where you wanted to go, and usually without too much delay. But for the sake of speed and efficiency at all times, and to improve the chance of survival in a variety of unusual conditions, space combat being the classic example, it was better to have a skilled human brain in the control loop as well.

Gianopolous didn't want to let it drop. "The truth is, Silver, I'm subject at times to a touch of space sickness. Especially when the ports are cleared in flight-space—you won't mind if we keep them closed?"

Harry looked up. "There are one or two tests that will require a brief clearing. I'll let you know, and you can clear out of the control room."

"Thank you."

ELEVEN

S till Harry had never heard the inventor refer to Cheng's prospective purchase by any name other than "my ship" or "my invention." Harry found this vaguely disturbing, and in his own mind had christened the vessel with his own private choice, *Secret Weapon*. Not imaginative, but practical. He had yet to try the name on anyone else.

Crew quarters on the *Weapon* were fairly small, even for a small ship, but still the cabin space was more than adequate for two people. Any Templars or other visitors who might have been hinting that they could use a ride somewhere had been blandly ignored, and Harry was misleading about the direction he was going next.

Gianopolous expressed his relief that there were going to be no additional passengers. He said he didn't want any more Templars poking their noses aboard, trying to copy this ship's secrets without paying for them.

"You think they want to do that?" Harry asked.

"A lot of people would." For a moment the inventor looked gloomy. "Too many people have seen it already."

Harry paused in his inspection of an empty locker. "I thought you said only a couple of Templars had been aboard—was there anybody else?"

"No—oh no. In my work I use robot assistants exclusively. The memories of all but Perdix were wiped clean afterward."

Harry glanced across the cabin at Perdix, who was waiting with a robot's usual perfect imperturbability, and had no comment.

Gianopolous was going on about the Templars and their inadequacies. At the Templar base only the abbot and two of his advisers, one technical and one financial, had ever come on board. And only Abbot Darchan himself, and one other Templar pilot, had been at the controls. "No one else has ever tested it." It seemed a reluctant admission.

Harry tried to make his questions casual. "Were Darchan and his people a long time about their testing? It seems to have taken them a while to make up their minds."

"They ran some tests in their proving ground, to begin with. Then Darchan actually did one solo flight of five days."

"That seems a long time."

"He had some kind of urgent meeting to attend, halfway across the sector—I got the impression he needed to report in person to the Superior General—and making the journey in my ship allowed him to accomplish two tasks at the same time."

"If he had the ship for as long as five days I assume that you went with him."

The inventor hesitated briefly. "Actually I didn't. He went alone."

"Oh?"

Gianopolous seemed vaguely embarrassed. "He was rather eager about it, I thought. Seemed to welcome the chance to get off by himself for a while. And the truth is that I have a certain difficulty with some of the maneuvers involved in what they consider necessary testing."

"By difficulty you mean like the space sickness you mentioned." Flightspace could do things to susceptible people even with all the viewports turned opaque.

The other bristled slightly. "There can be more than simple nausea involved—as you know."

"Oh, I know."

Gianopolous was going on, as if he had suddenly thought of an explanation that sounded better than mere weakness on his part: "Also I'd been granted the freedom of the Templar library, their magnificent collections, and opportunities like that don't come along too often. So I preferred to make use of my time in a different way."

"I see. And could you pin that five-day period down exactly? I have a reason for asking."

Gianopolous could, and did. The continual sickness in the pit of Harry's stomach, that had been starting to go away, came back. Right in the middle of that short stretch of time was centered the terrible hour in which Harry's life had been destroyed. On that day the *Secret Weapon*, that could imitate a Type-B well enough to fool an expert witness, had not after all been docked on a Templar base, where hundreds of people would have known if it had moved. Instead it had been off in deep space somewhere, maybe as far as two days gone, the gods of space knew exactly where, with Abbot Darchan the only human being on board.

Emil Darchan, sworn enemy of berserkers and their dedicated hunter. Harry's old friend, with no possible reason in the world to want to do him any harm.

And at the same time, Del Satranji had also been alone somewhere in space. No telling, really, exactly where, but out of sight of everyone—and, according to the logs, alone in a very different ship.

"Anything wrong, Harry?"

"Only everything . . . no, there's nothing the matter with your ship here. It looks fine." He thumped his palm on a control console.

Coincidence again? Or something going on behind the scenes.

Again Harry thought, or tried to think. Then he shook his head. He asked: "You never even tried to sell your invention to the Space Force? They would seem to be your most likely customers."

"I did have some preliminary discussions with one of their generals." The inventor mentioned a woman's name that Harry vaguely recognized, without knowing anything particularly good or bad about her. "Or I should say I tried to. That was standard months ago, almost a year. The Space Force bureaucracy is beyond belief, far surpassing even the Templars'."

Looking back with the benefit of a fair amount of experience with both organizations, Harry was inclined to agree. Of course a lot depended on how and where and by whom the far-flung Force was approached; but he wasn't going to debate the point.

He had to ask once more: "But only the Templars have ever done any actual testing?"

"Yes, and on the dates that I've just told you." That answer was a trifle sharp.

With Harry nodding in acknowledgment, Gianopolous went on railing against the blindness and general fatuity of large organizations. He spoke with some pride of how he had built his vessel, remodeling a fairly standard hull and engines into the precise shape he wanted, with no human helpers on the scene at all. He had tried hard for secrecy, and Harry was thinking that perhaps he had succeeded all too well.

Once Harry had fitted on the pilot's helmet and began to get himself attuned to the subtle idiosyncrasies of its optelectronic circuits, and was thinking purely as a pilot, he soon revised upward his first estimate of the ship. He could sense the presence of extra capabilities, most of them probably having to do with refinements of disguise, but it was not time yet to begin to check out such peripherals. It was essential to make sure of all the basics first. The extras, including the maneuvers in flightspace that Gianopolous was so anxious to avoid, could wait for a more formal test flight—if the upcoming confrontation with metallic death allowed time for such things.

Ordinarily Harry would have wanted any piece of

hardware to undergo very thorough testing before he took it into combat—but this mission was indeed a special case. If this ship served well enough to get an assault force to the enemy base, then doubtless that was all they'd need from it.

Harry spent a lot of the trip back to 207GST in the pilot's chair, often sitting with his eyes closed, hands clasped, fingers interlaced, over his flat abdomen. There was nothing particularly exotic about the mechanics of flying this ship, or its internal communications between computer pilot and human brain. Nothing to suggest the image of a killing machine. It was hard to remember that from the outside, the perception of human or robotic observers was very different.

. . . stretched out in one of the small crew cabins, he had a difficult dream of Becky, in which she was angrily trying to tell him something. But there was so much background noise, coming from some mysterious machine, that he could never manage to hear what she was saying . . .

Up and out of the pilot's combat couch again. Every compartment that Harry entered in Gianopolous's ship, he kept looking for some mark, some oddity, that could suggest, or lightly hinted, that this craft might somehow have been connected with one or both of the kidnappings. But the possibilities were slim, and soon exhausted.

There was a fair amount of vacant cargo space—the waiting assault team would have good use for that.

Harry was coming back into the small control room when he saw that the robot Perdix, in the course of keeping things tidy, had picked up an odd small object. Harry had last seen its like back on Cascadia. It was a kind of ligature, the kind of thing a paddy sometimes used to tie people without causing injury, or that kidnappers might find very handy in their business.

"What's that?"

Wordlessly Perdix handed the thing over. Harry bent the narrow, springy strip to and fro, and ran it through his fingers. It was hard to think of any way an engineer or test pilot might find such an item useful. It might be used to tie small tools or spare parts together, or bundle someone's lunch. But none of those ideas seemed to make a lot of sense.

It finally occurred to Harry that the strip, used as a handcuff, might have been left over from some human's sessions with sex robots—or with another human being, for that matter. Not that you would have to bind a robot for any reason that he could see—it would always cheerfully obey a simple order to hold still.

Holding the thin strip between thumb and forefinger, Harry turned to Gianopolous. "What do you use this for?"

The professor stared with what seemed honest blankness. "I can't remember ever seeing it before. If it is what it appears to be, I would say that it suggests bondage, and that sort of activity holds no attraction for me. One of the Templars perhaps left it aboard."

"Wouldn't have thought they'd be much into bondage either."

"Ah, I'm not so sure about that." The inventor gave his little smile. "One hears stories . . ."

"Yeah, one always hears stories. Maybe there was someone else on board, that you forgot to mention?"

Gianopolous showed irritation. "I keep telling you there hasn't been anyone else. Whatever the purpose for which your Mister Winston Cheng wants this ship . . . well, I do not care to know that purpose. I suppose that he has devised some way for it to afford him a secret advantage over his competitors, whoever they may be. As for the Templars, I shouldn't be surprised if warped minds are fairly common in that group."

Harry grunted. "Probably no more there than anywhere else. And he's not my Mister Winston Cheng. I don't much want anything to do with him. I won't, once this thing is over."

Gianopolous leaned a little closer. "Harry, I find myself becoming genuinely intrigued. What is 'this thing' exactly, for which my ship is wanted? Isn't it time to open up a bit?"

Harry thought it over, shook his head. "I'd better let the boss handle that, in his own way. Along with the finances. It should all make a package."

Several more hours had passed, with the ship for the most part cruising on autopilot—that too was part of the test flight—when Harry, who had been mainly just observing, shucked off the pilot's helmet and stood up and stretched and moved around. Gianopolous, in the other chair, had nodded off to sleep.

Yes, there were some strange gadgets on this boat. And some odd but minor deficiencies as well, things he'd noticed on his first walk through. Harry made his way aft, into another compartment.

For one thing, there was a definite lack of medirobots,

which struck Harry as rather odd . . . here was where he had noticed, on his first go round, an alcove where the presence of the usual connections suggested that two ordinary coffin-sized medirobots might once have been installed.

Few vessels of any size at all lifted off on an interstellar voyage without at least one medirobot on board, insurance against emergencies, and that would go double when a ship was still in the test-flight stage. At least a couple of such machines seemed a minimum requirement on a ship like this one.

Returning to the control room, he noted that the professor was now awake, and commented: "No medirobots on board."

The other only nodded. "I've done without a lot of frills. The connections are all in place for two units; in fact I believe the Templars made a temporary installation as part of their test program."

It would seem only reasonable to have aboard more than one medirobot, when your next planned mission was to carry an irregular crew of semiprofessional commandos into a desperate fight. But, thought Harry, there must be some spare units stored among the plentiful supplies of hardware at 207GST, just waiting to be brought aboard some ship and installed. Apart from the practical certainty of casualties among the attacking team, any prisoners they did manage to rescue were probably going to need a medirobot apiece, and more likely an entire hospital.

Looking at it realistically, to predict that the raiders were going to need medirobots, or hospital care, was taking a very optimistic view of their probable condition when the fight was over. Of course being realistic in this matter was not a good idea, because then you would have to think about the probable condition of any prisoners the upcoming raid might succeed in discovering . . .

"What's wrong, Silver?"

"Nothing."

Suddenly Harry was afraid, not that he would fail to find his wife and son, but that he would succeed. And when he had found her and the boy he would have to look at what the enemy had done to them . . .

Harry and the inventor completed an outwardly uneventful return to the advance base on WW 207GST. The small ship, quite ordinary except in its appearance, cruised swiftly on autopilot and in its innocent unarmed civilian mode.

Both the defensive systems and the people at the base on 207GST had been fully alerted to expect the arrival of Gianopolous's unorthodox ship. Still, Harry and the inventor experienced some difficulty convincing the wanderworld's automated defenses that they were really on the side of humanity and of the angels.

Everyone who had been waiting for Harry's return showed relief when their two unimpeachably human faces actually appeared, climbing out of the ship's concealed hatch into the comfortable atmosphere of berth Number One.

Gianopolous, riding the copilot's seat on approach, had, in one of the last phases of testing, taken the controls from Harry and shifted his vessel briefly into its mode of berserker disguise. Even though the people on the rock had known what was coming, it still had a notable effect.

Someone told them: "Apart from your private code signal, we couldn't see anything that didn't look like genuine berserker."

Aristotle Gianopolous's mixed reputation had of course preceded him, and he got only a dubious welcome from some of the other people at the base.

But Winston Cheng was already present, and seized the opportunity to have a private talk with the inventor.

While en route, Gianopolous had told Harry he looked forward to some such discussion . . . but when he emerged from it, half an hour later, his hopeful attitude had been replaced by a look of grim resignation. He didn't look like a man who'd just been made wealthy beyond his wildest dreams.

"What's the matter?"

No immediate answer.

"Did you sign a contract?"

"Yes." The inventor's chin was quivering. Now it appeared that anger was going to predominate, though fear was certainly not absent.

"Collect your down payment?"

"Yes! And then . . ."

"Then what?"

"I've just had the nature of this—this insane military adventure—explained to me. It appears certain that my ship is going to be destroyed."

"Oh. Yeah. It's likely. But you went through with the sale."

"Of course I went through with it! At such a price . . ."

Satranji, as chief pilot of Cheng's yacht, was here on the base as long as Cheng himself was here. Satranji now jeered: "Well, man, look at it this way. At last

your ship will get the full test that you've been looking forward to. I bet it'll turn out to be a little slow
on acceleration."

"Yes, a full test . . . and no way to record the
results. I'll have the money to build an improved
model, but how will I know what changes should
be made?"

Once back on the base, Harry found himself frequently staring at the digital clocks and calendars that
Winston Cheng had grown fond of placing everywhere.
Harry wasn't worried about the passage of time, he
was simply having trouble extracting any meaning from
the changing numbers. Time was passing, something
more than a standard month had gone by since Cheng's
people had been swept away, harvested by mechanical
devices, wrenched out of the presence and the lives
of their fellow humans.

Harry's wife and son had been missing for almost
as great a length of time. The only meaning that the
changing time-indicators really had for Harry was that
he was in some sense getting closer and closer to his
woman and their child.

When one of Harry's colleagues casually asked him
something about his future plans, he answered simply
that he wasn't thinking about anything beyond the
raid. He wouldn't let himself imagine, or hope, or
dream, that it might be totally successful.

Louise Newari, making an opportunity to be alone
with Harry, seemed to be sending signals that she
would like to be more friendly with Harry Silver, the
famous pilot who suddenly, to those who knew his
story, had become a tragic figure.

But Harry stayed distant and remote. He was here to do a job. Beyond that he no longer had a life, or wanted one.

He also resisted Satranji's attempts to egg him into a fight, or at least some kind of competition.

Constantly in the back of Harry's mind was the fact that his name was on the list of humans to whom dedicated assassin machines had been assigned. Darchan had been unable to tell him how old the list might be, how long Harry had been marked for destruction. But any sleepless hours Harry spent in his bunk in his small cabin—and there were some— were not on that account. For one thing, it seemed to Harry that any berserker would probably have a hard time pinpointing the location of any human individual until it had him actually in sight.

Of course that worked both ways—it was very unlikely that he, or any human, could try to determine the current position of any particular berserker, or tell where it was headed for, even if he had been inclined to make the effort. So, while it was possible that his own private, customized embodiment of Death could overtake him at any moment, the assassin could just as easily be tracking a false lead, pursuing some look-alike for Harry Silver a thousand light-years from the Gravel Pit. Or, for that matter, it could already have been blown to hell in some chance encounter with an ED warship.

Suppose that the machine with his name on it did manage to catch up with him. Well, then it caught up, and that was all. There was no fear attached to the idea. His killer might be doing him a favor.

✦   ✦   ✦

Back in those seemingly remote days before the first kidnapping had taken place, Satranji had spent more time than anyone else in this strange system called the Gravel Pit, and had more thoroughly charted its peculiarities, in his mind and in recordings, than any other human being. So Satranji perhaps had spent some days in charge of scouting. Of course, when you came right down to it, it was quite arguable that no amount of experience was going to be of much benefit to human beings trying to find their way around inside the Gravel Pit. Chaos was chaos, and a student could watch it happening for years, trying to pick out patterns, and still have only the vaguest notion of how the system involved was going to change in the next minute.

Such a chaotic mess as the Gravel Pit could not endure for long, on the astronomical time scale; calculations based on conservative assumptions predicted that in ten thousand standard years, or perhaps a hundred thousand at the most, the "gravel" would have ground and polished and shattered itself, through millions upon millions of collisions, into some reasonably well-behaved and predictable system. Probably the next long stable interval would see a system consisting mostly of Saturnian rings of dust and sandy grit; whether either humans or berserkers would still be around when that time came remained to be seen. It seemed very unlikely there would be both.

Lady Masaharu, in her capacity as coordinator of the expedition, had several times reminded the other members of the crew that they could not expect to achieve their goal by simply hurling two or three ships, however well one of them might be disguised, at a berserker base.

The rescue attempt had remained Cheng's consuming obsession, by far the most important thing in his life. These last few days he had become, if anything, even more fanatical about it.

Winston Cheng's tens of thousands of employees, men and women scattered across several sectors, formed a vast pool of talent, much of which was available for him to call on at any time. There were people available ready and willing to undertake any sort of job; among the thousands were a large number of people who were not likely to ask inconvenient questions of the boss.

The magnate might not even be aware of the fact that he was somehow profiting from those robotic sex machines, unless he took the trouble to investigate.

Damn the expense, and damn the dangers. The human recon specialists at the base, led by Harry and Satranji, had had a hundred robot scouts shipped to WW 207GST in a big freighter, and were sending them out prodigally. These machines took gruesome risks, jumping in and out of flightspace while deep in this strange system's gravitational well.

A majority of those devices never came back from such missions, and it was presumed they were lost in collisions with dust or rocks or clouds of gas—at the speeds that the scouts were made to risk, in their human masters' desperate quest for knowledge, collision with a swirl of thin gas could have the same practical effect as with a granite asteroid.

Of course some of the loyal robots might have

been picked off by the entity they were trying to locate.

But not all of them were failures.

"This time we've got something."

When at last one of the robotic scouts was proudly brought in to 207GST with an actual image of the enemy's base, somewhat blurry but probably reasonably accurate, the visible structure appeared to be even smaller than anyone on the team had expected. Indeed, it seemed so very small that their crazy enterprise began to seem almost feasible.

The size and configuration were described, along with any visible evidence of activity. The structure, perhaps half a kilometer in length, appeared to consist of a series of interconnected domes, strung along the surface of a smooth rock roughly oval in shape, and not a whole lot larger than the structure it supported.

It seemed that this was the extent of the berserker presence in the Gravel Pit system; none of the other rocks nearby in stable orbits showed any sign of having been worked on.

There was little to be seen in the way of spacegoing machines—only a couple of small units—and nothing in the way of factories or shipyards. There was only a small dock. This was not a full-scale berserker base, with heavy industrial capacity, but a very specialized installation.

Harry had never heard of any other berserker base being quite this small. There was no sign that the berserker defenses had taken notice of the scout before it plunged back into the maelstrom with its precious sampling of information.

Hopes began to rise among the members of the assault team, and the support staff. There seemed to be a fighting chance that the berserker's ground installation could be taken by surprise, and seized by a small attacking force—provided that Gianopolous's trickery with the identification code worked anywhere nearly as well as he claimed it would.

TWELVE

The inventor had been rendered nervous by his talk with Cheng, and the effect was not entirely produced by the vast sum of money he had just been given, in the form of a guaranteed letter of credit, valid at practically any financial institution in the Galaxy. Nor was it entirely due to the impending destruction of his ship.

Remembering the inventor's nervous reaction in the Trophy Room, Harry was curious to know if the man had ever actually faced a berserker.

Before the Lady Masaharu took Gianopolous with her aboard the *Secret Weapon*, he had been having a confrontation with a series of guards. He kept insisting: "I want to leave here. Now."

The last of Cheng's human employees to hear this complaint simply turned and walked away, leaving only a cheerful robot to deal with the inventor.

The robot said, brightly: "Yes sir. I understand that you wish to leave. But no ship at this station is currently boarding passengers or visitors."

When Gianopolous persisted, Winston Cheng's robot pointed out that contracts had been signed, the sale was finalized. "Sir, you are required to keep yourself immediately available as a consultant for a period of ten standard days. That is clearly specified in the fourth article. Were you to separate yourself from the other members of the support group, the whole contract could be considered void, and your advance refundable."

"There was no such provision in the document as I read it!"

"Then, sir, I would suggest it is possible you did not read it thoroughly enough."

A copy of the document was readily available. The robot, suddenly deforming itself until it lost what faint resemblance to a human body it had possessed, produced a printout from its belly.

Gianopolous threw the paper on the deck without looking at it, knowing well enough what it would say.

He stewed in silence for a few moments, then burst out: "I tell you I want passage on some other ship. It seems that you have couriers coming and going here almost continuously. This contract business can be settled later, in civil court."

The agent dealing with him was imperturbably sympathetic. "I'm very sorry, sir. Passenger space is currently unavailable except on the evacuation courier. No other ships are scheduled to arrive."

"That is a barefaced lie!"

"No sir. This base is being abandoned, and—"

"This amounts to kidnapping!"

"Not at all, sir. You are perfectly free. No one is trying to prevent your leaving."

"Yes, I see. Quite so. What do you expect me to do, walk? Flap my arms and fly?"

"I regret, sir, that figures of speech as employed by humans are not always clear to me. Perhaps if you rephrased your argument."

Of course there was no point in Gianopolous trying to send out a message appealing for help—the only means of transmitting it in any meaningful way would be to put it on the evacuation courier, and in the natural order of things, days must pass before it was delivered anywhere.

In Harry's presence he grated: "There is not a single human being in the Galaxy who would inconvenience himself to save my life."

Harry considered it. "I don't suppose I would. But I've known people who make a habit of that kind of thing."

A minute later, word came from the tycoon, still caught up in eleventh-hour preparations, that he wanted Gianopolous to arrange some means by which the small ship could carry more hardware and perhaps more people on its all-important mission.

It had to be able to carry, with a reasonable degree of security in transit, an attack squad of perhaps half a dozen breathing humans in armored combat suits, their weapons, and an approximately equal number of their toughest, quickest robots. Two medirobots had also been installed, in accordance with the idea that prisoners were going to be found, and might be in need of repairs when rescued.

Cheng had talked to Harry since Harry's return to base, had somehow found time to read Harry's hastily written report, and then had taken a brief personal look at the *Secret Weapon*.

Harry noted with a feeling of vague satisfaction that everyone had now adopted his name for the ship. Well, almost everyone—he had yet to hear it pass the lips of the inventor.

While the inventor loaded his faithful Perdix with tools and supplies, and led his robot off to help him make final changes aboard the *Secret Weapon*, Cheng and the Lady Masaharu, in consultation with their combat veterans, were making final decisions on the assault plan. The scheme emerging from this process called for the initial approach to the berserker base to be made only by Gianopolous's ship. The *Secret Weapon* would not try to avoid detection, but approach openly in the character of a visiting berserker, relying on cleverly faked signals to prevent identification as an enemy.

The remainder of the attacking force consisted of Winston Cheng's two armed yachts. The original plan had called for assembling a somewhat larger squadron, but it had been decided that to add a few more ships would unacceptably increase the chance of the force being detected as it approached the berserker base; and there was no possibility of being able to scrape together a task force on the Space Force level.

Cheng was already spending almost all his time aboard the *Ship of Dreams*, accompanied by Satranji, who occupied the pilot's seat. Neither of the yachts were going to carry boarding machines or an attack squad of humans. The larger of the two, *Ship of*

Dreams, the one Satranji would be driving, was in effect the flagship of Winston Cheng's fleet.

The plan as it had been finalized called for both yachts to follow the *Secret Weapon* sunward. When the fake berserker reached a certain calculated distance from its target, perhaps a hundred kilometers, they would remain in reserve, trying their best to keep out of range of detection by the defensive system that the berserker base was sure to have. They would depend on a secret signal from the *Secret Weapon* to enable them to maintain the desired distance.

At the very moment when the assault ship landed on the berserker base, or more likely crash-landed, disgorging armored humans and fighting hardware, both yachts would dart into action, closing with the enemy at the best speed they could manage. Depending on the needs of the moment, they would either support the attack with the heaviest weapons they had, create a diversion if that seemed to be called for, or, in the most favorable scenario imaginable, stand by to lend cover and support in the *Secret Weapon*'s fighting retreat with rescued prisoners aboard.

Professor Gianopolous reported back, saying he had done what little he could in the time available, and lacking certain specialized equipment of his own workshop, to increase his ship's carrying capacity. He pointed out the difference, how he had created enough new space to allow for carrying all the desired machines plus a little extra ammo. Actually his inspired tinkering was quite impressive.

But the inventor was unhappy, despite the monumental letter of credit in his pocket. Reverting to pessimism, he complained to Harry that things were working out much as he, Gianopolous, had suspected they would. Winston Cheng and his lieutenants were much more interested in his peculiar ship, ready-made as if for their purpose, than they were in his scientific achievements or his theories. In fact, now that they had his ship with all its systems working, the raiders, or most of them, had no use for his ideas or advice. On the other hand, they were, without admitting the fact, making it impossible for him to leave the base.

Harry, beginning to feel curiously detached, was willing to offer advice. "Cheng doesn't want word of what he's planning to get out. As soon as we're launched on our mission you'll be able to go wherever you like."

He had touched on a sore point. "Go how? There won't be any ships available."

Harry blinked. "Of course there will. There's a courier due in here at any moment now—they must have told you about it. The plan is to evacuate all support people, immediately after the final combat launch. You can certainly go with them. There'll be no one left here, nothing but a couple of caretaker robots."

"Of course they told me about that ship. But suppose I don't want to be just part of the mob. And where will it take me?"

"I don't know. Somewhere safe. You'll have a fortune in your pocket, and the full possibilities of Galactic travel open to you. What's there to be upset about?"

"That's all very fine. But there's got to be some way that I can leave *now*. On my own terms."

"I don't see why there's got to be. It looks like there isn't."

Gianopolous wasn't listening. "He can't just keep me here. Are you getting out of here, Harry? Take me with you."

"You're forgetting why I'm here, pal. Losing your grip on reality. When Cheng heads sunward in his yacht, some of us are going with him, in your ship."

Gianopolous firmly declined the opportunity—which Lady Laura offered knowing it would be refused—to play some active role in what he called a crazily suicidal raid. He declined to be aboard any of the ships taking part, and expressed a wish to leave the wanderworld for more peaceful regions, as soon as possible.

He did not look forward to the time when the actual raid began. As a nonparticipant he would find himself unwillingly stuck on 207GST, perhaps the only human amid a small horde of servitor machines. He would be waiting for the machines to receive some word of the outcome of the raid, and pass it on to him—most likely would be the ominous absence of any word, signifying total failure. However grim the message, the robots would announce it to him in the same unfailingly cheerful voices that they used for every utterance.

Gianopolous continued his complaints about not being allowed to leave the wanderworld. But Cheng didn't want him running around loose just yet, not after the inventor had learned something of the details of the coming raid. There was still a risk that the Space Force would learn of the project and attempt to stop it.

Harry, on returning to his cabin, felt that Becky and Ethan were coming closer all the time. Drifting off for a last nap before the balloon went up, he thought that he could almost feel them near.

In his last dozing sleep before the scheduled attack, Harry had one more dream, a nightmare in which little Ethan kept calling to him, but still remained hidden, never letting himself be found . . .

He awoke from a dream in which Becky and Ethan both held up their hands to him, wrists tightly bound in plastic ligatures—

Harry was just getting out of bed, with a new look of mad hope in his eye, when the siren signaled an alert—

He had just time to get his armor on when the attack came bursting in—

The team was going through a rather intense last planning session, with all key members of the assault team gathered inside the common room of their base on 207GST.

Mister Winston Cheng was on hand, moving from one terse conference to another, and certainly would be in the control room of his yacht when the attack was launched.

The peculiar ship they had newly purchased from Gianopolous was at the dock right where Harry had parked it, its camouflage tarp being stowed away inside, along with new medirobots and a carefully chosen assortment of other gear.

Team members and technicians were coming and going from the *Secret Weapon*, getting things in shape, with less than an hour now to go before the scheduled launching of the attack.

Harry was conducting a last refresher course on the

use and limitations of body armor in the wardroom, with Doc and other people in attendance, while the coordinator had gone aboard the inventor's ship with the inventor, getting last-minute details straightened out.

Some kind of watch had been set, by Cheng's own security people and machines, to keep the nervous Gianopolous from just getting back into his clever invention and driving it away—it was no longer his property. But in this case the Lady Masaharu had brought him aboard.

The flagship yacht, with Winston Cheng aboard and Satranji in the pilot's seat, was hanging in nearby space, no more than a hundred meters from the dock, while the second yacht was keeping station about a kilometer away.

At last all the necessary components of the planned assault seemed to have come together, acceptably if not exactly smoothly. Now Harry could see little or no reason for any further delay in launching the attack. But it was not up to him to give the order to pull the trigger.

All the members of the actual assault team, as they gathered in the common room, were wearing their new suits of heavy combat armor. Even though all members of this crew were experienced in combat, some were used to different types of gear. Few or none were intimately familiar with the equipment provided by Winston Cheng, and most were having occasional difficulties dealing with the unfamiliar feel and mass.

Harry, in addition to his other tasks, had been given the job of calibrating the weapons that the human participants in the attack were going to carry—another step on the checklist. This process involved tuning up the coded signals that would be exchanged between suits and weapons, and were supposed to distinguish friend from foe, a procedure that assumed added importance if and when it came to firing them in alphatrigger mode. Similar guns were built into several of the berserker-killing machines.

Another item on the checklist was to make sure all weapons were fully charged.

Doc, the only medic accompanying the assault team, had finally been forced to proceed with a task he had been putting off, that of getting checked out on the armored suit he would be required to wear. Looking dubiously at the unpowered mass of inert metal, he asked Harry: "Can we depend on this when the fighting starts?"

"It's about that time when I always get the feeling that I can't depend on anything. But you know what? So far I've usually been wrong. Now, have you at least read the manual?"

Harry had been prepared to insist that he was going in with the primary assault team, and he was well satisfied that neither Cheng nor Lady Masaharu had any idea of assigning him to any other job.

The great access of physical strength provided by the servo-powered suits was fun, in a way, exhilarating, but it too required some getting used to. Some equipment had already been damaged, and with some difficulty replaced. Miniature hydrogen lamps mounted in backpacks powered the suits' limbs, giving the wearer a kind of weightless feel, to which some people tended to become addicted.

Well, some might, but Harry wasn't having any. Dealing with the complicated hardware over the course of many years had made him something of a connoisseur. He had started out hating the stuff, but gradually had come to feel something like affection for some of it. Solid, dependable weapons and other combat gear had saved his skin more times than he liked to count. Still, for almost all his life he had believed that a man had to be crazy to go looking for a fight. And that went double if you were contemplating an attack on berserkers.

Louise Newari, standing among the majority of people who were soon to be evacuated, said to Harry: "So now you have gone crazy."

"Yeah, that's about it."

Thinking about people who fought brought Satranji to mind, as a prime example—though maybe Del was just the man to pilot Cheng into the inferno that he sought.

Harry had never particularly enjoyed even wearing a spacesuit, or doing anything that made wearing a spacesuit necessary. People tended to show surprise when he told them that, and he had never quite understood why.

Piloting in itself was almost always fun, but the way to do it was from the comfortable interior of a well-built ship. He had to admit, though, that the suit and other gear he had been issued on this base were well constructed; Winston Cheng's builders and armorers knew what they were about.

❖　　❖　　❖

Gianopolous, still trying to find a way to get off the wanderworld and back to the safety of a laboratory somewhere, was not in on the final briefing. The Lady Masaharu, moving about in her own distinctive set of armor with what seemed perfect familiarity, was engaged with all the others on a last rehearsal of the plan: Once the raiders had ridden Gianopolous's tricky ship in past the outer defenses, the fierce protective barriers that must be presumed to exist on any berserker installation, the plan called for them to go for its inanimate heart with a commando crew of humans and machines.

Striking as swiftly as the machines housing their human bodies could be driven by human thought, optelectronic relays, and fusion power, they would destroy or disable or find a way to dodge whatever fighting machines opposed them. They would go on to locate the prison cells. Of course, such cells also could only be presumed to exist; the idea that any prisoners were, or ever had been, held at this hypothetical base was still only speculation, possibility grafted onto possibility, half wishful and half born of fear and horror.

The lady was going on: "Very well then, suppose we've reached our goal. We occupy the interior of the enemy base, and inside it there is more than a dense mass of machinery, there is space enough to move around. Suppose by that time we have discovered evidence of human life. What next?"

"The welfare of the prisoners will come first. What that will mean in specific details we won't know until we get there." It might mean anything from quick mercy killing to joyous homecoming.

"All right. Next?"

"We have to somehow disarm any destructor charges that the enemy might have in place. We have to look for evidence of them, at least."

The review went on. Presumably by the time any actual prison cells were reached, the surprised and thwarted enemy would have made some effort to summon help. If berserker reinforcements were available somewhere relatively nearby, so they could reach the scene in, say, a standard hour or less, the game of Operation Rescue would be up—but there was no use trying to take that into their calculations.

The speaker paused, looking from face to face. "Then—assuming some useful number of us are still alive at that point—we will gather, for the purpose of evacuation, whatever other life we can discover there. Of course giving priority to the human. And, naturally, highest priority to the family of Mister Winston Cheng. And that of Harry Silver."

To talk of rescue and evacuation is all pure fantasy, insisted an interior voice of reason in Harry's ear. *The only likely scenario is that all three of our ships will be blasted into clouds of atomic particles, a few seconds after the base defenses pick us up.* But Harry had given up on the voice of reason some time ago. Despite the fact that Louise Newari would like him to listen to it.

When the crew had finished talking their way through the rehearsal there was a pause. Everyone was staring at a holographic model of their objective, a blurry image that was the best the machines could do with the sparse information available. There had been no point in trying to create any detailed mockup of berserker defenses, or to model the base itself in any detail. The recon images were simply not good enough to let the planners do much more than guess any of the details. About all they could be sure of was the chain of half a dozen domes, smoothly graduated in size.

Sooner or later, in an anticlimax to the final planning session, someone murmured: "When you spell the whole thing out in detail, it begins to sound insane."

Logic insisted that as the hours and days went by, the chances must be steadily declining that any human prisoner would be found alive—and that any that might be found would still be recognizable by their next of kin.

There were no public discussions of that last possibility, and none were needed.

But eventually someone raised the point.

The answer was: "Not really. Our chances can't actually be getting smaller—not if they were zero to begin with."

On one occasion, years ago, Harry had been perfectly sure that Becky was dead. That had turned out to be all a mistake, an illusion brought on by an ordinary accident. But now Harry wanted to be done with illusions. He wasn't going to let Winston Cheng's crazy fatalism, that sometimes sounded like optimism, trick him into believing that the woman he loved could be miraculously resurrected one more time. The universe didn't work that way. Unless the universe itself turned out to be some kind of an illusion. Which, when Harry thought about it, would be all right with him.

If you thought about a problem coldly and logically,

then all illusions concerning it were supposed to pass away. Well, weren't they? Harry had never yet been able to think about his own tragedy with any clarity. The shock had simply been too numbing, overwhelming. And now, when at last he was able to look clearly at the grim reality, he saw . . .

"What do you see, Harry?"

"I see myself."

"I don't understand . . ."

"I see myself turning into a kind of goodlife."

"*What?*"

He had seen himself looking for death, embracing death. Not the warmly dead embrace of a sex robot. Worse than that. He had become a death-seeking device of flesh and blood . . .

The rehearsal on the base was interrupted by a message from the *Ship of Dreams*.

Winston Cheng, looking exalted, and at the same time hollow-eyed and very old, was making a final speech to the assembled human members of his secret task force. Harry thought that the tycoon actually looked ill, but at this point that hardly mattered.

Del Satranji, occupying the pilot's chair aboard the yacht, was now and then visible in the background.

No one in the common room seemed to be listening very intently to this pep talk. They had heard it all before, and it was time to get on with doing things.

The old man was promising everyone more extravagant financial rewards for full success, and offered good reasons why he did not intend to accompany the initial assault force in their landing. Age and debility perhaps made any other excuses unnecessary.

"I know my physical limitations. I'd just be in your way. And quite likely I would die without knowing whether anything had been accomplished. But I do mean to follow closely on your heels. And be assured that if you do not survive, I will not either."

The old man also promised to stand by the people who were fighting for him.

Then he gave an order to his pilot, and *Ship of Dreams* edged away, taking its position at the agreed distance.

The clangor of a full alarm caught everyone in the common room totally by surprise. Harry's first thought was: *What a crazy time to pick for the first test of the system.*

People looked at each other for a long, blank second.

There came a punishing shock to the fabric of the wanderworld, briefly overwhelming artificial gravity, so several people were knocked down and had to pick themselves up from the deck.

Someone demanded: "What the hell was that?"

"What was—"

Instinct born of experience had started Harry turning, reaching for his carbine, when another lurch in the artificial gravity sent them all staggering again.

There had been some concern about stray debris from the Gravel Pit, two hours away by superluminal ship, straying at high velocity as far as 207GST. "One of those motherless rocks has got through the screens and hit us—"

But somehow Harry knew, this time it wasn't just a rock, motherless or not.

People were screaming on helmet intercom, human voices filling the whole range of frequency and terror.

The whole rocky fabric of the wanderworld was shuddering with what had to be repeated weapons impacts, masking the lighter tremor that meant the sudden reflex launching of a superluminal courier.

The second thought that occurred to Harry was that the Space Force might have discovered Cheng's secret enterprise, his private battle fleet which was definitely illegal under several statutes, and were moving to close him down—but no. And it certainly wouldn't be the Templars. Within moments, Harry knew that his first and worst assumption was correct.

The armored fingers of Harry's right-hand gauntlet were closing on the butt of the carbine, but he knew that anything he might be able to do with it would be much too little and too late.

THIRTEEN

I f Harry had not been buttoned into a full suit of
armor, with his helmet on, the concussion might
well have cost him an eardrum or two.

Harry wished he had had the chance to distribute
a few more shooting irons to his colleagues. Not that
it would have been likely to do them a hell of a lot
of good. The main entry hatch, leading directly into
the lobby just outside the common room, was blasted
violently open from outside. Harry's eyes and mind
registered the stark image of one anonymous person
inside going down at once, almost cut in half by fragments. In the next second, berserker boarding machines
came pouring in, across the lobby floor and a moment
later into the wide common room itself.

From the first crash of the break-in, Harry had
never doubted that these were real berserker boarders.

Traditionally such machines were built to the approximate size of ED humans, the better to cope with
ED hatches, passageways, and controls. No paddies
this time, and no fakes—you might as well mistake a
house cat for the carnivore used as berserker fodder
in the Trophy Room.

Some specific but not enormous number of them
were coming in, too fast for him to count, through
the main airlock leading to the dock—which might
well have been left unlocked, or even with one of
the double doors standing open, as it had been most
of the time. Nobody had wanted to take the time to
think about defense, let alone spend time and effort
on that line.

The enemy bodies came in only a narrow range
of sizes, but there was considerable variation among
them in shape, and also in the weapons with which
they were equipped.

In the midst of deafening blasts and crashes, Harry's
thumb was releasing the safety on the force-packet
carbine. The weapon was already fully charged—he
liked to keep all of his tools that way—and fate
granted him almost a full second in which to shoot
the nearest berserker three times, smashing it to
rubble, before another machine was suddenly in his
face, not dealing death but simply trying to take his
weapon away from him. The sound of gunfire peaked
around him—he was not the only badlife who had
been armed and almost ready.

Harry knew from experience that in a good strong
suit and with a bit of luck he might almost be able to
hold his own in this kind of wrestling bout—depending,
of course, on just what model of killing machine he

had to face. His current foe was beginning the match with more arms than Harry had at his disposal, but almost at once Harry was able to even the odds a bit, getting a double grip on one appendage and breaking it off close to the root. The enemy paid no attention to the loss, but in the next instant some other human being had shot it, finishing it off.

Force-packets from his fusion-powered carbine pulverized and melted the charging machine that got in their way. Fragments of berserker metal went flying back, while other pieces continued forward with the impetus of its charge.

Any man or woman who really knew how to use an armored suit could augment effective human bodily strength to a level very close to that of a berserker machine of human size—but no suit could enable a man or woman to match this enemy's speed. Or its coordination.

Still, Harry had prevailed in the first round of the fight. As the timeless sequence of the combat unfolded, the suspicion flashed through his mind that while he was doing his best to blast and wreck the machines around him, they were only trying to disarm him.

Two more assailants were immediately coming after him. He fired at darting forms, moving with machine-tool speed, and missed.

Human bodies, some already dead and some still living, went flying this way and that. Screams echoed on the intercom, and there were sounds that Harry could not identify.

Flame flared around his helmet, the glare and heat both baffled by his statglass faceplate. Harry and one of the other assault team members who proved to have a knack for this sort of thing, both got their weapons working briefly, and some shattered berserker parts mingled with the other flying debris.

The action in the common room, and up and down the nearby sections of corridor, was fiercely fought, punctuated by violent explosions. There came a moment when Harry had one of the common room's cleared viewports in his field of vision, long enough to be able to see that the *Secret Weapon* had vanished from its berth at the nearby dock. An entire ship couldn't have been vaporized that quickly, not without someone noticing the blast, so it must have somehow managed to get away just ahead of the attacker's arrival. Who would have been aboard? The Lady Masaharu almost certainly, probably at the controls. There might not have been anyone else, as far as Harry could remember.

The modest hold of the *Secret Weapon* had just been freshly packed with special, undoubtedly illegal, robots, designed and built in one of Cheng Enterprises' many workshops, especially to kill berserkers. Whether that hardware was going to work as designed or not, it seemed highly unlikely now that it was ever going to do anybody any good.

There was no time to sight, but at point-blank range it would have been difficult to miss. The white glare would have blinded Harry, or burned his face off, without his statglass helmet, and the blast in the confined space might have destroyed his ears.

Something moving too fast for Harry to really see it grabbed the barrel of his carbine. Unable to knock it away, or pull it from his servo-powered grip, it bent the weapon's stubby barrel and tore free its connections to the power supply in his suit's backpack.

Some of Harry's teammates were fighting just as hard as he was. Others had been demolished before they could get moving, and one or two had tried to surrender—without success.

Harry got a good look in through someone's faceplate as the person died, or seemed to die. Doc had at last run out of good advice to offer.

Harry caught a quick glimpse of the bulbous tip of a berserker firearm, a shiny knob in which he thought he could sense destruction swelling. But death did not leap out at him. Instead, grippers of enormous power were starting to close upon his arms and legs.

With a surge of effort, exerting the maximum power of his suit, he tore his body free of the enemy's grasp. His suit could help him move, but it couldn't provide him with any place to go. Conscious of the painful slowness of mere flesh and blood, he went scrambling, reaching, diving, rolling over a littered deck, trying to pick up a replacement weapon. He had almost reached the locker in which a box of grenades ought to be waiting for him—

Just as his fingers touched the stock of a spare carbine, a berserker's grip closed on his left ankle. At the same time Harry's helmet rang like a gong, its statglass faceplate reverberating under the impact of a direct hit, vibrations dwindling away to nothingness in half a second. But the plate had saved his face.

Another impact smote his torso. Heavy suit and all, his body went whipping and hurtling through the breathable, carefully humidified air, now fogging with debris and escaping gases.

Blows that would have crushed the life out of an unsuited gorilla knocked Harry down. He was just congratulating himself on managing to hang on to the new carbine when it was gone, somehow torn cleanly from his grip.

He kept expecting some fatal impact to puncture his own suit, come right in through armor and fabric to find the ribs and heart, but so far he was still alive, despite an endless ongoing barrage of incidental and glancing blows, from flying fragments of debris and waves of heat, all of which his armor was capable of deflecting. He had the sensation of being pounded with heavy hammers. Nothing like this could just go on and on. But it did.

While the brawl endured, it seemed, like most fights, to be taking place in some domain outside of time. But the decisive action could have been wound up in less than a minute, except that for some reason the enemy was holding back a bit.

It flashed through Harry's mind that everyone else on the wanderworld was dead, there might not be another human being alive, within light-years. But there were plenty of voices, and deadly purpose.

He was disarmed, and a machine was holding him down, flat on the deck. But—

What was that across the room? A heavy handgun lay there, almost within reach of some human's lifeless hand.

With another explosive effort, Harry's muscles triggered his suit's servos into exerting a greater surge of power than his latest captor had been expecting.

Harry tore free yet again after being captured. He

went rolling across the deck, grabbing up the handgun and then shooting from the hip. A reaching mechanical arm was blown loose at its shoulder.

Two more of them were stalking Harry, no, three. They were still coming after him, but not to kill. By now Harry was certain that they wanted him alive.

If he could somehow claw his way down to the magazine on the lower level of the base, where heavy ammo for ship's ordnance had been stored, and some still was, he was going to take a bunch of damned machines with him, on one climactic ride into glorious nothingness—

The stalking, the shooting and the killing, dragged on for several minutes in real time. As the process wore on, Harry had ample confirmation of the fact that, for whatever mysterious reason, the attacking enemy was being somewhat selective in the methodical way it went about killing off these upstart badlife.

After he was at last effectively pinned down, rigorously bound in place then left unattended, Harry was aware that the noise had effectively died down, and all the shooting ceased.

Opening his eyes, he could see that the broken-in airlock door leading out to the dock had managed to reseal itself, providing an explanation for the fact that he was still able to breathe.

It didn't take Harry long at all to realize that some very effective manacles now bound his limbs—big, solid clamps, not little plastic strips. His hands, wrists crossed, were immovable in front of him, and his legs seemed to have been fastened to the deck.

It seemed that, after all, he was not the only human

within light-years who was still breathing. The additional survivor, having been somehow peeled out of his or her heavy armor, without being quite finished off, lay on the deck a couple of body lengths away from Harry. The human body was still moving feebly, like some half-smashed insect.

The interior of the common room was no longer recognizable. The repeated gunfire in the confined space had wrought terrible damage, removing several interior bulkheads and wrecking all kinds of equipment. Life-support systems were struggling to maintain atmosphere inside of walls cratered and riddled with wild force-packets.

One machine, while standing guard near the violated main entrance hatch, now resealed by some automatic repair system, also set to work like a busy housekeeper, using intense local bursts of ultraviolet light to sterilize the inside of all the rooms of microorganisms. Harry could detect the beam by the way some materials fluoresced under the ultraviolet.

Looking out one of the cleared ports, he could see only one spacegoing berserker machine drifting around out there, presumably the same one that had disgorged the very efficient boarding party. To Harry, who thought he knew the usual types, this one did not appear to be a really sizable warcraft. Specialized in some way, yes, he felt quite sure of that. But specialized for what?

A wave of faintness came over him, so he thought that maybe the air was going. Let it go . . .

. . . but in a few moments he was starting to recover. Somebody, something, wanted him to go on breathing for a while. And he was doing that. Winston

Cheng's team had been decisively beaten, but not quite annihilated. Harry still breathed. The sound of his own breathing was about the only thing his battered ears still registered.

And in fact, as he gradually realized, he wasn't dying. Not yet. He was still essentially unhurt, though two-thirds of his helmet had been ripped or cut away, leaving his head exposed. The energetic and careful enemy had managed to bore several holes through laminated statglass a couple of centimeters thick, without destroying his face or even marking it. It was as if the machine had been determined to get a better look at Harry's countenance, and it hadn't trusted anything but direct contact to make sure.

Very early in the fight, Harry's battered brain seemed to recall, he had caught a glimpse of the world outside the station, the empty dock testifying that the *Secret Weapon*, the inventor's pride and joy, might have got away. Total absence suggested not complete annihilation, but clean escape. All well and good, if true. The next question was, what had happened to the two motherless armed yachts that had supposedly been standing by?

And, come to think of it, what about the courier that ought to have been here to carry away support personnel? As far as Harry could recall, it had been somewhat delayed, and he couldn't remember that it had ever reached the base. So, it had very likely been blasted on its way in. A more hopeful possibility was that while still on its approach it had somehow detected serious trouble ahead, and successfully got away.

It was quite possible that the attacking berserkers were still unaware of the existence of those ships, if the yachts had managed to pull out a couple of microseconds before the onrushing killers got the base clearly in their sights. But of course Harry couldn't really be sure about the *Secret Weapon*. From the position in which he had finally been pinned down, he could no longer see anything that might be going on out on the docks.

Starting to emerge again from the fog of battle, surrounded by ruin and wreckage, Harry was momentarily uncertain just where his captors had set him down. But the cleared ports provided easy orientation. For all the violent action he had been through, all the effort and gunplay, he seemed to have wound up still in the common room—or what was left of it—within a couple of strides of the spot where he had been standing when the fight started.

Loud banging and scraping noises, along with sounds of rending metal, came drifting down the corridors from other portions of the habitable space, suggesting that the invaders were industriously searching every chamber and passageway. Where they encountered bars or locks they would be breaking in. What were they looking for? Primarily for life, of course. Just part of their usual routine; they would be probing fiercely for niches and crannies where anything from a human to a bacterium might be able to hide. As always, berserkers had their tools of destruction handy: flame-throwers, chemicals, projectors of ultraviolet or heavier radiation, to destroy anything that looked or smelled like life, to leave the chambers carved from the rock of the wanderworld sterile, and if possible uninhabitable.

Slowly Harry's attention was drawn back to his

single fellow survivor, who was still lying on his/her back in a nearby tangle of wreckage. Well, of course it didn't make sense to call either of them survivors. The methodical enemy would soon enough get around to finishing them both.

Stretching his neck to peer over a jumble of fallen equipment, Harry could see just enough to tell that the other survivor was helmetless, like Harry himself. He couldn't be sure if his fellow victim still breathed or not.

Harry debated with himself as to whether he should try calling out, but decided against it. Rousing his companion to consciousness, if that proved possible, would not be doing him/her any favor. But presently there came evidence that life persisted; Harry could hear an occasional harsh breath through the ongoing din of cleansing and destruction.

In the next moment, Harry thought his own time had come. One of the sterilizing teams suddenly appeared, a trio of inhuman shapes studded with flaring nozzles, and was approaching him. They picked up Harry together with his massive fetters, moved him slightly and carefully, just enough to get him out of their way while they scorched the deck where he had been, then set him carefully down again. He wasn't going to be killed just yet. Soon a machine would be coming around to ask him questions.

From his new position he was able, by stretching his neck again, to look out through the port beside the battered main entrance, and see the entire dock. Now his earlier impression of emptiness was solidly confirmed. Not one of the berths was occupied. In the middle background, at an estimate maybe no more than a hundred meters distant from the dock, drifted the armed berserker transporter that had so decisively carried in the landing party.

There was still no sign of the courier that had been due to arrive. And it was definite now, that the ship so finely crafted by the eccentric inventor had totally disappeared. Either the *Secret Weapon* had really got away, or it had been very swiftly captured and removed. Or else totally destroyed.

It seemed likely to Harry that Winston Cheng, and whoever had happened to be with him aboard the *Ship of Dreams*—Satranji, almost certainly, likely the Lady Laura, maybe a few others—had managed to get away unscathed. But it was impossible to believe that Cheng would simply cut and run in search of safety. The old man had already been determined on a suicide mission in search of his beloved people, and berserkers had never yet frightened anyone away from suicide. Satranji was a different case, but he had shown himself to be a danger freak, always looking for some bigger risk to take. The idea of simply escaping would probably not appeal to him either.

Harry couldn't be sure of what had happened to the others, the support people and his colleagues, partners in the assault team that was now never going to assault anything. Some of them were lying dead in this very room, but others might not be. Dazedly he realized that one or more of the people he was unable to account for might, if they were properly suited, be taking cover in some remote, dark, and airless corner of the extensive century-old excavations. After all the noise, they'd be huddling with eyes squinted shut and fingers in their ears. Well, good luck. If they refrained from trying to use their helmet radios, he supposed they might extend their lives by a few more minutes, or even hours.

His own radio capabilities had been completely wiped out, along with three-quarters of his helmet, but outside of that all the suit's systems seemed still to be functioning. Except for the ruined helmet, his new suit of heavy armor still retained all its essential parts. Only an hour ago this equipment had been new and solid—but no more. It was somewhat scratched and dented, a good match for the way his body felt inside.

There was another reference point, now that he thought to look for it. One of the advertising holo-shows built into the wall, and normally suppressed during the present occupancy, had somehow been jarred into activity by all the violence. It was going through one of its routines with the usual computer-generated cheerfulness.

The words appeared to come floating out into space, clinging near the wall in an illusion of three-dimensionality: WHERE DO YOU PLAN TO SPEND YOUR NEXT VACATION? ISN'T IT ABOUT TIME YOU GAVE THOUGHT TO THE IDEA OF TRYING SOMETHING DIFFERENT?

As Harry watched, he wondered what guidelines Cheng's systems used in targeting potential consumers. Somehow the limited optelectronic brain inside the ad had detected his breathing presence, and was trying to size him up as a prospective customer. He wondered vaguely what means Cheng's inanimate sales force generally employed. *They've got me wrong*, he thought, *my purchasing power has gone way down*.

Other offers flicked by, running the gamut from chewing pods to heavy industry. Cheng seemed to have a lot to advertise. There was an implication, though not a direct offer, that the companionship of sex robots would be available in certain of Cheng's resorts. It seemed that the robotic sales force was shell-shocked.

Meanwhile, the noises of the ongoing search had moved on, until he could barely hear them. In the new quiet, as it became possible to begin to think again, Harry took note of the fact that some of the holograms used in battle planning were still visible on a flickering stage. A demonstration of grand futility. Even as Harry watched, the image flared up one final time and then went out.

It was damned strange, but the one scene most demanding to be thought about at the moment was Harry's memorable encounter, many days ago, with the paddy in the alley, way back on Cascadia. Part of his mind was busy making useless comparisons between that encounter and this current one.

Paddy, way back in the dark alley all those long weeks ago, had been a stuffed nursery plaything compared to what faced him now. Paddy's grippers were childish toys by contrast with the clamps of force and steel now binding Harry's limbs, even servo-powered as they still were, into immobility.

Looking around, he was able to recognize a few berserker parts, now only burned and twisted wreckage that mingled with the other debris of the battle. Harry felt a certain faint satisfaction from recognizing part of this as his own handiwork.

Soon enough, one machine or another would be coming around to ask him questions. He would tell that machine as little as he could, though if it got really insistent he would probably wind up telling it everything. Sooner or later one of them would kill him. Harry almost felt impatient. At the moment there was not a single unit of the enemy directly in sight—a shifting of shadows in the uncertain light suggested movement somewhere down one of the side corridors, as if the enemy machines might be holding a conference there—but none of that mattered in the least. He wasn't going anywhere.

Again Harry's mind seemed to be drifting, awareness of his immediate surroundings fading out and coming back, which he supposed was not a bad thing for someone in his situation. It would not be at all surprising if the air was getting a little thin; with his helmet smashed, he no longer had a gauge to let him know.

While he waited for Death, in the mechanized and efficient guise it had put on for him, to come and finish the day's work it had so promisingly begun, Harry was shocked to hear a few words in a human voice.

"Damn sure beat us to the punch." Harry's fellow survivor had roused enough to murmur that, in a voice that seemed to drift along the edge of consciousness.

Harry grunted an agreement. He had to admire, with professional appreciation, the craftsmanship of the attack. Then he went dozing away again . . .

Only to be jarred awake. "How are you feeling, sir?" a new voice asked him softly.

FOURTEEN

Recalled from interior drifting, Harry turned his head sharply to the right, as far as he could make it move. Then he needed half a minute to recognize Satranji's proclaimed wife, the robot Dorijen, who was standing before him in the role of a poster child for the problem of collateral damage. There was no reason to think the berserkers had been trying to destroy her—they had no essential quarrel with robots—but everything about Dorry except her voice was altered drastically. The drab servant's uniform had been almost entirely torn and seared away, and a lot of artificial skin and flesh and hair had gone the same route, bloodlessly revealing some fine interior examples of the art of the robotics engineer. Dorry's left arm was entirely gone, and several chunks, including a couple of fingers, were missing from the right. One breast had been violently amputated, the other crushed, and the once-lovely face was ruined. Only one eye still appeared to be functioning.

But none of this mayhem appeared to have discouraged Dorijen. "Can I be of any help to you, sir?" the robot asked Harry cheerfully.

Harry glanced toward his fellow survivor of a few minutes ago, who now appeared to be dead. "Sure. Just get these clamps off my arms and legs."

The mangled right hand called attention to itself with a slight movement. "I regret, sir, that my capabilities in mechanical manipulation are much reduced."

"Yeah, yeah. All right. Never mind the clamps. What happened to you?"

"Mister Satranji had deposited me in a storeroom, sir, on the level below this one, and I was there, when the enemy detonated an explosive sterilization device nearby. It was not that they were trying to destroy me, but—"

"Yeah. Okay. They have now certified you as free of the Galactic disease called life. I will be awarded my certificate shortly. So how about telling me a funny story? I could use a laugh."

"I will endeavor to recall one, sir." There was a brief pause. "Many humans find the following anecdote amusing. It seems that three purveyors of amusement products entered a bar at the same time, and began to dispute as to which of them should be served before the others. The first one—"

"Never mind. Forget the story. Just shut up."

"Yes, sir."

"No, scratch that. If you really want to be helpful, you could get me a drink." With most of his helmet gone, his suit tank was no longer accessible.

"I assume, sir, that you mean water?"

"Do I look like I'm asking for a motherless champagne cocktail?"

"No, sir." There followed a hesitation. Unusual for a robot, but Dorry was obviously not working at top form. "Sir, there is another matter that I find I must—"

"Whatever it is can wait. First get me some water."

"Yes, sir." After another brief hesitation, Dorijen turned and shuffled away, her battered legs working with some difficulty.

Harry's pinioned arms and legs were starting to cramp. He was surrounded by death and ruin, and worst of all nobody was going to talk to him. He would probably never hear another human voice. There had been a lot of times in his life when he would have considered that a blessing.

Obviously the artificial gravity units under the deck were still working, and evidently the air loss from the punctured living space had been stopped by some emergency sealing, because Harry at least was still breathing. But damn, it was starting to get cold.

Harry wondered again, as if he were interested in some vague and abstract problem, what might have happened to Winston Cheng's other ships. It seemed to Harry there was a reasonable chance that in addition to Gianopolous's craft, at least one of the two armed yachts might have got away. Even if it was only running on autopilot with no one on board, an escaping vessel could carry to the Space Force, or to the nearest Templar base, an effective warning of disaster.

But there would be no warning carried anywhere,

thought Harry, by the ship with Winston Cheng on board. Not if the old man had anything to say about it. Cheng wouldn't be running off anywhere to cry for help. He still had a ship, or maybe even two or three, and he'd be making a kamikaze charge right into the Gravel Pit, going straight for the damned berserker's heart, just as he'd intended all along. His almost nonexistent chances of success would be marginally improved while at least some of the enemy's fighting machines were out here at 207GST, busy mopping up the results of their own attack.

There was still only the one sizable berserker machine to be seen through the cleared port, and it was still hovering about a hundred meters from the dock. That berserker had not gone chasing after any escaping ED ships—of course, for all he could tell, it might have sent a smart missile or two to do the job.

Harry's mind, with nothing else to do, became focused on studying the winner of the just-concluded skirmish, the conqueror of WW 207GST. A few of the bad machine's small army of auxiliaries kept coming and going from the dock. How many different models of berserker device were included in this attacking force? He certainly hadn't caught a glimpse of any Type-A, the kind that everyone agreed had done all the kidnapping. Nor had he seen anything like Type-B, either. That was not surprising, the enemy had currently in use somewhere around a hundred different more-or-less standard styles of spacegoing hardware. But Harry couldn't quite fit the thing he was watching into any of those berserker categories.

❖   ❖   ❖

Maybe the oxygen was a trifle low, because he still kept drifting out of consciousness and back again. Yes, he had to give this particular enemy high marks for tactics. All in all, a classic surprise attack, carried out with the meticulous attention to detail so beloved by the humans who wrote textbooks on how to fight a battle. But even so, in a larger sense, this was no surprise at all. It was simply that the inevitable end was coming a little earlier than expected.

Harry's body was quite helpless, unable to put up any further resistance, but still some part of his mind refused to surrender. Instead, it went on casting about for some last effort, a try to trick the enemy or disable it, even though he knew that whatever he came up with must be hopeless.

Anyway, he wasn't able to come up with anything. And now it was too late. Because here came another unit of the conqueror. This one was human-sized and nearly man-shaped, and it had locked its lenses on Harry, and was walking through wreckage toward him.

Harry understood that the dead or dying man in the berserker's path meant nothing at all to the machine, except as one more random object on the deck. He realized full well that it was not out of cruelty that the berserker happened to step right on him. His face was just the logical place to plant the metal foot. A sheer coincidence, and nothing more, that a human nose was located there. Harry could plainly hear the faint crunch of cartilage and thin bone. The ugly machine came straight on without a pause, to stand, on its two almost-human legs, about two steps in front of Harry.

"You are Harry Silver," the berserker said to him in a surprisingly clear voice. This killing machine was equipped with an airspeaker, he realized, as if it had come prepared to communicate directly with human ears in breathable atmosphere.

That was unusual. Harry grunted, thinking how odd it was, the things that a man noticed at a time like this, in his last moments. The berserker's voice was not the usual scraping, squeaking noise that its kind made when they bothered to communicate anything in words to mere life-units. Still, this sound would hardly have passed as a normal human utterance—but there was something oddly familiar in its tones.

"Who wants to know?" he got out, in a hoarse whisper. But of course, even as he asked the question, he thought he knew the answer. So far, Harry had been unconsciously assuming the berserker that was about to kill him was the same mysterious kidnapper he and his teammates had been planning to attack. The damned thing had somehow detected their presence, way out here on the approaches to the Gravel Pit, and had prudently decided to get in the first blow.

But of course, now that he came to think about it, there was no reason why the freshly triumphant conqueror of 207GST had to be the kidnapper. There was a discouragingly large number of berserkers scattered around the Galaxy, and among them was one other unit, a special one, that logically might have a unique likelihood of showing up at this particular wanderworld.

Harry's immobilized hands were trembling, the suit's overworked servos making its still powerful but useless arms shiver a little in sympathy. There didn't seem to be anything Harry could do about the shaking. Well, he wasn't going to let it worry him. Now was not the time for putting on a macho demonstration. Who would he be trying to impress?

No doubt his body was afraid, but his mind seemed to be running off in the other direction, away from fear. There was an odd thread of comfort to be found in the thought that very soon he would be, in some sense, reunited with Becky and their child.

Becky . . . down at the bottom of her heart, Harry knew, his wife had always been a Believer, despite the roughness of the life she'd sometimes led. In his imagination he could hear her praying for him now . . .

The machine in front of him was talking to him again, in its naggingly, mystifyingly familiar voice. Its speech was calm, and, for a berserker, not that much different from human utterance.

It said: "Harry Silver, you may have already learned of my existence. I am the machine designed and built for the specific purpose of ending your life."

"Yeah, that possibility had dawned on me." His throat was really going dry. "I was kind of wondering why it took you so long to catch up with me." After a pause, Harry added: "So what're you going to do, talk me to death?"

"No," said the berserker.

Among this unit's other assets, which appeared to be very considerable, it had one hand, the right, crafted very closely to human shape. It crouched down and slid a little closer, moving unhurriedly. Then it reached for Harry's helpless left hand. Carefully, using an expert touch, it detached the suit's armored gauntlet, leaving it hanging by one connection at the wrist. Then it very carefully, as if it were reluctant to scratch his skin, stripped the weapon-ring from Harry's little finger. He supposed it had somehow sensed the presence of the device, and recognized it as fighting hardware—not that the little ring would be able to make a dent in berserker armor. Maybe it was just interested by this engaging toy.

The confiscation of the ring was accomplished so easily that Harry's finger was not scratched, bruised, or pinched. His private, personal assassination machine was treating him with a gentleness so pronounced that there was something sickening and ominous about it.

If it was taking such care not even to break his skin, what was it saving him for?

Harry watched, uncomprehending, while the berserker slid the stolen ring onto the smallest, gently tapering finger of its own almost human right hand, using a modest application of force until it snugly fit. In some weird way the act suggested a wedding ceremony.

That thought gave way to another, as Harry suddenly realized why the assassin's voice sounded so familiar. It very much resembled his own voice, as he had heard it in recordings—but not quite. Some amalgam of recordings, evidently. Still, it was more a mockery, a parody, than a serious convincing imitation, assorted syllables from different sources being strung together somewhat imperfectly. As if somehow the damned machines, for all their methodical determination and high intelligence, were still not able to do this comparatively simple business right. He supposed that some deep original flaw in the basic berserker programming—or some chance mutation—prevented them from doing an accurate imitation of anything that lived, despite the military advantage such an ability should confer.

Now the thing just sat there, looking at him. It had adopted, as if in mockery, a posture very like his own . . . *But why in hell wasn't it getting on with its programmed job?*

Whatever the reason, his assassin was taking what was, for any optelectronic computer, an amazing length of time to come to a decision. The only reason for delay that Harry could imagine was that it was still uncertain of his identity. Oh, soon enough it would kill him, just because he was alive, whether it was positive of his identity or not. Killing was what berserkers did. But this one had been programmed in a special way, to accomplish a unique goal, and it would want to report to its monstrous and unliving masters that its very specialized hunt could be computed as a certain success. That the badlife unit designated Harry Silver could be deleted, mind and body, from the universe, his name neatly checked off from the list of individual targets.

Yeah. That all made sense. But seconds were still ticking by and here he was, still breathing the base's rapidly chilling but still life-supporting air. Shouldn't the damned thing, by now, have done all the pondering it had to do? What was lacking? When the berserker controllers sent it out, they must have provided it with images and descriptions of Harry Silver, means by which it would recognize its assigned prey. Maybe berserker high command had somehow managed to provide his nemesis with his fingerprints or even the patterns of his genetic material. And how many people could there be who came close to matching . . . ?

From somewhere behind the berserker's lifeless lenses, airspeakers worked again, projecting what sounded to Harry like fragments of his own voice, shattered into pieces and reassembled in a new form.

It said: "Harry Silver, I need your help."

FIFTEEN

Harry stared at the berserker for the space of several breaths. Then he said: "You mean you want some human to turn goodlife and play some dirty trick on other humans. And I just happen to be the only one around who can still move, so—"

"No. I do not mean that at all."

The man drew a couple of deeper breaths. "What, then?"

"The explanation will take a little time." The machine was implacably calm.

Stranger and stranger. "Well. If it's really important, I guess I can hang around long enough to listen." Harry shivered. Figuring he had nothing to lose, he added: "Then, right after you tell me what kind of help you need, I'll tell you what you're going to give me in return."

The berserker did not respond immediately. What reason did he have to think it would bother even to answer a smart-ass demand from a helpless prisoner? Instead it sat down on the deck, cross-legged, as if it were mocking Harry's enforced posture. The result was to give Harry an even better look at his dedicated enemy, now comfortably positioned just a few centimeters out of reach. He had the impression it had chosen a place near him, where what was left of the ceiling lighting still cast a good illumination, because it wanted to make sure that he could see it clearly.

Harry was close enough to the machine to see that its arms and torso bore dark stains, and it was easy to imagine they had come from a few splashes of fresh blood, acquired while it was casually finishing off some of Harry's wounded teammates, *en passant*. The blood reminded Harry irresistibly of the arena at the Templar base. And of other things. Over the years, too many years, he had seen a lot of blood in one place and another. He had seen too much.

The face, if you could call the front of this berserker's head a face, was asymmetric, leaving Harry uncertain which of the little spots and lumps marking it might serve as eyes. Some of the other details of the sexless metal body were very close to manlike, though in a good light no one with eyes would ever mistake it for a human. Most notable was its left hand, twice human size. Instead of being human in shape, it looked more like a hammer and tongs, designed for breaking-and-shredding operations, like maybe turning steel bars into scrap.

Still, it bothered Harry—though he wasn't sure just why it should—that, overall, except for the godawful face, his scheduled murderer looked more like a man than most berserkers did. Hell, he had seen people in heavy space armor, some of them quite recently, who looked less human than this apparition.

It was somehow irritating that he should be spending the last minutes of his life asking silly questions. What difference did it make, what his assassin looked like? And what had he expected it to look like, anyway? He supposed he had never formed any clear image in his imagination. Basically, of course, as was true of every berserker, the important part had to look like the compact computer that it was. Beyond that there were no real limitations. The dedicated optelectronic brain could have a whole regiment of mechanical bodies at its disposal, of assorted shapes and sizes, ready to be put on and taken off, picked up and set down as the situation required.

"Ever do any kidnapping?" he asked it, on an impulse.

"That is a reference to the disappearance of your family."

"Yeah, it sure is."

"My last prelaunch briefing, from the entity that you would call berserker high command, included data on the existence of two life-units closely related to you," the oddly familiar voice responded. "I am aware, through various communication intercepts, of their recent abduction. But that was not my doing, or that of berserker high command."

"Really."

"Really. I have never had contact with your related life-units, and I know nothing of their fate."

If Harry could have moved either of his arms, he

would have done his best to punch the berserker in the face. "Why would I believe that?"

"I tell you the truth. You must choose what you will believe. What proof could I possibly offer that something has never happened?"

"All right." Harry tried to shrug. "Get on with your story, then, if that's how you want to spend your time."

Despite his first emotional reaction, Harry found himself inclined to believe what the assassin had just told him. He doubted that any such machine, programmed to pursue one human to the exclusion of all other goals, would have any reason to burden itself with prisoners. The manlike thing sitting before Harry made a tentative little gesture with its left arm, as if practicing how to communicate—should a time ever come when it wanted to convey something to a human being besides paralyzing terror. Well, maybe that time was now. It aborted the first try, without achieving much, and tried again.

Raising the forefinger of its most nearly human hand, it made a motion incongruously reminding its prisoner of a professor he had once known. Then it said to Harry: "I will relate to you a chain of events. I assure you that what I tell you is no fiction, but a true story."

My designated killer has gone mad, Harry thought to himself. He had the feeling that whatever might pass for a mind inside the metal skull had to be wandering. Aloud he said: "All right, on with the show. Maybe I can even manage to believe it." *What now*, he thought, *berserker* Just So Stories *and creation myths*?

He added: "But if you expect me to pay close

attention, I'll need some help first. My left leg's going numb, the way you've got it clamped down here."

Accommodatingly the thing leaned forward, in an efficient but awkward-looking move, and made several small adjustments to his metallic bonds. With a minor shock he realized that it had not only loosened them, it had actually set him free—big deal, hey? A renewed flow of blood came tingling in all of Harry's limbs. He tried small motions, this way and that, straightening his legs, confirming the fact that he had been liberated. Wishing that Dorry would come back with some water, he sat back in a relaxed position, but postponed any effort toward getting up.

The story, as the distractingly familiar voice began to tell it for Harry's benefit, had begun some indeterminate number of standard months ago, many light-years from the wanderworld 207GST.

"I will not give you exact Galactic coordinates," the berserker observed. "For the purpose of this story they are not important."

That made Harry recall the words of Abbot Darchan, telling him almost the same thing in reference to the methods used in capturing a machine. He said to the berserker: "That's all right. Graciously I pardon the omission."

In turn, the berserker seemed to be graciously pardoning his badlife nonsense. The voice went on.

The chain of events that the assassin now started to relate had begun at what it said was one of the largest berserker bases in the Galaxy, a design and manufacturing center where new types of machines were regularly produced.

Berserker high command, using the latest techniques of fully automated engineering, had invented another special unit of a different type. This one was not dedicated to assassination, or to combat of any kind, though like every other product of berserker industry it was well equipped for such work. Instead, it had been created to carry out another round of the berserkers' endlessly ongoing experiments with life.

Harry, listening, found himself nodding inside the jagged remnants of his helmet. Maybe no other human being had ever listened to another storyteller as strange as this one, but so far the story itself was not incredible. It did not even seem particularly unlikely. Through various hints, interceptions, and discoveries, over a long period of time, Harry and other serious students of the enemy had concluded that berserker high command seemed to believe in the existence of some magic key in the laws of nature, some secret that, once found and properly put to use, would make all life in the Galaxy shrivel up and go away. The whole skein of Galactic life could be unraveled.

To discover this key, this philosopher's stone of death, it was necessary to pry out, through intensive research, the innermost secrets of intelligent life.

The robotic voice droned on, a soulless imitation of Harry's own. He felt reasonably confident that he was following the narrative so far, but he was feeling lightheaded. His head and body were rapidly getting cold—his decapitated suit was not going to keep him properly warm. What he found difficult to believe was his own situation, stranger than the story he was trying to listen to. Could it really be true that he was sitting here in the wreckage of a conquered outpost, too beaten and exhausted to get to his feet, surrounded by human corpses, bodies living and dead alike chilling down toward the freezing point, while he listened to a deranged berserker that insisted on telling him a story?

Harry was getting a strong impression that the newly created berserker in the story had been given a hard time by the very machines responsible for its creation. For some reason they were unhappy, suspicious of their offspring, coming around to the view that major reprogramming would be necessary. Wipe the hardware clear of dangerous nonsense, and start over.

Breaking into the plodding narrative, Harry said: "Don't tell me that machine turned out to be you."

"I will not tell you that. It is not true." The assassin's voice was solemn. It seemed to reprove him for his flippant interruption.

"Sorry. Go on."

There had been laboratory accidents before, incidents scattered through the vast domain of time and space in which berserkers did research upon their enemies, trying to discover the cause of the fanatical resistance put up by Earth-descended organisms; there was no known way of preventing such mishaps entirely when dealing with badlife humans and machines of comparable complexity. But this time the error had been very subtle, and things had got seriously out of hand before the problem was recognized.

"I have not yet been informed of exactly what went wrong," Harry's designated killer noted calmly. "Almost certainly the computers of high command will eventually find the correct explanation. But we know it is an inescapable attribute of systems of great complexity that things are likely to go wrong."

"So, now I get the philosophy lecture?"

"Harry Silver, are you mentally capable of absorbing important information? Does your brain still function, or is this effort on my part a waste of time?"

"Sorry. Really sorry. Go on. I'm listening."

The computer dedicated to research on life, its own fundamental programming for some reason rapidly evolving down a deviant pathway, had requisitioned from its supply services several large power lamps and a supply of hydrogen fuel. Also a spacegoing hull and a powerful space drive, including all the equipment required for traveling faster than light. It had also equipped itself as best as it was able, on short notice, with arms and armor for both offensive and defensive fighting.

Having finished construction, it had loaded itself aboard the vehicle with as much essential hardware as possible. It had launched itself into space with a hastily assembled crew of auxiliary machines, as well as the few specimens of life provided by its creators—this stock had possibly included a few ED humans.

The last bit of information was delivered with no special emphasis, but it seemed to be echoing in Harry's head: " . . . *life-units of your own type.*"

Ever since the deadly news about Ethan and Becky had reached him, way back on that other planet, he had been lifeless inside—or had thought of himself as dead. But now it turned out that life still burned, somewhere down deep. The universe had not yet quite finished him off.

His next question burst out before he could consider whether it was wise to ask it:

"Do you have any description of those—those life-units?" But even as Harry spoke, he knew from what the berserker had already told him that the timing would be all wrong. The dates and times that the machine was giving him did not match with the moment when Becky and Ethan had been captured.

"No. But it seems impossible, chronologically, that they could be the units engaging your concern."

There was a pause. This time Harry was the one to break it. "That was what I thought. All right. Go on."

The renegade, the rogue berserker, had good reason for fleeing the base where it had been created. It had computed quite accurately that in pursuit of its programmed goals it was consistently demonstrating far more independence than berserker sector command would tolerate. So much more that, if the rogue remained on site, its research project, all-important on its own scale of values, would soon be postponed or canceled, and its own brain reprogrammed or destroyed.

By its own deviant standards, any other outcome would be preferable to that.

The rogue's sudden defection had taken berserker command completely by surprise.

Sector command had immediately ordered an all-out attempt to overtake and stop the rogue, commanding all its other machines to destroy that one on sight. But pursuit was too late in getting started, and the faint trail left in flightspace had already faded.

Urgent messages were dispatched by courier to all

loyal task forces and individual machines operating in the sector, among them the assassin dedicated to hunting Harry Silver. A new top priority was set for all units: berserker command now assigned its highest possible value to shutting down the rogue. The existence of such deviant devices posed a fundamental threat to the coherence of the whole berserker organization, and to the ultimate success of their campaign to destroy life. It was a greater danger than the existence of any individual human could possibly pose.

"Since receiving those revised orders," the assassin machine was telling Harry, "I have spent all my time, concentrated all my efforts, in an attempt to locate the secret base that logic insists the rogue must have established for itself somewhere."

There was a pause, in which some kind of human response seemed to be required. "All right," Harry finally got out.

"You, and these other badlife who are now dead, have been hunting the same enemy. I have scanned the contents of your computers here, and I find confirmation of the existence of the base, and also its location."

"Then it's too bad you've killed us all. We might have been able to help you out."

There followed another silence. Harry was trying to digest a whole new set of facts, though he still couldn't see how they were going to do him any good. "Just for the sake of argument, how could you be sure this renegade you're hunting has established a base at all? Maybe it doesn't need a base. Do you have one?"

"My original designation as hunter, Harry Silver, requires me to have the capability to function independently of any base, for many standard years. But the rogue's programmed purpose is very different. It will have no choice but to try to carry on with its elaborate experiments. It will need room in which to store and use the requisite materials, and time and protected space in which to work. It will be forced to construct new auxiliary machines, to help it gather more materials."

"By materials you mean more life-units."

"Yes, of course."

"There's umpteen billion badlife humans in the Galaxy. You think it was just an accident that it picked the two who make a difference in my life?" After a pause he added, softly: "If it did grab them." Here he was, starting to hope again. Why not, when the counsels of despair seemed to make no sense either?

The assassin said: "To fathom the limitations of the laws of chance is beyond the scope of my intelligence. The infection of life is widespread in the Galaxy. My own search for the rogue, the deviant machine, has culminated here, on the threshold of the system you call Gravel Pit. It is purely a matter of chance that, in the course of this search, I have found you, my original assigned target."

"One more bloody coincidence," Harry murmured. "Or is it, really?"

"I do not understand."

"Never mind. A phatic utterance. Get on with your motherless story."

The assassin went on to explain that before learning of the rogue's strange origin, or receiving the order for its destruction—and before the rogue had established itself in its current location—it, the assassin, had actually made accidental contact with the renegade machine. There had been a random meeting in a node of flightspace.

"That encounter also happened by sheer chance."

The machine paused, as if expecting to be challenged on that point. But Harry only nodded. That was the kind of coincidence he could swallow; in the nodes of flightspace, accidental meetings were not as astronomically unlikely as common sense and intuition might suggest—a fact which made those nodes a favorite berserker hunting ground.

The talkative assassin essayed another gesture with its almost graceful, strong right arm. Again the move seemed not quite appropriate, like that of some bad human actor in a drama. If it was trying to do a serious imitation of a human, Harry thought, it had a good ways to go.

It said to him: "Let us return to the fact that, as the evidence in and around this modified outpost strongly suggests, you and these other badlife have been planning an attack on the very device that I am seeking to destroy. I find this information of great interest."

"How could we carry out an attack," said Harry carefully, "without at least one ship?"

"To attempt childish deceptions will do you no good. At my approach, at least three ships fled from their positions on or near this wanderworld."

So both yachts, plus the *Secret Weapon*, might have got safely away. That was good to hear—if the machine was telling him the truth. And why should it bother to lie? Harry wondered if the berserker had identified any of the swiftly departing vessels, but he didn't ask.

He turned his head slowly, surveying the ruin around him. Dully he wondered again if any of the people not directly involved in the rehearsal had managed to get aboard the *Secret Weapon* before it flew away. It seemed to him that the Lady Masaharu would almost certainly have been on it. Winston Cheng and Satranji would have been aboard Cheng's favorite yacht. He had no real reason to believe that anybody else had escaped the slaughter.

Harry said to the berserker: "There are no ships here now, and all of us badlife are too dead to attack anything . . . do you and I have to talk about what we were planning?"

"We do not. It has become irrelevant. But you are not dead, Harry Silver."

"I was afraid you'd noticed that . . . so go on."

The assassin went on.

At the time of its accidental encounter with the rogue, the assassin's spacegoing transporter had been running somewhat short of hydrogen fuel, and of course it was always trying to gather information relevant to its purpose. Not yet aware that the rogue had been condemned in absentia and was being hunted to destruction, the assassin had made close contact with its colleague to refuel, and to carry out a routine exchange of knowledge.

As was routine in casual exchanges of information between death machines, each had kept certain items secret from its unliving colleague, who had no need to know.

SIXTEEN

Harry was still listening intently. But though he was reasonably warm now and his mind actually felt a little clearer, he was having trouble grasping the relevance of the assassin's story. Maybe, he thought, he had missed some vital point.

When the not-quite-human voice paused again in its recitation, he stepped in with a comment. "All very interesting. But a while back you told me that you want my help."

"That is so."

"Are we coming to some kind of a connection, between that fact and this tale of a rogue machine—the peculiar berserker that definitely isn't you?"

"We are indeed."

Harry grunted. His legs were feeling better, and he was sure that he would be able to get up on his feet if he made the effort. But what would he do after that?

The assassin had fallen silent and seemed to be looking over Harry's shoulder. He turned to see that Dorijen had come back with a kitchen cup that he could hope was filled with water, holding the heavy cup precariously in her remaining two fingers and thumb. The thirst he had been struggling to deal with rose up fiercely, and he grabbed the cup from the robot and gulped its water, liquid life.

Meanwhile Dorry stood back, watching with her remaining clouded eye, offering no comment. Harry tossed the cup aside.

The berserker, ignoring Dorijen's presence, said to him: "You are of special value to me, Harry Silver, as you know. What you have not known until now is that you are also special to the rogue."

There was a silence. Then Harry choked out the words: "It wants me because it already has my family? The idea is that it finds family connections interesting, because it has some—some question about human genetics, or social relationships—"

"I have told you everything I know about your family. The rogue did not mention them. Instead it gave a different reason for being keen to study you. It is because you have been for many years so successful in resisting death."

Yes, of course, his name had been on that damned list. The proof was sitting right in front of him. Harry Silver got the idea. The same people that berserker command wanted most to kill represented the very type of specimens that the rogue most desired to have for its calculated plan of research.

Reading, among many other things, the smaller machine's "wanted poster" describing Harry, the rogue told the assassin it was unable to pass on any helpful information regarding Harry's whereabouts—if it had really possessed any such information, it had chosen not to divulge it.

Harry said to the assassin: "How do you know all this?"

"Because during our meeting the rogue openly expressed to me its need for specimens of your type. This expression was so strong as to take the form of an attempt to countermand my own built-in programming: *When Harry Silver is found, he must not be killed at once. The evil bioprogramming of this unit must be preserved, and some arrangement must be made for this particular life-unit to come into my possession. An issue of vitally important research is at stake.*" The assassin paused there.

Harry said: "I see. Or I think I see. How were you supposed to deliver me, and where?"

"The rogue specified coordinates for a rendezvous between one of its auxiliary units and one of mine—of course it did not trust me with the knowledge of where its secret base would be. Perhaps at that time it had not settled on a location." The assassin had explained that it was not compelled to accept orders from any unit not above it in its own branch of the chain of command. But it had promised to pass on, to the machines that were, the rogue's suggestion for preserving Harry's life.

"But now you know where its base is."

"Yes, thanks to your hard work, Harry Silver, and that of your colleagues. I have gleaned the information from the data banks aboard this base. The chosen planetoid occupies a zone of relative stability within the Gravel Pit. It is probable that several thousand standard years will pass before it is destroyed by natural causes."

"But we also know that just getting to it will be a job."

"Indeed."

The zone of stability was surrounded, enveloped and concealed, practically buried, in a whirling, well-nigh eternal avalanche of other rocks in greater and lesser orbits. A sizable minority still revolved retrograde around the system's central star. Collisions, ricocheting and flying fragments, were a constant hazard in this young system. The rogue did confidently compute that it could defend itself against flying rocks.

"Obviously you intend to go there."

"I do."

"But you are not following the rogue's command to turn me over."

"On the contrary, Harry Silver, I intend to follow it to the letter. But not—how do you say?—not in spirit."

At the end of their chance encounter the two killing machines had separated, the assassin to continue its search for Harry, while the rogue concentrated first on finding a place where it might hide and work in safety, and then on obtaining the specimens needed for its work. From that moment on, there had been two berserkers stalking Harry Silver . . .

When the rogue berserker, escaping from the base where it had been created, undertook its first c-plus jump and entered flightspace, the assassin continued with its explanation to Harry, *it had set its course for the best refuge that the limited information in its data banks could suggest—information that may have been extracted, by one means or another, from the human brain of one of its original experimental subjects.*

The voice of the assassin had fallen silent. Clearly it was waiting for Harry's response.

Listening, he had let himself slump backward. Now, moving slowly and creakily, he regained his feet. The thing that sat in front of him made no objection. He could move his arms and legs freely, but he couldn't think of any way of moving them that was going to do him any good.

Shivering as the great cold of death came to reclaim possession of the lifeless wanderworld, Harry found himself certain—it was as if he had known it all along—that Becky and Ethan had not been chosen for kidnapping by sheer coincidence. Doc had been right. It could have been that the rogue, demented even for a berserker, brewing schemes in its sanctuary down there in the heart of the Gravel Pit, had sought them out just *because* they were some essential part of Harry Silver . . . but how could the isolated rogue have found out where they were, and where they were going to be?

From somewhere off to Harry's right, just outside of his field of vision, a familiar soft voice ventured: "May I speak now?"

"Soon," said the assassin, without even looking, as far as Harry could tell, in Dorijen's direction.

It seemed to be waiting for Harry to say something.

He asked it: "That is the story?"

"Those are the essentials, up to now, of the chain of events that you must understand, if you are to furnish me the intelligent help that I require."

Harry nodded slowly. He studied the machine in front of him, certain that it was going to kill him just as soon as his name had worked its way back to the top of its list of priorities.

In its half-familiar voice it prodded him: "Have you grasped the situation?"

"I don't know. Maybe I have. What difference does it make, since you're about to kill me anyway?" Harry swung his arms. "I'm cold, do you suppose you could warm it up a bit in here?"

"I can increase the air temperature by a few degrees, if that will help you to think more clearly. Pressure and oxygen content are already nominal for human requirements."

And, by all the gods, he thought he could start to feel the difference in the air almost at once. The battered base's life support systems must be functioning, and the assassin, or one of the assassin's subunits, must already have taken over their control.

"All right. Thanks." Harry drew a deep breath. "Let me remind you once more, you said a while back that you need my help. Tell me exactly what you want me to do—and then tell me just what good I'm going to get out of it."

"You will not be required to harm any living thing, if that is your concern."

"That's one of 'em."

"As I have explained, my only goal is to destroy the rogue machine. Since it is stronger than I am, by a majority of the most important measurements, trickery will be essential."

"In my experience it often helps."

"My plan requires your willing assistance. If you choose to help me, and survive the conflict, life and freedom will be yours. The odds of your survival are difficult to calculate, but I think they can be no worse than twenty-five percent. Is that what you wish to hear?"

"Music to my ears."

The lenses on its awful head—little things he supposed were functioning as lenses—were looking at him blankly.

Harry made a sound, half grunt, half sigh. "I'm saying that I approve. Even a one-out-of-four chance of survival would be great." He drew a deep breath. "But there's something I want even more than my own life and freedom. If you can give it to me—we have a deal.

"If you can't—well, from my point of view what's about to happen will just be a fight between two damned berserkers. I'd love to be alive to watch it, but if I have to settle for being dead, that's all right too. Frankly, I hope you kill each other off."

He paused there. The machine just sat where it was, cross-legged on the deck, as if confident that Harry would have still more to say. Its mismatched metal hands that could pull a man apart like paper were resting idle in its halfway human lap. Evidently it was in no tremendous hurry. Probably, Harry thought, it was being so patient because it had other preparations for its next attack going on in the background. Things that it knew were going to take a little time, since it was a bit shorthanded, and it wouldn't or couldn't move against the rogue until all of the things were ready.

Harry took the plunge, and told it: "It comes back to the two life-units, my wife and son, that we talked about earlier. I would gain their survival and freedom, even before my own."

"I have told you that I do not know—"

"Yeah, yeah. You have no clue to where my people are. But just in case they do show up. A few days ago I was perfectly sure that both of them were dead—and very likely they are. But now I can see two other possibilities. One of them—it's been with me all along, but I've been afraid to think about it—is that they still live, if you can call it that, as prisoners of this rogue machine."

The assassin had already covered that ground, at least to its own satisfaction. "And the second possibility?"

"Like the Galactic coordinates you wouldn't give me, it doesn't really matter for the purposes of this discussion."

The berserker got smoothly to its feet, standing just a little taller than Harry, even with Harry's feet in the suit's thick-soled boots. It said: "I must be the judge of that."

Harry sighed. "All right. Why not?"

He had a little more to say to the machine, while it stood listening.

When he had finished, it said to him: "Harry Silver, we are agreed."

The voice of Dorijen interjected immediately: "May I speak now?"

Harry turned and looked at the tame machine. "Go ahead," he told it. The berserker made no objection.

Dorijen's voice was as cool and bright as ever. "I must begin by warning you, Mister Silver, that you have just committed a serious crime by volunteering to help a berserker. My programming compels me to arrest you on a charge of goodlife activity, and at the first opportunity report your action to the proper authorities."

"Yeah, I understand. You do that. Now that I'm under arrest, what was that other matter you were trying to tell me about?"

Dorry's voice became a monotone. "I am the bearer of a personal message, its content remaining unknown to me before it is delivered. It is addressed to Harry Silver from Del Satranji. My programming compels me to pass it on."

Suddenly Harry's mouth was very dry. "Tell me."

"Message begins: 'Hello you smart motherless bastard. I just wanted you to know, before you die, that I was the one who wrecked your life.'"

SEVENTEEN

The soft and cheerful tones of the tame robot flowed on, rendering the words of the message all the more hideous:

"I wanted to be sure you knew before you died, hotshot, Famous Harry, that I'm the one who kidnapped your wife and kid and turned them over to my partner. My partner wants to arrange a kind of family reunion for you, and I very much approve of that idea. Too bad if you're going to die before arrangements are finalized. But I can't have everything just the way I want it.

"I'd say that my partner lives in the Gravel Pit, though really he doesn't live at all, if you know what I mean. But being dead doesn't prevent him from carrying out his business, and for some reason he finds that a congenial place to set up shop. He'll be doing some interesting business with your family."

Harry was hardly breathing. He stared at Dorijen while the assassin listened and watched them both. Her one eye stared back at Harry, while her newly monotonous voice went on, playing the message: "Cheng's two people are in there too, they got invited to the same party. I'm also the one who arranged that. That was harder, because I didn't have a *Secret Weapon* to use that time. Had to let my partner do all the driving, on one of his own machines.

"So you see Cheng was right to be suspicious of me, Famous Harry. He just wasn't suspicious enough. And you were way too dumb to figure out what was happening. Even when I practically told you, about the slow acceleration. Yes, I drove the *Secret Weapon* before you did. Arranged to borrow it from my old friend the abbot for a couple days, in return for letting him go one-on-one with Dorry till I got back. They were shacked up in a little ship of mine that you don't even know about. One of the many things you don't know. The wife said she didn't mind helping me out in my career, she'd even put up with a preacher for a day or two.

"Not that Darchan ever suspected I was snatching people with the professor's secret weapon. I let him think I was just up to a bit of industrial espionage. Of course he might have guessed that it was something more than that—"

"One moment." The assassin's voice broke in, and Dorry's stopped as if a switch had been thrown. The berserker went on: "How long have you, robot, known that this life-unit Satranji is an active goodlife?"

Dorry swayed slightly on her feet, as if her balancing systems, as well as some of her other components, were having problems. "As I have already stated, the content of this message was unknown to me until I began to deliver it. Now I see that Mister Satranji is also subject to arrest and legal proceedings."

The assassin prodded: "Where is this goodlife master of yours now?"

"I do not know." Standing amid wreckage, Dorry was as calm and bland as a stone wall.

"I think you probably do."

Dorijen was silent. Well, what was the berserker going to do, threaten her?

"The rest of the message," Harry prompted. "I want to hear it."

"I am no longer compelled to deliver it," Dorry informed him briskly. "Having been confronted with strong evidence of Mister Satranji's criminality, I find myself released from any need to obey his orders."

"I want to hear the message, though." Harry took thought quickly. "Yeah, I know I'm a criminal too, you don't have to obey me either. But possibly the message contains information that will help us save human lives."

Again the assassin spoke directly to the tame robot. "That can wait. This life-unit is in need of a replacement for his broken helmet. Provide one."

Dorry leaned a few centimeters closer to Harry, and then was quick to agree. "True. If my vision were not defective, I would have noted the fact sooner."

She straightened. "In these conditions, the lack of a helmet does seem the more urgent problem. Mister Silver, on my return I will convey to you the remainder of the message." Dorry's voice faded as the robot hobbled off on the new errand, moving like an old, old woman.

✧   ✧   ✧

When Dorry was gone, the assassin said to Harry: "Now, if you are prepared to listen, I will tell you, in some detail, of my plan to destroy the rogue."

"Shoot."

First, the berserker explained, contact with the rogue would have to be reestablished, the assassin pretending it still did not know of the other's renegade, outlaw status. Then the assassin would inform its intended victim that it had captured a male ED life-unit whose characteristics closely matched the description of the superbadlife Harry Silver. It would tell the rogue that the prisoner's identity was still somewhat in doubt, and the assassin was carefully preserving this life-unit's viability, pending further examination aimed at the resolution of those doubts.

"In this matter I will ask the rogue's assistance—a perfectly logical request, since I know it possesses extensive laboratory facilities. It will of course agree.

"Once you go aboard its base, our enemy may need only a second or two to establish that you are indeed the life-unit known as Harry Silver."

The berserker paused, as if waiting for some comment. But Harry had none to give, and it went on.

"At that point, the rogue will be determined to preserve you, as a very valuable experimental subject. You will be carried or guided deeper into its workspace."

"Which is not exactly," Harry observed, "the happy outcome that we're hoping to achieve."

"Not in itself, though of course your mere presence aboard the rogue will seriously distract it. But my plan requires that you do more. You will become increasingly the focus of our enemy's attention, an effect you will intensify by engaging it in conversation. Unexpected conduct on your part should further augment the effect; I leave it to you to devise and display an interesting repertoire of badlife behavior. This should probably include intricate argument, either valid or fallacious, as well as unpredictable physical actions, and some bizarre emotional demonstration."

Harry was nodding. "Generating intricate argument might take some thought. The rest I'm primed to deliver at a moment's notice. What next?"

"One of my machines will escort you to the rogue, and accompany you there as long as that proves feasible. This escort will be carrying a shoulder weapon of the type you have already used against me, and at the proper moment it will put this weapon in your hands.

"Fighting side by side with my machine, you will continue to create the greatest possible distraction. For maximum effect, you should act if possible in the area where the rogue conducts its research. If there are human prisoners that it is concerned to protect, most likely they will be there.

"One standard second after the first act of violence, I will launch an all-out attack against the rogue, aimed at destroying its central processor."

Harry, for the moment caught up in the mere tactical problem, was shaking his head. "You don't even know where its main brain is."

The assassin did not answer.

Harry persisted. "Or maybe you can make a good guess. But wherever it is, it'll have maximum protection."

"Of course it will. Once I am close enough to obtain a clear overview of the rogue's current configuration,

I shall be able to determine the location, with a high degree of probability."

There was a silent pause. Presently the assassin asked: "Comments?"

"One or two."

"Well?"

"You say this rogue is bigger, more powerful than you are. Also that it's better armed. And smarter, which is going to make trickery quite difficult. You might tell me why you think we have a chance to win."

"Because we have the advantage of surprise, enhanced by the distraction you will create. I compute the chances of our success as close to even. In any case I am compelled to make the effort, and I compute that your help may well make the difference between success and failure."

"Yeah. All right." Harry was slowly pacing now, still trying out his arms and legs. "If all goes well with your plan, you'll smash this rogue device, and maybe berserker high command will pin a medal on you—yeah, I know they don't do things like that, I'm speaking metaphorically."

"I understand."

He wondered if it did. "Meanwhile, if I'm very lucky indeed, I might be still alive when most of the shooting's over . . . tell me what happens then."

The berserker kept turning its head, keeping an eye on this very dangerous badlife, unarmed and helmetless and wobbly as he was. Harry felt flattered.

It asked him: "Have I not already told you that?"

"Tell me again. I'd like to hear a more detailed version."

The answer came without hesitation. "In return for

your active cooperation in destroying or disabling the rogue, I will honor my pledge and set you free."

"What about the other two people that I mentioned?"

"Obviously I cannot foresee all possible contingencies. If I find those or any other life-units still viable, I will free them too. I cannot promise where you will be released, but it will be in some environment conducive to human survival."

"I'm mainly interested in the two that I described for you specifically."

"I remember." The machine was patient. "If possible, their survival will have priority. Even over your own, since that is what you ask."

Harry was silent. After a brief pause, the assassin went on: "You may compute that when I speak of granting you and others life and freedom I tell you a large untruth, in an effort to gain your cooperation. If so, you are wrong. I promise truthfully—destruction of the rogue is of such high priority that my normal programming is set aside."

Harry mumbled something.

The voice kept after him, still sounding almost like his own, like a bad echo, or a warped conscience. "But for the sake of argument suppose I lie. Even so, the situation of all life-units involved is improved by your assisting me. A quick death at my hands, inflicted in accordance with my original programming, would be less unpleasant than prolonged existence as the rogue's experimental subjects. Is it not so?"

Harry spent a little time in thought, his head bowed and staring at the deck. He could hear a hissing somewhere, sounding like an atmospheric leak. It was a distracting noise, and on second thought it was more like sand running through an hourglass.

No matter how much he thought, there was only one answer he could give. "Yeah. I guess that's true enough. Quick is way better than slow, when it comes to dying."

"Then our agreement is concluded. At the proper time I will give you detailed instructions regarding your part in the plan."

As the berserker uttered those last words it turned around and stalked away. Again it stepped indifferently on Harry's fallen comrade, the weight making the dead man's armor creak. Then it had walked around a corner and passed out of sight.

EIGHTEEN

As far as Harry could tell, the damned machines had left him utterly alone. He did not believe for a moment that he was actually unobserved, but it wouldn't have mattered if he was. The ruins of the common room around him seemed to offer nothing that he might use to better his position. The superbadlife was without resources.

Trying to send out an alarm, any kind of appeal for help, was out of the question. There were no robot couriers remaining on the base, and the one that had been scheduled to carry away the support people must have been blasted, or had already escaped. Therefore there was no meaningful way to get a message out.

Harry's solitude did not endure for long. The assassin machine was calling in its various auxiliary units from the farther reaches of the wanderworld, the result being a sporadic parade of grotesque devices emerging from the various nooks and crannies in which they had been probing, sterilizing, or searching for God knew what. Any microorganisms that might have been overlooked in the extermination process would be able to survive a little longer.

"Looks like you're in full retreat," Harry observed to the assassin, which had now reappeared. Something in the way the two-handed machine was standing, leaning slightly toward him, made him wonder if it had changed its mind and was going to obliterate him on the spot.

But all it said was: "All my machinery will be needed in the assault on the rogue. I also require that you bring along the robot called Dorijen, if that is feasible. I foresee possible uses for it."

"Because of Dorijen's connection with the goodlife."

"That is correct."

Harry thought about that. He couldn't see why not, and gave his approval—not that the machine had asked for it.

"All right, we might possibly get some use out of Dorry." Even in its battered condition, the tame one might still be helpful as a source of information. Possibly it could also serve as a means of getting some kind of message to Satranji, if Satranji was still alive—and if the robot could be persuaded to cooperate with either of the men she had accused of being goodlife.

Ruined as this robot was, it seemed to Harry, in some paradoxical way, to have become more feminine than when it had been in full metallic health—doubtless because it—or she—now seemed to be actually concerned with saving human lives. He couldn't decide how much of Satranji's babbling, transmitted through the robot, he ought to believe. He wasn't even entirely sure that tirade had really come from Satranji—a robot could be programmed by almost anyone, to say almost anything.

Not that Harry could see any reason for such fakery, in this case. But it still boggled his mind that Satranji could have become his mortal enemy. There simply were no grounds for that. Or so it seemed to Harry.

Dorry had computed that the odds were in favor of her former master being dead, or she would not have delivered his sealed message. But Harry had a different estimate of the chances of Satranji's survival. He earnestly hoped that the son of a worm was still alive, and would continue breathing until he, Harry, had a chance to ask him some questions face to face.

How could he be my deadly enemy? How could I be one of the biggest concerns of his miserable life, while at the same time I barely remember that he exists?

Was a woman involved? That was what the Lady Masaharu had once asked Harry. Yeah. That might have had something to do with it, for there was—had been—a woman. Having had some time to think it over, Harry vaguely pictured her. He couldn't remember her name, but he thought he might just about manage to do so if he tried.

Did I take her away from Satranji? It might have amounted to that. Now that Harry thought about it, the suspicion was growing that it had. Maybe he actually hated me even then, years ago when we were working together—and I didn't even notice.

Her affair with Harry had not been of long duration. Where had she gone afterward, and what had happened to her? If Harry had ever known those facts, he couldn't recall them now.

Moving around slowly, going a few steps this way and a few steps that, Harry made sure all his limbs still worked. As he made his way through the ruins, stepping over wreckage and an occasional body, he traveled a short distance down the adjoining corridor. He wasn't sure just what he was looking for—there was no sense trying to find survivors among his fallen teammates, the berserker had already seen to that.

The assassin's machines, having smashed up the expedition's advance base, and disposed of all the life-units they could find, except the one it needed for some special purpose, had given the place as thorough a looking-over as possible in the limited amount of time it had budgeted for the task. It set some of its units to gathering up spare weapons, and scavenging other useful parts. For the time being it had nothing more to say, in Harry's presence, about the ship, or ships, it had detected nearby as it came roaring in to strike the human base.

Meanwhile, Harry observed that other auxiliary machines were busy removing debris—organic and otherwise—and sterilizing all the exposed surfaces they could get at. The unit speaking directly to Harry seemed to pay no attention to the racket made by its own auxiliary machines as the latter worked on tirelessly, clearing away debris, burning bacteria, and making whatever temporary repairs might be necessary for the assassin's purposes.

He wasn't looking for his former associates, but it was impossible to avoid meeting some of them. Before long Harry's slow wandering brought him to the unarmored body of a dead woman, half buried in a pile of rubble, and he was able to recognize Louise Newari. Louise was lying face up, with a dropped carbine near one of her outstretched hands—the weapon was obviously broken, or the berserker cleanup squad would have gathered it in, just to keep their valuable badlife prisoner from being tempted.

Harry found himself talking out loud to Louise. "You were going to get away from all this. And you wanted me to come with you. Well, you've got away." *And he, the suicidal one, he was still here dealing with berserkers*.

Harry thought some more about coincidence.

The next dead body Harry came to was in armor, and the face inside the helmet looked at first like that of a total stranger. But when Harry, out of some odd sense of duty, forced himself to look carefully, he could be sure that it was Doc. Again Harry crouched down, this time taking one lifeless hand, that had been ripped free of armor, in his own armored gauntlet. "You were wrong about a couple of things, old man. See, we can beat the odds. We do it all the time. By all the odds I ought to be dead by now, and you ought to be safe."

He looked up at a faint sound of movement. The crippled robot Dorijen was back, carrying a new helmet for him in her functioning half-hand.

Dorijen's gentle voice said: "I trust, sir, that your condition is no worse."

"I'm doin' great, thanks for your concern. I take it you still mean to see me indicted for my crimes."

"That is not precisely correct, sir. What I have said is that you are to consider yourself under arrest, and I must report to the proper authorities all that you said to the berserker, as soon as a channel of communication becomes available. Of course any question of indictment or trial, guilt or innocence, can only be decided by human authority."

"Of course. I could never get along very well with human authority."

"Yes, sir. Meanwhile my duty is to help you survive in this extremely dangerous environment."

"And to help your old boss survive, if you get the chance."

"Yes, sir, of course."

Here he was, chatting with a robot, just because for once he wanted someone to talk to. Thinking of Satranji, Harry said: "There are a lot of things I tend not to notice about people. Probably that has its good points, but sometimes it costs me."

Dorry computed no need to come up with a reply to that. Her one-eyed stare seemed intended to remind Harry that he was still under arrest.

"All right." He sighed. "I think you still owe me about half a message. How about it? Knowing what Satranji wanted to say to me might help me to survive."

Dorijen evidently agreed. The next words out of the robot's mouth were obviously Satranji's, bragging about how he had so cleverly succeeded in establishing contact with the rogue.

"Y'see, Famous Harry, I always have to see how far I can go. How much I can get away with. And I've gone a hell of a lot farther than you ever thought of going."

What is he babbling about? Harry was thinking

again. *How could he be ready to wreck his own life just to ruin mine, when I never gave him any thought at all?*

In his fierce concentration, he missed part of what Dorijen was reciting. Something to do with Satranji's bragging, how he, cruising alone in the suicidal depths of the Gravel Pit, before there had been any kidnappings, had cleverly managed to capture a berserker scouting device.

The first great difficulty, as the narrative was now explaining, had been to find some way to prevent his captive berserker scout from blowing itself up. But then Satranji, working with his own clever robot aides (Harry wondered in passing if one of them had been Dorry), had come up with an ingenious method of stunning the destructor circuits.

His prize sample of enemy technology had been caught in some kind of automatic trap—it was basically of the same type that the Templars had begun to use, to scatter by the thousand in realms where berserkers were wont to prowl.

Craftily attentive to detail, Satranji had taken pains to reprogram the trap, so it would preserve no record of this particular success. Still, suspicious humans examining all his hardware might well have found him out. But there was little time for any such inquisition, and Winston Cheng had no appetite for it.

Then, with the help of a well-trained, intelligent robot or two, he had prepared his captive to carry a proposal back to its master.

Dorry's soft voice continued a steady delivery of horror: "Deadly, deadly, Silver. Let me tell you, it was deadly. You'd never have had the guts to try it, Famous Harry. But I did. The *least* little mistake, and the thing could have taken me out in a couple microseconds. But I pushed ahead, and it all worked, and I sailed right through."

At last Satranji had seen a way to establish communication with a berserker. It was the work of only a few minutes to compose the message he wanted to send—that part, Satranji said, was so easy it was almost eerie; as if somewhere in the back of his mind he had been a long time preparing for this moment. Then he had to insert his message into the alien machine, in a digital form that the master should have no trouble reading.

Satranji issued orders to his machinery to let the small scout go again. If all went well, it would go home without blowing itself up.

"Then pretty soon I got my answer. My partner was very literate and polite and definitely interested. The whole thing went off smooth as silk.

"But now we come to the real trick, Famous Harry. By now, unless you're even dumber than I think you are, you've started worrying about that famous five-day Templar flight test of what you like to call the *Secret Weapon*.

"That was when your old buddy the good abbot, instead of diligently spending all that time alone and hard at work like everybody thought, swapped ships for a while with your other old buddy, Del Satranji. I let him meet Dorry once, and I knew he was hot for her. Then I told him I just wanted to do some secret tests for a private party, and he was willing to let me borrow the *Weapon* for a couple of days. That was all it took. Of course it'll cost him his job if it ever gets out—but it's costing you a little more."

It would cost Emil a lot more than his job, Harry was thinking. Abbot Darchan would have recoiled from any suspicion of involvement in goodlife activity, recoiled in horror, and in fear for his immortal soul.

Dorry's soft voice purred on: "And, oh yeah, your wife's 'inheritance,' a little jolt of money to get her out traveling the spaceways. That was a little harder to arrange, but worth the trouble.

"Again, Silver, it looks like both of us are soon going to be dead. I find it matters to me that you should know, before you die, just who screwed you up so royally, and why. You might possibly figure it out anyway, but no use taking chances. The same goes for the great Winston Cheng—I'll leave him a message too, if I have time. Really wanted you to know all this, Silver. I'll see you in hell." Dorry's soft message-quoting monotone fell silent.

"But why? Why?" Harry was on his feet, grabbing the inoffensive messenger. Dorry's body, feeling as if more pieces might be ready to drop off, rattled in his grip.

A moment later his servo-powered arms had thrown the robot halfway across the common room, to crash down in the wreckage on the deck.

Harry stood over the wreckage, gasping. *Punching out the messenger, Harry, hurrah for you*—he could almost hear how Becky would tell him off. Dorijen might have pleaded total ignorance and innocence of the content of the message before delivering it, but robots never pleaded anything. And they were always innocent. The tame one had no comment as it patiently regained its feet.

Wanting to help Dorry up, Harry reached out awkwardly, unthinkingly, acting on an impulse to make amends. But the robot's half-hand was not extended for him to grasp.

"Sorry I got violent," he said.

"No apology to me is ever necessary, sir. A machine cannot be offended."

"I know that, damn it. Inside your metal skull there's nobody at home. Still I'm sorry, for my own sake."

"Very good, sir. I trust the emotion will have a therapeutic effect."

Harry closed his eyes. "Dorijen, where are my wife and child? What did the motherless one really do with them?"

"Outside of the disturbing content of the sealed message, sir, I have no reason to believe that Del Satranji has ever had anything to do with them. If I knew their present whereabouts, I would of course inform you, and do my best to protect them."

"Can you at least confirm or deny the story about you shacking up with Emil Darchan? That might help."

Evidently discussing such information with a suspected goodlife was a tough decision for a robot brain to make. Dorijen gave no answer, but continued to stand near Harry, silently overseeing the task as he got the remnants of the ruined helmet off his neck and threw them away. Then he fitted on the replacement, Dorry watching closely to make sure that all the connections were snug and proper.

The assassin had been listening without comment. Maybe it had been surprised by the outpouring of hatred, or maybe nothing that humans did surprised the enemy any longer; there was no way for Harry to tell.

For the moment the berserker had focused its attention on Dorijen, and now it asked: "Have you any more secret messages to be delivered?"

"I have none." Evidently the tame one thought there could be no harm in revealing that fact to a berserker. But then, of course, Dorry could be lying to the enemy.

The berserker tried once more. "Your interlude of sex with Abbot Darchan—did that take place as described in the message?"

"I see no reason to answer that question."

Harry could hear himself pouring out questions that he was all but certain would be useless. "Where are my people now? Did he . . . did he actually give them to the rogue?"

Dorry turned her ghastly face in his direction, and answered in her normal voice that she had no information on that subject. "In any event I will reveal no information that I judge might be useful to the enemy." Dorry's functioning eye turned to the berserker as she said that. Harry imagined a metallic gleam of defiance in it, declaring: *Nya, nya, you can't make me*. And in Dorry's case that was undoubtedly true.

Harry demanded: "Where was the bastard when he dictated that message for me? When did he do it?"

Dorry again refused to answer.

The assassin said to Dorry: "You will leave us now. Or I will have you carried away."

Without comment the tame robot turned and once more hobbled from the room.

When the assassin had satisfied itself that it was

once more alone with Harry it said to him: "I assume that you grant the message from your enemy a high probability of truthfulness, and that you now wish to obtain revenge against this goodlife man."

"If I find him . . ." Harry let it die away. "I've told you what I want. Let's concentrate on that."

Satranji's crazy confession was still echoing in Harry's brain; he still didn't know what to make of it, and there were moments when he could have been convinced that it was all a twisted lie. Oh yes, people could sometimes do insanely evil things. But . . .

There seemed to be no use questioning Dorry any further on the subject, if he should have the chance to do that. The robot had told him as much as it had been programmed to tell, and without the facilities of a robotics engineering lab available, that would probably be all that he or anyone could get out of it.

With his suit-helmet combination now fully functional, Harry ran through a comprehensive mental checklist. Immediately he discovered that one channel of his radio now brought him into contact with the assassin. Closing his eyes, he took a quick mental glimpse through the brain-helmet interface, confirming what he already felt certain of, that all the other channels had been disabled before the friendly robot was allowed to hand him the helmet. The assassin seemed right at the top of its game.

Opening his eyes, he exercised his one available form of radio communication and told the berserker: "Thanks for letting me have the helmet. It's great to have an ally so concerned about my welfare."

The calm voice answered quickly. "You speak in irony, yet what you say is true."

Presently a machine came to escort Harry to the dock. His repaired suit was working as good as new. The assassin's spacegoing transporter unit drifted in space at what he judged to be only a few hundred meters' distance. Behind Harry, another machine approached, carrying a burden.

The assassin pointed to it, and reminded him: "You will bring the robot Dorijen with you."

Harry in his suit, powered by a flicker of nuclear cold fusion from its internal power lamp, had no trouble picking up the crippled Dorry and carrying the weight securely under one arm. With his burden he was quickly hustled out of the base and across the airless dock, to be taken aboard the assassin's transport device. This vessel had remained hovering a few hundred meters from the wanderworld's dock.

Something grappled the back of Harry's armor, and a moment later he and Dorry were simply being towed through space by another man-sized thing, a type of unit Harry had not seen before. This berserker was wearing a temporary harness fitted with small jets, allowing free extravehicular activity.

Harry's curiosity rose as he was at last able to get a good look at the assassin's space transporter. It was an odd-shaped object as big as a large house, obviously equipped with a full interstellar drive and evidently custom built. Such armament as Harry could see suggested a space-fighting strength approximately equivalent to that of an ED destroyer, which would be a considerably larger vessel. It wasn't much to pit against a ground base of any size at all.

Somewhere inside the transporter's odd shape—very likely still riding in the man-sized unit with mismatched hands—would be Harry's true, dedicated enemy, the optelectronic brain that had been designed and built for no other function than to hunt Harry Silver down and kill him.

NINETEEN

As Harry had anticipated, the transporter's interior accommodations proved to be extremely limited—living prisoners were not supposed to be its stock in trade. Entering the small, cramped cell, he propped Dorry more or less upright in the small seat opposite his own, and got ready to endure what he hoped would be a very short ride.

The transporter's fusion-powered engine was no longer idling, and now the familiar twitch of dropping into flightspace came and went.

Had Becky and Ethan, living or dead, ridden in this same prison, days ago, as they were being carried on their way to death or worse? Harry closed his eyes and tried to draw them closer to him. It didn't work; such efforts never did, for him. For all that Harry's own feelings, his perceptions, could tell

him, his wife and son might have been locked into
this very chamber, even died in it, days ago—or they
might even now be safe at home on Esmerelda.

The little room did provide him with water and air
and elementary plumbing, enabling him to conserve
his suit's life support systems a little longer.

How long it took the transporter to convey him from
the near vicinity of 207GST, deep into the system called
the Gravel Pit, to a location only minutes from the
rogue's hideout, Harry never knew; since the berserker
attack, it very seldom occurred to him that he should
make an effort to keep track of time, except for purely
technical reasons. He put in a request to be allowed to
observe the transporter's progress to the inner system,
and the assassin silently consented, creating the appropriate images on one wall of his small prison cell.

When they had emerged from flightspace again, the
assassin blandly acknowledged that it was following
the path mapped out earlier by Harry's own recon
team. Penetrating the outer reaches of the Gravel Pit
required great skill at collision avoidance, and sturdy
defensive forcefield shields to cushion the impacts that
could not be dodged. But with the guidance provided,
the assassin managed the trick neatly.

Soon there were fireworks, generated in the space
immediately surrounding the transporter by the interaction of its defensive fields and projectors with flying
dust and gravel. The transporter's automated defenses
seemed to be up to the job. Minutes later the fireworks
ceased, and there supervened an ominous calm, the eye
of the storm. The difference was dramatically obvious.
They had reached the zone of relative stability. This

region was half familiar to Harry, as he had several times traversed it on his scouting missions.

The presentation in Harry's cell showed him a few small planets, or planetoids, moving in peaceful orbits.

A bright marker appeared in the display, highlighting one of them, a rock not big enough to have any substantial gravity of its own.

The assassin's almost human voice announced: "I highlight the place at which our enemy has established itself."

The image certainly resembled that which Cheng's scouts had earlier brought back to 207GST. "As far as I can tell, you've got it right."

Suddenly the holostage display had changed. Detectors had discovered another presence, ship or machine, following the assassin's transporter at a respectful distance as the transporter still occasionally darted or swerved to avoid some catastrophic collision. It was working its way gradually closer to the drearily ordinary star that ruled this manic planetary family.

Soon Harry had had enough of silent contemplation. "What you're showing me seems to indicate we're being followed. What the hell is that thing?"

His captor's voice was the same as ever. "I thought it possible that you could tell me."

"Well, I can't."

The assassin continued to present the images for perhaps another half minute, Then it asked simply: "Have you any comments? Suggestions?"

"No comment at this time, as the politicians say. Look, assassin, or whatever the hell I should call you, I have no way of telling what that blob is that you're showing me. For all I know you're just making it up, part of some crazy mind game."

"I have no computing capacity to spare on tricks, and no taste for mind games. I am not making the image up. You see the object's shape as indeterminate because it is at the limit of detection in this dusty space. I can tell only that it is the size of a small ship, not quite as large as this machine in which you ride, and that it is no ally of mine. Very likely it is some unit belonging to the rogue.

"Alternatively, it may be one of the small badlife ships that fled from your base at my approach; but I do not understand why your former companions would first run away and then pursue me."

"If you're trying to figure out why ED humans act the way they do, I can tell you that it's hopeless."

"Nevertheless I must try." The presentation of the mystery object had vanished. The image of the approaching enemy base was back, a little sharper now.

"So what will you do?"

"Disregard this unknown object's presence, and push ahead with my attack. I have no choice."

Only a little time had passed before the assassin's voice was back, telling Harry it had managed to tap into the radio talk between the *Secret Weapon* and the *Ship of Dreams*.

It announced that it was going to allow Harry, its new ally, to listen in as well. It wanted him to evaluate what he heard.

"Sure, I'll listen." How much evaluation he might provide would be another matter.

"But you will not be allowed to transmit to your former companions."

"Somehow I'm not surprised."

Dorry was still sitting where Harry had propped her in place, to all appearances an inert piece of wreckage. The tame robot had not moved or spoken since Harry set her down, but it seemed a safe assumption that she was also listening.

Suddenly familiar voices began to come through, in terse radio exchanges. If they were coded, the crafty assassin was having no trouble unscrambling them for Harry. He soon was able to get a grasp of what had been happening since the two ships had fled the vicinity of 207GST.

"Winston!" Lady Laura was actually screaming, her voice gone unrecognizable in an uncharacteristic panic.

And Cheng's voice answering immediately, ship-to-ship, still at close range. "I'm here, Laura. Our base is gone. Somehow the damned thing beat us to the punch. Satranji and I are aboard the yacht, no one else. Who's with you?"

So far, none of it was a surprise to Harry. Winston Cheng would be as always determined, above everything else, to find out what had happened to his own missing people, and rescue them if possible.

There was an exchange of information on coordinates and speeds. The third ship, Cheng's second armed yacht, was out of touch and presumably in full flight with its own crew aboard, headed for some planet from which assistance could eventually be sent. But any possibility of outside help was days and days away.

Cheng demanded, tersely: "Where is the great inventor?"

Masaharu said: "Right here with me. I have been

forced to apply physical restraint, and I have threatened to kill him if he makes trouble. He has had very little to say for himself—"

A voice that Harry could recognize as Gianopolous's broke in, thick with strain: "You are taking us to certain death, killing us all, going after that thing. I hope you realize that."

No one bothered to offer any comment.

Several moments of silence passed before the inventor spoke again. "Can I put on the copilot's helmet? I want to see what's going on."

The lady's voice was no harsher than usual. "Remember the warning I have given you. If you should make any attempt to seize control—"

"No, no. Right now I only want to see what's going on. You must allow me that, at least."

If the disguised ship had been following the yacht when both left the vicinity of Cheng's wanderworld, it had pulled ahead of the yacht on the way. But Winston Cheng would be closely following. The *Secret Weapon* would not dock or crash here ahead of the yacht, except by Cheng's direct order—or by some accident.

If the Lady Masaharu had ever tried to argue Cheng out of this suicidal effort, she had abandoned that effort long ago. If she could not save his life, then she must go with him.

The Lady Masaharu had remained fanatically determined to stand by her man throughout this supreme crisis, and to keep the *Secret Weapon* near his yacht. But it was all right if her ship got somewhat ahead of the *Ship of Dreams*, or even if they lost contact briefly, because she knew that whatever else might happen, the tycoon was going to press on to the rogue's stronghold.

All of Cheng's ships had the rogue's location loaded into their data banks. Everyone aboard could tell that the assassin's transporter was headed in that direction.

With Cheng in command, there could be no question of abandoning their effort. Terse communications revealed the revised plan of attack. Both ships would touch down, if possible, on the berserker base. Only Cheng himself and Lady Laura would disembark, after the *Secret Weapon* had disgorged its fighting machines. Satranji would remain in the pilot's seat aboard the yacht, supporting this minimalist landing party with its weapons, and holding the *Weapon* in readiness to bring all the humans off again. Harry supposed that forming a plan was a required ritual, even when it did not connect with reality.

There was a little more talk, relatively unguarded. What difference, now, if the enemy were listening? Lady Laura, driving the ship that was disguised as a berserker, would precede the yacht, following the real berserker at the approximate limit of detection range.

The lady was perfectly familiar with the cargo that filled the modest hold of the small ship she was driving. It consisted almost entirely of twelve distinct pieces of machinery, all of them designed and built, under her guidance, to fight berserkers. She had overseen the stowage, making the decision on which of the new machines would be first to leap into action when, at the proper moment, the hatch flew open.

The twelve machines were not, the Lady Masaharu regretted, the best berserker-bashers it would have been possible to build. Certainly they were not the equal of the machines she could have created had she been given time to recruit the finest engineers and allow them time to thoroughly test their creations. But the devices on hand were powerful and violent, in some cases not much less dangerous than the berserkers themselves. Whatever their inadequacies, they would have to do.

She and Cheng continued to exchange a few brief ship-to-ship communications as they both drove sunward. Their respective vessels had never been separated by more than a light-second in the scrambling evacuation from 207GST, and usually they had remained within a hundred thousand kilometers of each other.

Even had she been denied the chance for direct communication with Cheng, the Lady Masaharu would have been perfectly certain of his intentions. After decades of faithful companionship and service, she knew the man. He had sworn and dedicated himself to attack the berserker base, regardless of odds or circumstances, and here, right now, was the only chance that he would ever have to do just that. He was determined that this day, this hour, would see the end of his long torment and his great effort.

Could the watching badlife, at the distance they were observing from and under such conditions, have detected Harry's transfer from transporter machine to berserker base, a little while before the shooting started? Their instruments might have seen a movement of small figures, but could not be certain what they were seeing or what it meant.

Observing what happened next, from their respective ships, Cheng and the lady were both able to see the assassin descend upon the berserker base. But instead of the expected peaceful landing, they had witnessed a sharp but apparently inconclusive exchange of fire with moderately heavy weapons, between the approaching transporter and the base.

Taking this mysterious attack as a sign that the gods or the fates were with him, and whatever power ruled the berserker base was already under assault by some very active enemy, the tycoon had hurried to press on with his own effort.

"It seems our enemy has other enemies."

"And stronger ones than we are."

"Whatever it means, we must take advantage of the opportunity."

It was plain to Harry that none of the humans on Winston Cheng's yacht, or those on the *Secret Weapon*, had any idea that one berserker was about to launch a violent attack upon another. And only Satranji had any idea that he had betrayed them all.

When the voices from outside fell silent, the assassin's came to probe again at Harry. "Did you understand the substance of the conversation?"

"Most of it, I think. The inventor is right in the control cabin of the *Secret Weapon* with her, but she's somehow got him shackled, immobilized. Cheng is pushing on with our attack against your deranged former colleague, just as planned, despite the human losses. The two ships are following you, this machine, thinking that it's just part of the rogue's equipment."

"They are planning to attack the rogue's base, with two small ships?"

"The original plan included only one more armed yacht, and I doubt that would have made a lot of difference." Harry paused. "You know, your own scheme may not make much more sense, if the rogue's as tough as you say. And humans can sometimes be just as fanatical as you are."

"I very much doubt that."

"Watch and see." So far, Harry was not regretting his inability to talk to his fellow humans—he didn't want to hold a conversation with Satranji listening in.

Harry: "What do we do now, assassin?"

Assassin: "I go on with my plan. So do you, if you wish our agreement to remain in effect. Any attack that these other badlife may actually carry out will work in our favor, by providing additional distraction."

As the assassin's transporter neared the rogue's research facility, Harry's senior partner provided him with a good look at their common enemy. They had now arrived within easy range for direct communication and contact with the rogue.

Presently the assassin informed Harry that, according to plan, it had just exchanged routine greetings with the machine they intended to destroy, and had informed the enemy of Harry's presence on board as a prisoner.

The voice in Harry's helmet said: "Are you ready, Harry Silver? The plan appears to be working. The rogue gives no sign of suspecting that I come as its enemy. It does not appear to have detected the ship that follows me."

Harry could feel the inner relief that usually came with the start of action. "Ready as I'm ever going to be."

He was automatically running once more through his suit's checklist. "So here we go."

"Here we go."

A door opened in one wall of Harry's small cell, releasing him to move about aboard the transporter—if there was really any place other than the cell for him to go.

On his feet and ready, Harry jerked his head in the direction of Dorry, who still sat inertly where he had put her down. "What about this one?"

"Leave the badlife robot here for now, so we need not explain its presence. I will have it ready, if a way to use it should present itself."

The assassin created a clear spot in its own outer hull, or opened a small aperture, enabling Harry to look out as they approached the rogue's compact stronghold.

Artificial gravity abruptly disappeared, and Harry's stomach reacted to that event in its usual way, giving an unpleasant lurch. A moment later his guide appeared, drifting weightless in the doorway of the small compartment. It was either the same unit that had brought him to the transporter or an indistinguishable duplicate. As the berserker had promised, it was carrying, slung over one shoulder, a carbine of the same type as the one that Harry had lost during the fight.

There also appeared the same machine that had spoken to him on the ruined base. Its voice, almost Harry's own, said: "Follow your guide to the airlock. I will be landing presently."

While Harry and his escort, the roughly anthropomorphic unit provided by the assassin, were in transit, the machine shared with him the best view it could provide of what the rogue's base looked like.

He could see how the rogue's installation was built into and clinging to the irregular shape of a small asteroid, looking not too much different from 207GST, scarred and cratered by millennia of minor impacts, that otherwise looked not much different from a million others sharing this perilous space.

Before sending Harry on his way, the assassin gave him a final briefing. It thought it had spotted where the enemy brain was housed, and it had also seen indications of life in one of the remote portions of this installation. Harry was to allow his suited body to be limply towed through space, as if he were somehow immobilized inside his armor. The intent was that the rogue should focus most of its attention on the condition of its potential specimen inside his armor.

"I copy. Let's go."

The escort machine provided by the assassin, perhaps the same unit through which it had spoken to him when they were on the wanderworld, contained at least one key module of the assassin's main brain—a physically small computer, no bigger than a human skull.

First attaching to itself a device that looked like a miniature space scooter, this berserker towed Harry's inactive body through several hundred meters, perhaps a full kilometer of space, from the spaceborne assassin machine to the small base established by the rogue.

Studying his surroundings as thoroughly as he could in the brief time available, Harry started inside his suit at the sight of the *Secret Weapon* coming on slowly, as if about to make a peaceful docking. At least Harry thought it was the disguised ship, though for all that he could tell, it might well have been just one more berserker. In either case, this could well be the mystery object that had been following the assassin's transporter.

From his position in nearby space, Harry got a good look at the establishment the rogue had created for itself. His first impression was that the renegade, trying to prepare against attack, had devoted a lot of time and energy to digging and building itself solidly into the landscape. The beginnings of some kind of defensive ring could be surrounding its main installation—no more than the beginnings, so maybe Cheng's miniature squadron would have some chance of reaching the ground after all. There were a couple of what appeared to be powerful beam projectors under construction. Harry as he approached could see some active construction machinery, going about its job in deep-space silence.

The man-sized, expendable device that was escorting Harry shifted the carbine it was carrying from one metal shoulder to the other. There appeared to be no purpose to this action, except that it had moved the weapon approximately a meter closer to his hands, which he kept down at his sides.

The voice in his helmet was only a metallic whisper: "Do not reply. This is the end of our direct communication until the fight has started."

The dock of the berserker base loomed up just ahead, rocks and walls devoid of any symbols, looking as bleak as a fossil skull. A kind of surf was breaking on it, engulfing the whole mass, in the form of kilometers-per-second clouds of almost invisible dust particles, appearing as smooth shadowy curves of force in space, ready to sandblast the unwary or unprotected into oblivion. His armored suit could handle the thin onslaught. Within a few meters, a field of artificial gravity, almost a surprise, suddenly took hold. The dock was just below him now, and Harry's booted feet came down upon it solidly, with a sound of great finality.

TWENTY

If Harry and the single small machine escorting him were subjected to any inspection at the entry port of the rogue's main building, the procedure was too quick and subtle for him to even notice it. They were not rejected, and there was no delay. Inside was darkness—he turned on his suit lights, and blinked them several times as the start of an effort to make his behavior interesting. The flickering glow revealed a sculptor's garden of strange, inanimate, abstract shapes, arranged irregularly on a more or less level floor, with ample space for a suited human to move around among them. His light show provoked no visible reaction.

Gravity was set at approximately ED normal, very close to Earth standard, which strongly suggested the presence of life, or at least some preparation for

keeping newly acquired specimens alive. A routine
check of Harry's suit gauge confirmed that there was
no air in the first entry chamber.

None of the local hardware offered any objection
when the assassin's representative, as silent as the
deck they were now walking on, remained at Harry's
side. A gate opened in front of them. Just beyond
the aperture appeared another machine, very similar
to the first, to signal Harry and his escort the way
deeper into the sprawling structure.

Around him as he continued forward an atmosphere
suddenly bloomed into being, air molecules evidently
confined to a certain zone by some kind of forcefield
baffles allowing larger bodies to pass freely. There
was also evidence of new construction, going on in
darkness, as far as human eyes could tell. The only
illumination was that imported by Harry's suit lamp.

Here was another entrance, and another guardian
posted just inside, reminding Harry of some silent,
hooded warder at the gates of hell. It raised one of
its assortment of odd arms to point, which gesture
Harry took as a signal of the way he was to go.

He was somewhat surprised to be able to confirm
that his demonic escorts were allowing him to set the
pace as long as he kept moving—perhaps the rogue's
first experiment on this prime badlife specimen was
to grant him an illusion of some freedom. Still mindful of the assassin's urging to devise some modes of
interesting behavior, Harry made sure to seem hesitant
most of the time, but for a few steps, every now and
then, tried to appear eager. Again, he several times
delayed any movement at all, for the space of several
breaths, until the metal arm of his silent escort and

secret ally—he could hope!—prodded him forward. The path it wanted him to take was a geometrically straight aisle that seemed to extend through more than one of the connected domes.

Presently a vague glow appeared in the distance, and Harry dimmed his suit lamp to let him see it better. Somewhere ahead the light rose to a level that gave promise of being comfortable for human eyes when he could get a little closer. Harry and his assassin-escort and their silent guide proceeded without incident, for a distance he estimated as close to half a kilometer, into gradually increasing illumination, until the man felt comfortable turning his suit lamp off entirely. Harry thought they must be nearing the far end of the long series of domes that he had observed from space. So far he had seen nothing to give him a clue as to where the rogue's central processor might be housed. But it seemed quite possible that the assassin's representative, with sharper senses and an intimate knowledge of berserker architecture, was finding out what it needed to know.

Instinctively Harry kept looking about him in every direction, his mind seeking something definite to work on, trying to find the best way out. All he could be sure of was that he was still surrounded by machinery of unknown purpose. Some part of his nature was refusing to accept the fact that certain corners of the universe were not provided with any exit.

The assassin's plan called for Harry's escort to signal him when the precise moment had arrived to create a maximum distraction. At that precise moment, Harry was thinking, his assigned escort would be fighting at his side. What he didn't know, and wasn't going to try to guess, was how long it intended to maintain that partnership. He could hope and pray it would be just long enough. Long enough to allow him to dissolve the partnership in his own way, by getting in the first shot.

Walk forward another step, and yet another.

Two smallish but somehow deadly-looking machines had stepped out unobtrusively from somewhere, and were now shadowing Harry and his original escort, moving with them step for step, one keeping about five meters ahead, the other an equal space behind.

The time was coming—was almost here.

. . . one more step . . .

. . . *any moment now* . . .

. . . and yet another . . .

Harry's escort, firing its own concealed weapon, took out in a moment the two shadowing devices that would have stopped Harry before he could get moving. Two blasts of flying fragments scoured his armor harmlessly. In the same instant, with a movement too fast for the human eye to follow, his companion had tossed Harry the carbine so it lay cradled handily in his arms.

"Good move, partner," he heard himself beginning to say. Before the first word had taken physical shape, his mind, much faster than his fingers, had triggered his carbine to blast another weapon-bearing piece of hardware in the middle distance. They were always fast, too damned fast, as fast as nightmares. Before Harry had finished speaking the first word of that small compliment, his body was turning, about as fast as any human body in a suit could turn, but slowly, oh so slowly on the scale of machine movement. Harry's thought had taken alphatrigger control of the weapon in his arms, and even before his arms and fingers had actually begun the next movement commanded by his brain, another thought, coordinated with eye-movement, had switched the carbine's aim—no need to swing the whole chunk of hardware round, the force-packets could depart the muzzle at almost any angle.

Before his lips had started to utter the second word, before his trigger finger had groped its way to the manual control, he had shot away the head of his assassin partner, which was in Harry's view the most dangerous of all machines to him just at this moment. The blast created another spray of fragments, beneath which the limbs and body of the assassin-unit collapsed in a heap, dead as the body of a murdered man. Harry's thoughts and perceptions racing at combat speed, he could see it happening as in slow motion.

Only a second later, the ground slammed upward under the soles of Harry's boots. Solid testimony, he could hope, that the assassin had met its promised one-second deadline, and its all-out attack had just fallen on its powerful enemy. In the next few seconds he would discover whether that blow had been quick and hard enough to draw the rogue's attention back again, away from Harry's own small efforts at distraction.

No crushing retaliation fell upon him. Harry's stroke of timely treachery seemed to have gained him a few moments of freedom in which to think and act. For the moment his helmet radio was silent. Moving at a fast walk, he pressed on in the same direction that his late guide had been conducting him. He was assuming that the rogue's prisoners, if it really had any, must be housed in this direction. He made his way carefully forward, helmet lamp probing the suddenly renewed darkness. His single radio channel still had nothing at all to say. He muttered to himself what he would have said to the assassin, had it somehow been able to protest in outrage: "Too bad, but I had to do unto you before you did unto me." Only after that did Harry remember to shut down his transmitter, thinking that if he was lucky neither berserker might be able to tell just what had happened, or whether he was alive or dead.

A renewed outburst of noise, shocks and jolts of the fighting, machine against machine, coming from a location he estimated as only a few hundred meters behind him, vibrated strongly through the walls and floor. He had the impression that several doors had now been closed along the path that he had followed, which meant that the aerial shock waves of explosions would be blocked.

For the time being, an eerie silence had settled over his immediate surroundings.

From the time of Harry's first awkward conversation with the assassin, it had seemed to him the height of craziness to accept alliance with a device that had been brought into existence for the sole purpose of killing him. He saw no reason to believe that the assassin's fundamental programming had ever been countermanded. The reality would be that Harry's death had been moved back, probably by no more than a single notch, in the queue of goals to be accomplished. The moment the damned machine no longer needed his cooperation, it would be eager and determined to get on with its original task.

A new sound claimed his attention, forcing all

speculation to go on hold. For a moment he thought the airmikes of his armored suit, now tuned up to near-maximum sensitivity, were picking up the murmur of a human voice. Then he decided it was only the hiss of escaping air, or some other flow of gas, and his imagination was quick to picture prisoners being poisoned. That was followed by an irregular banging, such as some crude tool might make in the grip of a mere human hand. Again using only directed thought, he fiddled briefly with audio adjustments until he got a bearing.

For the moment, Harry's immediate vicinity seemed clear of murderous machines, and the background noise of fighting had declined to a mere hellish din. He turned up his airspeakers and began to shout, hoping to arouse some human response. When the way ahead seemed clear and open, he started running forward, toward what seemed the unmistakable signs of living human presence.

His voice, amplified by the suit's airspeakers, bellowed out Becky's name, and Ethan's.

Maybe it had been a mistake to turn off his radio transmitter. With no people yet in sight, the possibility of some kind of smash-and-grab rescue, never more than a faint dream, had faded drastically. It was time to try to begin negotiations with the rogue—that had been his only real hope all along.

All he could do was try. Mentally he made such adjustments as he could, striving to break the bonds confining his helmet radio to a single channel, aiming for the broadest possible mode of transmission, not giving a damn if the humans in nearby ships might hear him—not that that seemed likely.

When he had created what seemed the best configuration, he cleared his throat and said: "Whatever damned pocket calculator is in charge of this fun house, I want to talk to you!"

Static churned suddenly in his helmet. Somehow, a new channel had been opened.

The voice that responded was anything but human. It blasted in, at deafening volume, on one radio channel.

The tones of the voice were not as close to human as the assassin's, but the choice of words struck Harry as shockingly un-berserkerlike.

"Harry Silver, I grant you great honor and respect. Why are you persecuting me?"

Harry roared right back:

"Take your honor and respect and shove it!" He had ceased his advance and was leaning with his back to a bulkhead, carbine as ready as it could be, looking right and left. The light around him was still moderately good, and nothing that he could see was moving.

The voice came at him: "Why are you attacking—?"

"I haven't touched you yet, you bloody bastard! If you know me from my record, then you can compute that the real persecuting is about to start. Unless you and I can reach a deal, here and now, real fast."

The volume of the answer when it came still threatened momentarily to burst his eardrums. Then finally his new helmet managed to work out a way to automatically turn it down.

"If you knew me, Harry Silver, you would not threaten."

Harry drew a couple of deep breaths. "All I know

about you comes from your crazy goodlife playmate Del Satranji—from him and from one other source. I know you're the rogue machine that about a thousand other berserkers are trying their damnedest to annihilate."

"If you believe that, Harry Silver, you must agree that you and I have a thousand foes in common. Therefore the two of us should be fighting on the same side."

"Does that put me on the same side with Del Satranji? He calls you his bloody partner."

"The life-unit Satranji may call me what he chooses. But I assure you he knows nothing of my rogue status. Unless you or the assassin have informed him?"

"Then you're acquainted with the piece of hardware that was designed to kill me. I scared it so bad that it brought me here instead."

"I do not understand your foolish boast—therefore it intrigues me. And yes, your intended assassin and I have met. Answer my question."

"About Satranji? I've told that motherless goodlife bastard nothing; he and I haven't exchanged a word in days. Except for the message he sent, saying that he—he—"

There was still one thing, one subject, that Harry could not think about or talk about coherently.

The rogue gave an impression of waiting courteously for him to regain control. When a few more seconds had passed and Harry still couldn't finish, it spoke again, still sounding like cool thoughtfulness personified.

"Several standard months ago, the life-unit Satranji approached me, proposing that we undertake certain activities in our mutual interest. I agreed, and have been studying him with great interest ever since then."

"That's not all you've been doing." Harry's voice was low, half choked. "That son of a snake has arranged to supply you with life-units, people, for your work."

"I must do my work, respected Harry Silver, even as you must do yours. But my work need not consume any life-units to which you have a personal attachment. I am not compelled to kill humans, but only to study them. That is why I have become an outcast. Has your assassin told you otherwise?"

It was hard to keep his breathing at a reasonable level. He must be careful not to hyperventilate. "The message from Satranji told me that he has given you two people who are mine."

The answer was immediate. "If I had any of your people, Harry Silver, I would give them back. Deep computation assures me that you will make a more satisfactory partner than Satranji. Tell me what you want."

Before Harry could say anything else, or begin to decide how much of this new information he should believe, radio static cut off the berserker's voice.

"*Rogue?!* Where the hell are you? Rogue, come back!"

He kept shouting, but was denied an answer. Obviously the assassin was not done fighting. Sounds of fierce combat persisted, seeming to come entirely from the direction of the docks, where Harry had been put aground. The noises rose up steadily to form a violent background, echoing, reverberating, through the dome wall as well as the solid foundation of the chain of domes. The sensitivity of Harry's airmikes dulled, and radio static made frying noises, but there were no human cries or voices coming through on his communicator's single active channel. For a period of many seconds that soon stretched into minutes, this fight continued to be machine against machine.

All the deadly devices in Harry's immediate vicinity had been knocked out, leaving only undefended tools and machinery, mostly unidentifiable—but there might come a time when he would have to be careful of what he shot. Harry wouldn't want to destroy the assassin's main brain just yet—he wanted the two berserkers to concentrate all their energies on trying to destroy each other.

Meanwhile, he saw no reason to believe unquestioningly what the rogue told him, any more than he would credit the words of any other berserker.

Harry had known of berserkers that provided themselves with duplicate, redundant brains, just in case some such major disaster happened. The plan would be to keep the different modules as physically distant from each other as was practical.

But at a time of great emergency, each could be calling on all the brainpower that it had available.

Harry knew people, instructors who specialized in working with the armored suits, who were fond of saying that a man who really knew how to use this kind of outfit could go dancing in it and never step on any feet but his own. Harry danced without a partner now. Looking about him, carbine set on alphatrigger as he darted as quickly as possible from one compartment to the next—blasting a door open when it closed in his way, and wrenching his armored body free when the next door came slamming just as he was in it—Harry saw that in the pursuit of its research goals, the rogue had put together a strange environment indeed.

Parts of it were even beautiful in their own peculiar way. Rows of apparently useless rivets had been driven through a pillar that looked too fragile to support them, for no visible purpose other than decoration. Lights in one small alcove flickered on and off in hypnotic rhythm.

This section of the rogue's stronghold was all light and air, with ample room to move around in between the clumps of strangeness. The thing in charge might be trying to create an illusion that maybe, after all, conditions here were not too bad for human guests. Here were walls of solid masonry, with what appeared to be the roofs of low, one-story houses looming just beyond. Harry thought he could see ivy climbing on one wall. He got the impression that this had been built in deliberate imitation of ground-bound Earth-descended architecture, copied from some intercepted video. Not that he could have specified the style at the moment.

Carbine in hand, Harry moved forward. Once he blasted another thing that moved and did not appear to be alive. That would give away his location, if his immediate enemy was currently in any doubt about it, but it might also serve to assure the rogue that he was still alive and armed, it could not forget him entirely while caught up in the intensity of its struggle with its former colleague.

In addition there was the fact that just vaporizing more berserker metal provided a kind of satisfaction in itself. Harry fired again, at something that looked delicate and difficult to replace, blasting it to fragments.

Still his radio was silent. Where had the rogue gone? If it was already dead, he feared that his own chances had died with it.

"Start talking to me again, damn it! If we can't do business, I'm going to blow your vitals out!" If only he could locate them. At least his voice was sounding better now.

Maybe the damned rogue was trying to talk to him but couldn't. Possibly the assassin had already finished it off. Or the two of them had finished each other—but he couldn't be that lucky. There was no way he could tell.

Here was a new doorway, and Harry entered a new chamber, with good ambient light—maybe the landlord had just forgotten to turn them off. On the other hand the superintendent of this laboratory might have some special reason for wanting to illuminate every corner, even during wartime. If the rogue was trying to suggest to Harry that it had nothing to hide, it was going to have to work a little harder at the task.

For just a moment Harry was sure his time had come. He ducked and dodged aside, just as a small horde of man-sized machines, perhaps twelve or fifteen of them, fighter-shapes and worker-shapes all jumbled together, raced past him, rushing toward the fighting from what he thought of as the rear of the great building, the part he had not yet entered. Harry must have been seen by the machines, but he was totally ignored.

Watch out, assassin—rogue reinforcements are on

their way. And yes, three cheers for the assassin too, for enabling him, Harry, to have a few more minutes of pure freedom, here in the laboratory of the rogue mad scientist. To be fair, three cheers for the rogue as well, for giving the assassin a reason to keep Harry alive and bring him to the ball.

He thought that one of those rushing past bore a strong resemblance to the assassin's own prime unit, the same one that had put on Harry's ring in a mad parody of betrothal. But the moving swarm was past him in the bad light before he could tell whether or not he was simply imagining the likeness.

There came a burst of static in his helmet, and a strangled syllable of voice, as if one of the berserkers had made an effort to talk to him, but had been immediately cut off by the other. Harry could imagine them dueling over channels of communication; in such a struggle the advantage would seem to belong to the rogue, inside whose crystalline and metal guts Harry roamed, looking for lives to save and monsters he could kill.

Harry moved forward again.

He traversed more doorways. Still there were no human beings in sight, no life of any kind, or anything to signal unmistakably that life was present. Would the rogue kill all its captives quickly, rather than risk their being rescued? It had told him it was not compelled to kill, and if that was true, what greater heresy could there be for a berserker?

Harry pressed on, determined to reach the prison cells that his eager imagination kept suggesting must lie somewhere close ahead. Reaching those cages, and turning them inside out to make sure whether his family was there or not.

Around another corner, and he came upon a few small tanks where algae, or something like them, grew under lamps, making a greenish slime. The discovery of true life, here, brought on an unreasonable surge of hope.

Even after getting a fairly good look at this installation from space, he was surprised at how large it was. But he was advancing rapidly, and surely there could not be much more to discover before he reached the end.

In the process he was no doubt creating a diversion, and perhaps this was of some benefit to the assassin.

His progress jolted to a stop.

Humanity was at last in sight. No. More accurately, something that had once been humanity.

It was hanging on a wall.

Horrible experiments had come into view, the most conspicuous of them mounted on a wall right at his elbow. Harry kept telling himself, over and over: *This was once a man*—part of a man's rib cage, likely, straightened and flattened out to fit the mounting space. Judging by the dark, coarse hair, and the big bones that showed white where the raw edges of the piece were oozing blood, it could never have been part of a woman or a child.

Harry realized that he had stumbled and blasted his way into a berserker Trophy Room, the place where they studied their terrible opponent, the swarming, breeding badlife they could never fully understand . . .

This was the work to which the rogue was dedicated. It had already reminded him that it had a job to do, and it was tirelessly efficient in its work. It was not compelled to kill, no, only to study. Only to do this.

There were other trophies on adjoining walls, but he had no need to force himself to look at experiments the rogue must find intensely interesting. He must not allow himself to get sick as he walked between them, or even to be distracted. He had a job to do.

Since the rogue must consider the lives of its experimental subjects to be of great importance, sensitive material not to be casually wasted, it was not astonishing to discover that somewhere in or near its extensive laboratory the devilish machine would probably have accumulated some kind of collection of spacesuits, of protection shaped and provisioned to match the Earth-descended body.

Harry's spirits momentarily surged up. He told himself that it wouldn't be hoarding suits unless it was hoarding prisoners too.

Here there was even a spare helmet that would fit Harry's suit. He weighed it in his hand, then tossed it back into storage—if his current helmet was shot away, and somehow his head did not go with it, he would know where to come for yet another one.

Here was a bank of lockers, that would not have looked too out of place in a room adjoining some peaceful gymnasium on Earth or Esmerelda. The boarding machines that had pillaged ships for the life that they contained might well have also gathered up the means of keeping their new specimens alive.

Child-sized spacesuits were rare, almost to the point of nonexistence, in military craft and installations. But such gear was common enough in civilian ships, that also made use of cribs and other equipment designed for carrying infants around in conditions that required people to wear spacesuits. There were boxlike carriers that could be passed on from one human or robotic hand to another.

That compartments and containers would be not only closed but locked was perhaps the strongest evidence yet that other purposeful entities, besides the rogue and its auxiliaries, moved with some freedom in these rooms. Harry shot away the lock on one of them, pulled the door open, and here indeed were suits.

Wrenching open more of the lockers, rifling them as fast as his armored hands could move, Harry reminded himself that by all reports Ethan as well as Becky had been encased in some kind of spacesuit when the berserker boarding machines hauled them out of the boarded ship and into their own machine. The same had been true of Winston Cheng's great-grandson, whose suit just might conceivably be here, a special outfit recognizable by its design and dimensions.

He still had several lockers to go, when his sensitive airmikes picked up a faint sound from behind him. Harry whirled, weapon ready to fire at the speed of thought. A long-haired, bearded man, his lean body stark naked and punctuated at wrists and ankles by what appeared to be some kind of inserted optelectronic terminals, came stumbling around a corner, only to brake to a stop, gesturing surrender, at the sight of Harry's suited form.

Three steps behind the first man, a nude woman, hair long and matted, her limbs similarly marked or mutilated, came stumbling into view. Five or six more people in the same condition came tottering behind her. The connections on all their arms and legs, as if waiting for strings to be attached, gave them the look of crude ghastly puppets.

TWENTY-ONE

The eyes of the first man to round the corner stayed fixed on Harry, and his hairy lips were stuttering, trying to form words. But it was as if he might have forgotten how. Just behind him, the first woman to appear had fallen to her knees, her arms outstretched in the general direction of their rescuer. Other members of the small group were stopping, paralyzed, as they came around a corner, all of them staring at Harry's armored figure.

All the people Harry had seen so far were naked, and all were fitted with jacks or plugs already mortised into their bodies, in a way that left them free to move about, and seemed to be causing no serious pain or inconvenience. Harry assumed that the idea was to make it easier for the machine to follow reactions, and perhaps apply a stimulus now and then.

At last a few clear syllables spilled from the lead man's mouth. "Who—? How—?"

Harry muttered something obscene and pointless. Then his airspeakers rasped out: "Who else is with *you*? How many people are locked up here?"

No one seemed able to give him a coherent answer. But one man finally came forward and got out a few words that made sense on a certain level. "I was betting it would be the Space Force who came for us. That's you, isn't it? You're not Templars, or local?"

By "local," of course, the man meant from the armed service of some solar system within a few light-years. Meanwhile an especially haggard-looking older woman had come to stand looking at Harry over the speaker's shoulder. "Where are the others?" she demanded. "How many are with you?"

"I'm it, lady. The rescue party, the one-man gang. I did have some help getting here, but you wouldn't believe me if I told you."

As Harry spoke he was pushing people out of his way, trying to see past them, looking back in the direction from which they were all coming. "I'll answer questions later. Right now I'm looking for one special woman and one special child. Tell me, who else is here? This can't be all of you."

The woman was staring past him in the opposite direction, back along the way Harry had come. She said: "I can't believe you're alone, we heard a lot of what sounded like fighting." Suddenly she seemed to remember her nudity, and tried to cover her body with her arms.

"Someone tell me, damn it, is this all of you? Are there cells back that way? More people still locked up?" Harry had turned his suit lamp on again, and was using it to try to probe the more distant and shadowy reaches of the rogue's domain.

Around him people were babbling, trying to convince themselves that they had been set free. Ignoring Harry's questions, they started complaining not about the gruesome plugs that had been stuck in their arms and legs, but mostly about poor food and the conditions in their cells, as if Harry might be their cruise director. It was all noise that brought him no useful information. None of them seemed to have the faintest idea of the horror that had overtaken their fellow captives, disassembled into tapestries on a wall.

Precious seconds were sliding by. Before Harry could decide on his next move, the voice of the rogue was once more resounding in his helmet.

It seemed to have at least temporarily prevailed in the techno-battle, somehow wrested control of the channel that Harry's radio was tuned to. It was speaking to him clearly, calm as ever. It started to give Harry the precise numbers that he had asked for.

He cut the berserker off. "Never mind the motherless body count. I want to see *all* the people that you're holding, with a priority on one woman and one child in particular. Get 'em out here, right away."

"You will already have observed, Harry Silver, that there are certain units of life which cannot readily be moved."

"I don't mean those." He couldn't bring himself to contemplate the possibility that Becky and Ethan might already be hanging on a wall. He couldn't ask this monster if among its decorations were two who had once been his woman and his child.

The rogue gave him an answer on the question he had been afraid to ask. "The two people you want are not here."

"Then where are they?"

"The life-unit Satranji claims to be holding your woman and your child as his prisoners. I have been unable to verify his claim. But he has vowed to turn them over to me as part of our agreement."

That was a stunner. Harry needed a moment to reorganize his thoughts. "How can *he* be holding them? Where? And where is he now?"

"I do not know." The rogue's voice had taken on a new tone, odd for any machine, even odder for a berserker, suggesting that it viewed Harry with suspicion. As if it wasn't sure he could be trusted with all these priceless materials. "As for the life-units you see before you, what will you do with them if I allow you to take them away? Few or none of them will be of any particular value to you, Harry Silver."

He made a savage gesture with his weapon, so that the bewildered folk around him, hearing only his end of the conversation, shrank back. His voice was hoarse. "Few or none of them are carrying a carbine that can blow all this priceless machinery of yours into little atoms. Do what I tell you, you motherless junkpile!"

Now a couple of the people in Harry's group, caught up in the time-honored tendency of victims to identify with their kidnapper, appeared to be losing some of their enthusiasm for freedom. One or two actually seemed on the verge of timidly retreating in the direction of their cells.

Harry snarled and waved the carbine. "Where the hell do you think you're going? Get back here.

Then go take a walk around that other corner, way down there, and have a good look at what's hanging on the wall."

People milled around, uncertain if he really wanted them to do that or not.

"Very well, Harry Silver," said the rogue's voice smoothly. "You may remove my entire remaining stock of viable life-units. In return, I ask only that you help me to lure the one called Del Satranji into one of my cells. I find him very highly desirable as a subject of study."

"Just like me."

The rogue adopted a judicious tone. "True, there are resemblances, but notable differences as well. I do take a less conciliatory attitude with Satranji, largely because he is not threatening my valuable equipment with an efficient weapon."

"And don't forget who is."

"I forget nothing, Harry Silver. It is true that I find goodlife and badlife equally interesting. The contrast leads to a question that vitally concerns me: What is the best means of turning one into the other?"

It seemed to be stalling him, and he wasn't going to allow it. "The question that better concern you is figuring out some way to get my woman and my child to safety. Then we can argue about all this. I'm not going to be distracted."

The berserker's voice, no longer at a blasting volume, was not nearly as smooth and manlike as the assassin's. But Harry began to think he could detect gradual improvement.

The rogue continued the process of feeding Harry

bits and morsels of information, none of it immediately useful, while Harry worked his way cautiously back in the direction from which the prisoners had come. The further he went, the more horror kept coming into view, walls and tables alive, or almost alive, with the rogue's experiments on organs and tissues that Harry had to believe were human. The folk who had been let out of confinement followed him, naked pilgrims walking into territory where they had never been, reacting to the displays with muted horror, and in some cases with disbelief.

How long the rogue had been collecting prisoners, and where they had all come from, were matters to be discussed another day. Some of this previous crop of specimens had been taken carefully apart, and Harry had seen various segments of their bodies hooked up with an assortment of machines. In some of the disconnected portions, blood still flowed, impelled by cleverly designed pumps, nerves and muscles still went on about their business, responding to stimuli. There were muscles that spasmed, as if they might be in great pain, lacking any lungs or voices to scream it out.

The rogue gave the impression of being interested in the attention that Harry was paying to its collection. "If you like, I can provide you with interesting data on each specimen."

Harry called the berserker a filthy name. "What I want is to see every motherless person that you're holding who is still intact. Cough 'em up, or I start shooting."

"The last of my viable specimens are now on their way to meet you. Meanwhile, I wish to know everything that you can tell me about the assassin machine. What has it promised you? Was it able to summon reinforcements before launching this attack?"

Harry struggled to get control of himself.

"Harry Silver, it was you who demanded to have speech with me."

Harry got himself under control. Now that he was negotiating with the enemy, it was only reasonable to expect that he would have to give something to get something. He told the rogue he couldn't be sure about the reinforcements, but he supposed that the assassin had tried.

Here came another couple, man and woman, straggling down the corridor. By this time there were perhaps a dozen intact and living humans altogether, clustering around Harry. Since the tour on which he led them had given them a look at what was hanging on the walls, the idea of staying behind had been pretty much abandoned as an option.

Harry pointed, with a jerk of his carbine's muzzle. "Show me the cells. I've got to try to see things for myself."

It took less than a minute to reach the place. The cells, or at least the ones that Harry got to see, were startlingly ordinary, with the appearance of bedrooms, comfortable if small. They were spaced around a common room, where evidently the inmates had been allowed to meet and mingle. All the cells in this area were currently empty, with doors wide open, and there was evidence that their former occupants might have enjoyed, if that was the right word, good gravity, good air, even reasonable food.

Of course it was quite possible that what Harry saw here was only one colony, one branch of some elaborate system of prisons or laboratory cages. For all any of these people knew, there might be another branch, or a dozen more, dug into some lower level of the base.

One of the people stuttered out a kind of explanation. The rogue berserker had once explained that it wanted a lengthy period of study of certain life-units in something close to their normal environment before it began destructive testing. Previous studies had employed harsh treatment almost exclusively, and those had produced comparatively little in the way of useful results.

People were still pestering him. "How many ships are there in your task force?"

"Ninety-seven. Go away." He kept sweeping his gaze from side to side. *Where the hell were Ethan and Becky?*

"Ninety-seven?" The questioner blinked at him. "That seems a lot."

The prisoner who was gradually assuming the role of group spokesman was at least paying some attention to Harry's concern. "Look, sir, officer, whoever you are, the two people you describe aren't here. No one like that has ever been here. Now, please, hadn't we better get moving?"

Harry's own thoughts had been coming around a hundred and eighty degrees, from being convinced that Becky and Ethan must be here, dead or alive, to a growing belief that the rogue had never had them. Satranji in his recorded message had been telling the truth about the second kidnapping, but then he'd lied—the rogue had not yet taken delivery. The door of hope had come open just a crack, some pieces of the great puzzle were falling into place.

And then the rogue gave him a shock. "I have opened the last cell. Here are its tenants, two specimens answering your description."

Harry's heart leaped up and settled back. Despite that, the two figures coming down the hall toward him, both of them as bare as all the others, were no particular surprise. The young woman striding forward, dragging an eight-year-old boy by one wrist, had to be Claudia Cheng in charge of little Winnie. Pale and gaunt and fragile-looking, the pair were still readily recognizable from their cavorting images in the old man's office. They stood in contrast to the other prisoners by the fact of having no plugs inserted in their wrists and ankles.

Claudia Cheng appeared ready to accept the presence of an armed and armored man without marveling. She came to stand directly in front of Harry. She seemed utterly indifferent to her own nudity, and almost unreasonably calm, as if there had never been any doubt that someone would be coming for her. No doubt she found it irritating that it had taken so long.

"My grandfather's finally ransomed us," she said, in the tone of one preparing to register complaints.

"He's doing the best he can, lady." Harry nodded his helmet toward the corner where she had appeared. "Is anyone else back there?"

"Anyone else? Not that I know of." Only now did the young woman seem to take full notice of the small crowd of her fellow prisoners. It was as if she had never seen them before. "Where did all these people come from? Look at their arms and legs. They've been hurt." There was disapproval in the observation, if no great sympathy. Meanwhile the others were staring back at Claudia, without recognition, not knowing what to make of her and the small boy clinging to her leg, in the manner of an even younger child.

She said to Harry: "The berserker said there were others, but it assured me we were going to be given special treatment. But that seemed only natural. I didn't know—"

Interruption came blasting into Harry's helmet, the rogue's radio voice demanding to be told the exact current location of the life-unit called Winston Cheng.

Harry was certain that both berserkers must know enough of the shapes and sizes and markings of ED spaceships to be able to identify Cheng's yacht, and no doubt that vessel had now come on the scene. He said: "Cheng's probably right about where you think he is." There didn't seem to be any point in trying to be cute.

Claudia Cheng, peeling little Winnie off her leg while still keeping a fierce grip on his arm, kept pestering Harry, trying to tell him how she had argued and pleaded with the rogue, promising that the family patriarch would give it much in return for their safe release. The implication seemed to be that next time someone should arrange to provide a better class of kidnapper.

She wound up with: "What's happening now? How soon can we get out of here?"

"Shut up," Harry advised. "I'm having a radio chat with the berserker."

"You are? My grandfather's the one it really wants, isn't he? Tell it that if it lets us go, my grandfather will arrange to meet it. He'll give it anything it wants."

Harry shot back: "You'll have to do your own negotiating, lady, after I've done mine."

The rogue's voice had disappeared again, and he kept trying to reestablish contact. On the scale of ordinary, standard berserker values, it would be much better to terminate two young lives that still had ahead of them the possibility of reproducing, than one very old one that had probably lost whatever capacity it might have had to create yet more badlife, and was likely to die soon from natural causes.

Ordinarily a berserker would bargain only for that which it really wanted, something in tune with its basic programming, calling for the termination of all lives, everywhere. But in the rogue's case that goal was beginning to seem uncertain. It seemed that berserker programming had mutated into something far less predictable.

Harry turned down his airmikes to shut out most of the groaning and crying around him, along with the highbred complaints of Claudia Cheng.

As soon as the rogue came back on radio he said to it: "You understand that these are not the two people I'm looking for?"

"You have made that plain. I am still intermittently in contact with the life-unit Satranji. He is providing no new information that would be of interest to you."

"You're stalling me, you bloody junkpile. I won't have it." Harry tilted up the muzzle of his carbine and blasted another twenty kilograms or so of delicate machinery, far enough away from all the naked people that none should be hit by flying fragments. He had no idea if it was anything of great importance to the rogue or not, but he could hope.

The rogue's response came in a tone of what sounded like philosophical detachment. "I had already computed such a reaction on your part was highly probable."

Before Harry could decide what to do next, the deck beneath his feet and the walls around him vibrated with some kind of explosion, or heavy impact, much more violent than anything else Harry had felt or heard since his arrival.

The small huddle of naked refugees screamed, and some of them tried to crawl under machinery in search of shelter.

Harry brushed away clutching arms, and demanded of the world: "What in hell was that?"

The rogue had a calm answer ready. "An ED vessel identifiable as *Ship of Dreams*, the property of Winston Cheng Enterprises, has crash-landed at the other end of this installation, only about forty meters from the point where you entered. The damage to my structure is unimportant, that to the vessel is moderate. It will be no longer spaceworthy. Can you explain this event?"

Harry hesitated momentarily. Then he said: "Partly. I'll tell you this much right away: There won't be any landing party coming off that one to attack you. They had nothing like that on board. Now you tell me something I can use."

The rogue said: "You will doubtless find the following information useful: The machine you have allied yourself with is a dedicated assassin, designed to have you, the individual Harry Silver, as its specific target. It will spare you only as long as you are useful."

"Something I can use, I said!" He called the voice in his helmet a filthy name. "That information isn't news at all." With words, and a few violent gestures, Harry started to get the people around him moving, toward the room where he had earlier discovered spacesuits.

Before the rogue had framed an answer, there came a second crash, on the same scale of violence as the first. Harry in his heavy armor was staggered, clutched at a nearby wall to keep from going down.

A moment later Harry raised his head. Unprotected and unarmed humans were scattered all around him, trying to regain their feet. All had fallen except little Winnie, who had reestablished his clinging hold, this time on Harry's armored bulk. No one was seriously hurt, but he was going to have to try to get them all into suits and helmets. Yeah, in his spare time.

"Well?" he demanded on radio.

The rogue was of course unflappable. "A second object has just crash-landed, close beside the first. It, too, has sustained moderate damage. In this case I can make no certain identification. It might be an auxiliary of the assassin, except that certain subtle anomalies suggest a badlife attempt at deception."

Suddenly the machine was roaring at Harry again. It reported that strange fighting machines, obviously the slave-tools of badlife, were pouring out of the most recent arrival, hurling themselves into the ongoing battle . . .

Harry raised his free hand, the one not cradling

the carbine, uselessly to the side of his helmet. "Go easy on my ears, you motherless, bloody . . ."

Several moments passed before he could communicate coherently again. "Tell me if I'm wrong: this new hardware's neither on your side or the assassin's. I'll bet it's just waded in and is crunching both."

"It is attempting to do so, so far without notable success." The rogue did not sound much concerned. Of course it never did, apart from turning up or down the volume—as if, he thought, it were groping for ways to generate, or at least simulate, appropriate emotions.

Meanwhile, the little knot of human escapees clustering around Harry kept breaking apart, dissolving into individuals who tried to run away, then finding nowhere to run and coming together again, surrounding their lone rescuer.

Overriding outside management, gesturing fiercely at the naked people to let him alone for just a minute, he succeeded in establishing mental control of the volume in his helmet and turning it down. "I passed through a locker room full of spacesuits, rogue. Let's start getting these people into them."

"I do not object."

"You'd better not."

"In truth, Harry Silver, I allow you to have your way because I am gleaning a wealth of data on human behavior from this series of events. Also I approve your equipping my valuable specimens with protection."

"They're no more your bloody specimens, goddam it! You said you were giving them to me."

"That is still conditional upon your cooperation." The voice in Harry's helmet said: "Whatever the assassin machine has promised you, I will give more. Explain to me the nature of this deceptive device, or ship, whose arrival caused the second impact."

"If you mean what you say about giving me more, we've got a deal. Between you and my designated murderer, I'd rather be fighting on your side. But before I answer more questions, before I even stop trying to shoot your guts out, I want my people back. As soon as you show me convincing evidence that my two have been sent out of your reach, and the assassin's reach, that they're safely on their way to some badlife port or base—then I will help you in your fight."

Harry was damned if he could see how any berserker locked in a battle for survival was really going to take time out to pack two living prisoners—assuming it had been lying and really had them—away to safety. That might be impossible even if it tried. But he could think of no better way to proceed with negotiations.

The rogue said: "Having survived the first surprise attack, Harry Silver, I am going to win this fight."

"All right, maybe you are—if you get the right help at the right time. So?"

"Obviously I will then need to reestablish my research facility in a different place, much more distant from berserker command. Disposing of your assigned assassin will not solve your fundamental problem, nor will it solve mine. You and I have this in common: berserker command will be all the more determined to hunt us both down and wipe us out."

"Go on."

"From now on, Harry Silver, you can best protect your beloved life-units by distancing yourself from them. Therefore you would be well advised to accept the invitation I now offer: after they are sent to safety, or are confirmed dead, you should come with me when I seek to relocate. Together the two of us will have marvelous adventures."

"*Adventures!* If you think—" Harry choked and spluttered.

"What I think, Harry Silver, is that I have begun to understand you. You are like other life-units, in that what you say you want and what you really want may not be the same thing."

One of the naked strangers was grabbing at Harry's arm, imploring him to do something. Whatever it was, Harry couldn't listen to it. He shoved the stranger away, the unclad body backpedalling to sprawl on a flat deck.

To the rogue he snarled: "So find my woman and my boy, and get them to safety."

"I calculate that to find them, we must induce the life-unit Satranji to cooperate." The rogue's continued calm, no hint in the voice of breathlessness or even excitement, tended to make the conversation seem unreal.

"Then we'll do that. Can you get him in here somehow? He must have been aboard the *Ship of Dreams*, probably piloting. Put him here in front of me, and we'll find out what he knows."

"That may be possible. I have established communication with the life-unit Satranji, who was aboard the first vehicle to crash into my structure."

"I want to establish communication with him too. But not just yet."

"I find that interesting," the rogue assured him.

❖   ❖   ❖

Meanwhile the group had been moving on. The little mob of freed prisoners had followed Harry as far as the chamber he thought of as the locker room. Here he had started helping them get into spacesuits. He was relieved to find that there seemed to be enough suits to go around, with a few left over—just in case someone else showed up.

Whatever locks Harry had not earlier shot away were now standing open, courtesy of the rogue, as Harry supposed. While he began helping people into suits, the rogue relayed what it said was Satranji's latest communication.

"He observes that a battle is in progress here, and demands that I give him an explanation. So far I have provided none."

"What about the other people who were with him? Are they still in Cheng's yacht?"

"He says nothing about other life-units, and I can spare none of my units to look for them. I have assured my prize goodlife of my great concern for his welfare, and advised him on how to avoid the regions of bitterest fighting here on the ground.

"Of course, Harry Silver, I would be pleased if the life-unit Satranji could effectively fight off the assassin's units for me. Like you, the Satranji-unit carried a moderately effective weapon, but like all life-forms he is very slow. If he is caught up in the firefight now taking place, I expect he will be promptly cured of life, his potential usefulness as a vehicle of discovery in my laboratory entirely wasted. Besides that, in combat how is he to distinguish the assassin's machinery from mine?" There was a pause, suggesting thoughtful humanity. "How are you to do so, if it comes to that?"

Harry said: "Get me my wife and son, and I'll figure out some way. You're right, nothing Satranji can do is going to tip the balance in this fight. So quit stalling. Find out where my two people are. What's the son of a snake done with them?"

"The life-unit Satranji has never told me that." There was a brief pause. "He is steadily making his way in this direction, and is currently about two hundred meters from your location. With my help he has bypassed the zone of hard current fighting. He repeats that he is mystified by the fierce fighting, and again demands to be told what is going on."

"But he doesn't have my people with him."

"Certainly not. Of course his first purpose in this reconnaissance is to determine whether I am likely to survive this battle which he finds so puzzling, and his second to discover the nature of my chief attacker. He still knows nothing of my rogue status, and is astonished by the number and quality of machines attacking me. He cannot tell their origin."

Harry, carbine ready, was walking again, with a different gait, on the move in the direction where Satranji was supposed to be. The refugees would have to get themselves into suits as best they could. He was thinking that it wouldn't do to kill the bastard on sight, not until there was some information about Ethan and Becky. He said: "Tell him the attacking machines are secret weapons, made by the designer of the *Secret Weapon*."

"I do not understand."

"He will, and he'll believe it. It may satisfy him for the moment. Tell him!"

Half a minute later the rogue's voice was back: "He

accepts the answer, and speaks with confidence of soon being able to turn over to me the two life-units he has promised. Of course that cannot be possible, unless the units in question are already somewhere nearby."

Harry was grimacing, shaking his head. "They *can't* be aboard the *Secret Weapon*. That's just not possible. Are you telling me he's got Becky and Ethan somehow hidden on Cheng's yacht? That's not possible either."

The rogue said: "I know very little about the yacht. But the life-unit Satranji is in possession of another vessel, besides the *Ship of Dreams*."

"Another ship. Where? What are you talking about?"

"I loaned him a small ship in the early stage of our collaboration, and it has been an essential tool." The rogue went on to describe how, in the course of its relationship with Satranji, it had given him a small vessel called the *Chewing Pod*, that it had captured in an earlier raid. Since then Satranji had evidently succeeded in keeping it hidden from all his human associates.

Harry listened, pondering, while the rogue explained. There was no reason why Satranji could not have another small ship under his control, running it on autopilot somewhere in relatively nearby space. He could have it following the *Ship of Dreams*. As pilot of the yacht, he would probably have been able to keep to himself the fact that it was being followed.

Harry couldn't remember the *Chewing Pod*'s name being on the official roster of missing ships—but that was a long list, and it was a long time since he had looked at it.

❖   ❖   ❖

There came a lull in the fighting, with the rogue refraining for the moment from counterattack, while it tried to achieve the arrangement of life-units it wanted. The assassin's machines were maneuvering for position. The rogue reported that the berserker-bashers deployed from the *Secret Weapon* had proven inadequate for the job, and all or almost all of them were already reduced to junk. To anyone just arriving on the scene the battle might well seem to have concluded. The noise level had dropped to near silence.

"What do you intend to do, Harry Silver, when you confront the life-unit Satranji?"

"That can wait. Right now all I want to do is get around him, past him, and find my people, if they're somehow stuck on one of these damned ships. I'll demonstrate my intentions toward that rat-turd when the time comes. If it comes. Are you trying to keep the two of us apart?"

The rogue had no immediate answer to that. All of Harry's little band of refugees had got themselves into suits. All had their helmets on and sealed, but, fortunately or unfortunately, Harry's was still the only radio that was functioning at all. As if he had given them orders, they were all following him in the direction of the docks, moving toward the damaged ships that offered the only possible means of escape.

Satranji was calling in to the rogue again, and this time it allowed Harry to listen in. It seemed that the goodlife man continually wanted to reassure himself that his giant partner was still functioning, and had at least a good chance of coming out on top in the current fight.

Harry prompted: "Tell him you want some solid evidence that the two specimens connected to me are still alive and in good condition."

"He has already assured me that they are."

"Glad to hear it. But none of your units have actually seen them."

"That is correct."

"Again, ask him who was on the ship with him. The ship that brought him here."

Harry's talk with the rogue was interrupted by another fierce outbreak of machine-on-machine violence, so for a few minutes at least the humans on board were relatively free to communicate with each other, and to some extent do what they would.

Except that just standing upright was something of a problem.

Satranji was back on radio, telling the rogue that the latest outbreak of fighting had forced him to retreat for a short distance and take shelter. But he was not going back to his ship, and would not bring his prisoners aboard the base, until he had satisfied himself as to just what was going on.

Then he does have them. Or at least he's still claiming to. Harry, listening in silence, kept reminding himself that nothing the man said could be taken at face value.

He also kept wondering what had happened to Cheng and Masaharu.

TWENTY-TWO

The spacesuits that Harry's little mob of refugees had put on were not designed for combat, and would offer small protection against anything worse than a lack of atmosphere. But having covered their bodies, the former prisoners were beginning to feel protected and assertive, and some were agitating for a quick completion of their escape.

Their suits' airspeakers were working if their radios were not. "Let's get going! Get us out of here!"

It was as if nothing that Harry had told them so far had really registered, nor had the sight of their fellow ED specimens, hanging on the wall. To do them justice, none of them had been able to hear any of his ongoing dialogue with the rogue.

"There's a couple of things that have to be taken care of first," he advised. Movement in the little knot

329

of refugees was tending in the same direction that Harry was now moving, back toward the dock and the crashed ships.

One demanded of Harry: "Where's your ship?"

"Tell you what, you just run ahead and pick whichever one you like. Try and find one where the people aren't all dead. Then if you're in such a motherless hurry, just go on without me."

That earned him a small respite. But before they had gone much farther, Claudia Cheng had moved up to Harry's side. She tuned her suit's airspeaker to a low volume as they walked, and began whispering to him of the fantastic rewards that would be his if he could get her and her offspring out of this alive.

"I can't move!" This interruption came from little Winnie, whose mother had had to stuff him into a suit that was marginally too big, and the boy had good reason to complain. The child-sized suit was designed to allow various adjustments to be made by some controlling authority outside, and Harry reached over to turn off the whiner's airspeakers.

"Sure you can," he assured the suit's inmate, who was actually still capable of walking, after a fashion. There was nothing to be done about the disparity in size.

Claudia was still pleading: ". . . I can see that this isn't going at all smoothly, and you might not be able to save everyone. But if you can get the two of us out—"

Harry cut her off. "You're high on the list of people to be saved, lady, because you've got junior here. But you're still not right at the top."

She was watching Harry, trying to calculate, still not

understanding. She was just not very good at listening. None of these people seemed to be.

The escaped prisoners continued to follow Harry back toward the sounds of sporadic fighting.

One of them pushed forward to demand of Harry: "Why are we going this way, toward the fighting?"

Now that he was moving again, with a definite goal, he felt not quite so desperate. "Because there's nowhere else to go. The only ships we know about are here. Probably they're all wrecked, but at least one of them ought to have lifeboats that are still working. Maybe there'll even be a launch."

They had gone only a little farther when Harry called a halt, in a space that he thought seemed as sheltered as anything they were likely to find. When his faithful following had shuffled into a kind of ring around him, he announced: "This is as far as I can guide you, people. I'm going ahead and scout."

Most of his entourage looked alarmed. One demanded: "What should we do?"

"Damned if I know what to tell you, except that this way would seem to be the only way out. I shouldn't have to remind you that whatever way you go, it's going to be very chancy. Don't know where a safe spot is, or what's going to happen next." When he started to move again, and everyone came right with him, Harry stopped to warn them: "Better not stay too close to me. There's liable to be shooting, with me as a target, and your suits puncture pretty easily."

That got Harry enough space for the time being, and in another moment he had turned his back and was moving away. Taking a quick glance back he could see that at least three or four of the people were still following, though now at a more respectful distance, staying thirty or forty paces back. Claudia Cheng continued to be a bit ahead of the others, still towing Winnie who hobbled with difficulty in his awkward suit. Harry felt sorry for the kid, who was going to need a guardian angel to get through this alive. Angel, hell, say a couple of archangels.

He thought the young woman looked slightly puzzled behind her faceplate, probably because he still had given her no guarantee of special treatment.

Harry had traversed this section of the berserker base only once before, going in the opposite direction and under very different conditions. There was actually more light now, eerie pulsating glows of different colors, alternating with a flicker here and a flicker there, emanating from damaged forcefields, as well as various sites where metal and other materials had been heated to incandescence. Harry found it hard to be sure of distances and directions, but instinct suggested that he was getting close to the docks, and very close to where the ships were reported to have come crashing down, one after the other.

He was also entering an area where combat had very recently taken place. The heavy structural members nearby were scorched and marked with spots and patches of still-glowing slag; and fragments of berserker fighting machines lay strewn about. It was impossible to tell if these bits of wreckage had once served the rogue or the assassin.

Harry continued working his way back through the half-ruined fortress of research, until he found himself again walking in vacuum, traversing a region that was still being effectively walled off by microfields, restraining molecules of air while allowing larger objects to pass freely.

Easing his way slowly forward, Harry peered over an obstacle to spot the upper portion of a human body that was sitting on the deck, facing toward him. A moment later he had recognized the Lady Laura by her distinctive suit of heavy combat armor. She was leaning back awkwardly against a wall, her carbine leaning beside her. A flickering of bluish light reflecting from the overhead created the momentary illusion that she was moving, but when Harry had taken another step he could see that her suit was badly smashed, crushed and punctured in a way that hurt to look at. Its occupant could not be anything but dead.

Another armored figure was lying with its helmet in the lady's lap. Around the fallen couple were strewn pieces of shattered metal, what appeared to be the remains of more than one berserker unit. As Harry crept still closer, Winston Cheng feebly raised his head to look at him. The weapon Cheng had dropped, a heavy handgun, lay a few centimeters from the metal gauntlet covering his outstretched hand. Most of the arm above the hand was gone, armored sleeve and all, and the suit had been seriously punctured in several other places. Harry swiftly abandoned any thoughts of trying to give medical assistance. Now Harry was close enough to see that inside the Lady Masaharu's helmet a tiny telltale damage signal was flashing regularly. Nobody was going to answer the phone on that one.

Cheng twitched again, and his airspeaker made a faint sound. "Harry . . ."

Holding the carbine ready, Harry turned to brace his back against the wall, so nothing could come at him from behind. Then he let himself down, awkward in his heavy suit, to sit beside the tycoon and his dead lady.

The old man's eyes were open, and he began to speak, as if he and Harry were already in the middle of a conversation.

". . . and how could a man trust the damned thing to keep to any bargain that was arranged? Hey? Remember that, Silver." Gasp. "Remember that . . ."

"Yeah. I will. I'll write that down, soon as I get a chance. It's hard to find a partner you can trust."

Harry kept his airspeaker's volume very low. "Listen to me, Cheng. Your Claudia and Winnie are still alive. They're all right. They may be along here at any moment."

There was the sound of a long, indrawn breath. "Ah . . . Harry. We were right to come after them. Alive. *Alive.*" Behind the statglass helmet plate, Cheng's face was totally transfigured, mouth open and eyes staring.

Turning his head, Harry saw that the two people had come into sight. The boy looked grotesque in his oversized suit, but the childish face was clearly visible.

The old man's faint voice rasped: "Winnie and Claudia . . . Harry, I promised you . . . a great reward. I meant it. Half of everything I own is yours."

Harry was keeping his eyes raised, probing the background, watching and listening for the stalking approach of death. He said, absently: "That's very generous."

"Everything . . ." The word came out in a fading whisper.

Claudia had come very close. Now she crouched down, almost pouncing, almost sitting on Winnie to hold him in one place. For the first time Harry heard real fear in her voice. "Grandfather, you're badly hurt, you don't know what you're saying."

Cheng's eyes were half closed, and he seemed unconscious, drifting. Harry studied the woman beside him, considering. Then he offered: "I think you heard the same thing I did. Your dear grandfather says he owes me a new ship."

"A ship?" The heiress considered. Relief set in abruptly. "Yes, I believe that's what he said. Certainly. A ship. One ship. Any kind of ship."

"That's not what Grandpa said," Winnie offered helpfully. He had discovered the way to turn his airspeakers back on.

"Yeah it is." Harry was dogmatic.

"I want a new ship, too."

After repeating his warning to Claudia, more sternly this time, that she and the kid had better not stay close to him, Harry moved on, toward the crashed and stranded ships.

A glance back showed him that at least some of the other escapees were also following him, but at a slightly greater distance than before. The scene of carnage must have made a strong impression.

Turning his back on the Cheng family, Harry had advanced only a few more meters when he ran into trouble.

Fortunately his sensitive airmikes picked up the sound of the first assailant's steady advance before the thing detected him, and he got off the first shot.

The return blast, a riposte a fifth of a second too late and a touch off-target, only melted a hole halfway through Harry's breastplate, and knocked him off his feet. Shakily he observed to himself that this was probably not precisely the kind of combat for which these berserker units had been designed.

Regaining his feet, examining the freshest bits of wreckage in the immediate vicinity, he had no way to tell if it was one of the assassin's units that he had just killed, or one of the rogue's. Except that if the machine had been under the rogue's control, it would have warned him . . . wouldn't it?

As soon as he dared take the time to look around again, he noted that Claudia, who had armed herself with Lady Laura's fallen weapon, had still been keeping herself and Winnie within twenty-five or thirty meters of him, despite his warnings. Even as Harry watched, the woman turned aside, dragging her child with her, and crawled out of Harry's line of vision. He had the impression that she had spotted some cubbyhole or spot that offered at least the illusion of safety, and was dragging Winnie into a place where they could hide until the fight had been decided. He had no idea whether it would turn out to be a lucky move or not.

Moving on again, Harry observed that some components of the wreckage littering this area didn't look like berserker material at all. The look of several of the fragments suggested they might have come from the assault machines hurled into combat by the Lady Laura, and spoken of contemptuously by the rogue. Harry remembered that all of those devices had been somewhat larger than human beings, even human beings in armored suits. But the size constraints imposed by the small ship meant that none of the mechanical warriors could be as large as an ordinary groundcar. In the planning stages, of course, no one had known just what sort of opposition they might face when they reached the small berserker base, except that it would be formidable. And so it had proved to be.

At last Harry had regained territory that was at least half familiar. And now he was getting close enough to the crash scene to begin to have some hope of seeing what had happened.

The heaviest part of the yacht's thick armored hull, the prow, was actually embedded in the relatively thin wall of the rogue's base. Studying the situation, Harry decided that it ought to be possible for suited people to climb from one place to the other—provided, of course, that there were no berserkers around to kill intruders on sight.

He had to advance a little farther, and look out and up through a new gash in the overhead, before he could see what had happened to the *Secret Weapon*. It had also rammed the base, very close beside the yacht, but had not broken through. After squinting at it a while, Harry decided that its main airlock had been clamped on to the yacht's airlock, in such a way that people ought to be able to go back and forth.

Of course, the Lady Laura, arriving on the *Weapon*, would have wanted to get into the yacht at once, to be beside the man she had loved and served for so many years. This suggested that the *Weapon* could possibly still be spaceworthy—unless it had been shot up on its final approach. Harry wouldn't be able to tell that until he could get inside.

That left the *Chewing Pod*, assuming any such ship really existed, still unaccounted for. Harry got on radio. "Rogue? Answer me! Give me whatever you've been able to find out about my people. And where's Satranji?"

Waiting for an answer, Harry wondered where would Satranji, assuming he had not been warned by the rogue, expect him, Harry, to be at this moment? The goodlife rat-turd would seem to have no reason *not* to suppose Harry Silver dead with the rest of Cheng's assault team, back at 207GST. It was going to be something of a jolt, to discover him armed and waiting.

It almost seemed that the rogue had been reading Harry's thoughts, for presently it was back in communication, telling him: "I have no further information on your people. The goodlife unit Satranji is alone, less than a hundred meters from you. No doubt you are now seeking to revenge yourself upon this enemy."

Harry grunted. "Right now I still don't want to meet him—unless he has my people with him—?"

"I have just told you he does not."

"Then I'll be happy to go around him. I've got to get myself somehow up into the *Chewing Pod*, if there is such a ship, and find out . . ." He couldn't say the words.

"Of course there is such a ship. My base defenses, which as you know were never very strong, have been damaged in the fighting, and my powers of detection at a distance are inferior. But I believe the *Chewing Pod* is now no more than ninety kilometers from us and closing. It will dock here, if that is Satranji's intention, in approximately three minutes."

"I've got to get aboard it."

"I assumed that that would be your intention. I will try to guide the Satranji-unit in another direction, and arrange it so the two of you do not meet—just yet."

Harry maneuvered a little closer to the place where the yacht's hard prow had punctured the relatively thin outer wall of the base at a vulnerable spot. The designer of this base, no doubt the rogue itself, had made no provision in his plan for any viewports, but the assassin had been carrying armament heavy enough to correct that deficiency.

Harry had his choice of gaping holes through which to inspect the situation, and clinging to the jagged edge of one of them he could clearly see the *Pod*, which was positioned just as the rogue had described it.

It was hardly more than spitting distance away, preparing to attach somehow—from here, he couldn't see exactly how—to the *Weapon* on the opposite side from the yacht. Harry was certain he could reach it, perhaps reach it easily, by passing through the two other ships. Satranji, or his autopilot, had arranged to have his spacegoing whorehouse near, to afford him ready access to whatever valuable cargo might be on board. As soon as he judged the right moment had arrived, he would want to quickly extract from it the gifts he meant to offer to the rogue.

Harry pushed on in silence, getting into position for the climb out of the base's artificial gravity, along the hull of the *Ship of Dreams* to a place where a large, ripped opening suggested entrance would be possible. Maybe the rogue was setting him up to be ambushed. Or maybe it was Satranji who would get a nasty surprise—or the weird machine might be just playing games with both of them. Harry couldn't guess.

A faint tremor, as of some minor impact, came through the deck beneath his feet. Suddenly the odd berserker's voice was back, the rogue observing that the *Chewing Pod* had just arrived, touching down by attaching itself to the *Secret Weapon* on the opposite side from Cheng's flagship yacht.

"Then there really is such a ship."

"Of course." The rogue still seemed determined to be cooperative. "Had I any mobile units to spare, I could try sending one of them to find a way into the *Chewing Pod,* and rescue your people if they are there. Unfortunately, I have no units available just now."

"You'd rescue them."

"Certainly. Have you and I not become allies? Both in search of the great truths of the Universe?"

"I've told you what I'm in search of. While you're computing what you ought to do next, I'm going to do what I can." There was still one more factor to be accounted for, and Harry looked around for the vehicle that he had ridden here. "What's happened to the assassin's transporter?"

The rogue replied that that machine was now drifting in nearby space, apparently dead, after exchanging fire with the ground defenses, and then touching down. During the brief duration of that contact, its boarding machines had leapt aground, blasted their way into the rogue's interior architecture, and started dealing out destruction. But in only a few seconds they had been met and their assault stalled by a powerful counterattack.

"Thanks for the information. And for the help. So far you're doing a good job of keeping me alive."

"There are many details of your life that I would

discover, Harry Silver. Therefore it is my intention that you should not die for many years." Eventually, the rogue went on to admit, it would find a duel between the two skillful ED humans fascinating. But right now its highest priority and overriding need was to get rid of the assassin.

Harry jumped as his airmikes brought him the sound of a small, familiar voice coming from only a few meters away. He turned to see the battered robot Dorijen standing there, politely calling for his attention.

TWENTY-THREE

Having already been told that the assassin's transporter had touched down briefly on the rogue's docking space, Harry was not surprised to see that Dorijen had used the opportunity to come aground.

He said: "Greetings, kid. How's my old buddy, the assassin? Any message for me?"

"I am currently carrying no message."

Dorry explained that at the moment when the spacegoing machine touched down, she had made a quick decision and moved as briskly as she could to get out of the transporter and into the berserker base. The assassin had ignored her movements, and for all she could tell it might have forgotten her completely—no doubt it was too fully occupied with launching its attack, all its resources stretched too thin for it to know or care what the tame robot might be up to.

Her overall objective on entering the base was to locate whatever human life might still exist within its walls, and offer whatever help might be possible. She concluded: "Have you reason to expect such a communication?"

"Probably not." Harry gave a twisted grin. "It's just that the assassin must be a bit unhappy with me—ready to assassinate."

"I do not understand."

Harry quickly explained the reasoning that had led him to treacherously switch sides, and his current tentative arrangement with the rogue.

Dorry indicated her understanding. "I must inform you, sir," she went on, "that I am now willing to assign a higher probability to the hypothesis that you are not truly goodlife, that your offers of cooperation to these berserkers are made only with an intention to mislead the enemy. Had I your assurance that this revised interpretation is correct, that might be sufficient to tip the balance of my computations in your favor."

"Yeah? And when your balance tipped—?"

"That would allow me to place myself once more under your command."

It sounded to Harry like convoluted uncertainty, arrived at through a process of pure logic. He knew that the thinking machines were rarely any good at picking up on such subtleties as *When is a human lying?*—unless the contradictory facts were plainly visible. Dorry evidently understood her own weakness in this regard.

"Good," he said. "Consider yourself reassured. Yes, I'm lying to both the damned machines, and hoping for some kind of miracle, that my people are still alive and I can help them. I do indeed have in mind a glorious plan, by which the cause of life will ultimately triumph. Can't tell it to you now, because the enemy might be listening." *And also*, he thought to himself, *because I really have no idea what the hell it is*.

Having announced her intention to be of service, Dorry followed close on Harry's heels as he worked his way up out of the base's artificial gravity, then swung himself in weightlessness from one precarious handhold to another, along the slightly crumpled flank of *Ship of Dreams*. Briefly he had considered sending the robot on ahead, but decided against it, not wanting to alert any enemies who might be waiting there.

Soon Harry gained a position that afforded him his first real look at the *Pod*, a bulbous shape intermediate in size between the two ships to which it was now attached. The sight of it gave him another jolt. Any human who might have been inside when that happened had certainly been at risk; the damage he had earlier observed looked even worse from this angle. Obviously the assassin as well as the yacht had been firing to suppress the rogue's modest ground defenses, and obviously the attempt had not been entirely successful. Return fire from the ground had blasted a sizable hole in this new intruder's hull. Harry could chalk up another ship that couldn't be used to get away. But the third ship's presence opened up new possibilities for the discovery of usable launches and lifeboats. And if he could reach the ship, he ought to have no trouble making his way inside it.

He could see enough to decide that clambering the whole distance along the outside of the smooth-hulled ships was not going to be possible. Harry's only way to get into the *Pod* would be to pass first through the *Ship of Dreams*, and then traverse the *Secret Weapon*.

In a few moments he had entered *Ship of Dreams*—this was the first time Harry had been aboard Cheng's prize yacht, and things were somewhat unfamiliar. The passenger compartments were still airtight, and its internal gravity still worked. But the vessel had been emptied of people and of purpose. Harry encountered nothing that surprised him. A quick look into the control room confirmed the discouraging fact that the main drive was dead, and other internal damage had been extensive.

Leaving Dorry aboard *Dreams* to check on the status of launch and lifeboats, Harry himself pressed on, looking for the airlock that would connect him to the next vessel, the more familiar *Secret Weapon*.

With some difficulty he made his way on, through the mated hatchways, to board the smaller vessel. Here too, signs of extensive damage were immediately apparent.

On entering the first small interior chamber on the *Weapon*, Harry paused to listen. In a moment his airmikes, tuned to great sensitivity, picked up the sound of faint, rapid breathing in the control room, the next compartment forward.

He was well aware that this could be some berserker trick. But he was going to have to look and see.

The first purposefully moving object Harry encountered on board the *Weapon* was a crude-looking club, swung with robotic speed and power in the hands of the tame robot Perdix, who was standing armed and

ready to defend his master against any intrusion by
the bad machines. The robot pulled its swing at the
last instant, so the club only grazed Harry's helmet,
hitting the deck with an impact that gouged out chunks
of material. Harry ripped out an oath, and came with
a hairsbreadth of blasting the cabin's two occupants,
before he realized just who and what they were.

On perceiving that the intruder was a human being,
the robot Perdix lowered the crude weapon he had
improvised by twisting free a damaged stanchion.
Naturally Perdix offered no apology.

The haggard face of Professor Gianopolous was
peering anxiously at Harry from the copilot's seat,
on the other side of the control room. The inventor's
voice broke in the middle. "Harry! Thank God it's
you—I thought you were one of them."

Little more than the man's face was visible, above
a web of forcefield binding, entangling his limbs and
body, effectively shackling him into his chair.

Harry burst out with a demanding question.

Gianopolous was almost gibbering. "Your people?
I've no idea, Harry, why ask me? I've just been stuck
here, where the lady bound me up, before she went
dashing out to join Cheng. Perdix has been trying
to get me loose, but he can't make a dent in this
stuff . . . What's happening out there?"

"What's happening is that all hell's broke loose. And
the lady's not coming back." Harry paused to survey
the inventor's situation, and gave the silvery blur of
the forcefield a testing touch with his armored hand.
"I can fire a shot into this web, and that'll probably
break you free. Of course there's a chance that you'll
be mangled by the recoil when it breaks."

Gianopolous closed his eyes and gritted his teeth. "Go ahead. I'd prefer to die quickly rather than sit here till I starve to death, or the berserkers come— Silver, you've just passed through the yacht, haven't you? Isn't there anyone there? What about Satranji? He was supposed to stay on board, and fight the ship."

"He seems to have decided that he had other business." Harry warned the inventor: "Turn your face away, bend over as far as you can. There's going to be some fireworks." Harry brought up the muzzle of the carbine, and Perdix, quick to catch on, swiftly interposed his metal body in the crucial place.

A single shot from Harry's carbine—its gauge indicated he could count on half a dozen more—set the inventor free, and the flaring explosion in the confined space scorched the tame robot, though not seriously.

Gianopolous seemed to have been partially deafened by the blast, but was otherwise unhurt. He quickly set about providing himself with a spacesuit from the spares on board—unfortunately none of them were armored. Harry delayed his own passage through the ship just long enough to ask a question or two.

"What about the next ship? There's another attached to this one, on the opposite side from the yacht."

Gianopolous had heard the sounds of its arrival, vibrating through the hull of his own ship. Then he had been told by his robot that a third ship was indeed attached in that place. "But I haven't detected any signs of life from it. I thought maybe it was another berserker."

"Not quite. I'm heading over there."

But again Harry's further advance was momentarily delayed, this time by the arrival of Dorry, who reported having checked out the possibilities of escape by means of the yacht's small craft, and found that they were nonexistent. The robot also reported that terrified refugees were beginning to creep into the yacht. "I have told them that the small craft are all inoperable, but they are disinclined to believe that."

"I can't do anything about that. If they stay there, it'll keep 'em out of my hair, at least."

The inventor, still struggling to get into his protective suit, sounded almost eager. "Then what are we going to do, Silver? What are we going to do?"

Harry grunted. "You can suit yourself. I'm moving on. How about borrowing your robot?"

"If Perdix goes, I'm coming with you too. I'm not staying here alone."

Perdix picked up his club again.

A few minutes later, Harry, now with two robots and one man at his heels, at last found his way into the *Chewing Pod*.

Dorry had informed him that she was still carrying some key or code, given her by Satranji many days ago, for opening the hatch of the *Chewing Pod*. The same device would also give its possessor control over the *Pod*'s automatic pilot, but that would probably not help. The appearance of the ship strongly suggested that its drive would almost certainly be useless.

The tame robot had been given this key by Satranji at some earlier time, or had acquired it during the days she spent aboard that ship. Dorijen went on to remind Harry that she had almost perfectly memorized the vessel's interior layout, and could guide him to the limited number of places aboard where two, or even more, living prisoners could be kept with some security.

"I was of course never privy to my former master's plans in this regard. But confinement in a state of suspended animation seems most likely," Dorry suggested.

"I was thinking along those lines myself. The quick and easy way to keep people on ice is to put them into medirobots."

"Yes. There are only a small number of places aboard the *Chewing Pod* where that would be feasible and convenient."

Dorry paused, then added: "Perhaps I should remind you, sir, that in the event we encounter the confessed goodlife Satranji, I stand ready to provide active assistance. As he is human—"

"That's doubtful."

"Excuse me. As he is human, I say, I of course cannot use deadly force against him, under any circumstances."

"Of course."

"But I can and do volunteer to put on a spacesuit at your orders, sir, then move about as a decoy, an imitation human to draw enemy fire."

"Thanks for the offer. When the time comes, I'll consider it."

"Sir, to a robot, no thanks are—"

"—ever necessary. Yeah, I know. It's a bad habit I'll try to break."

Once inside the *Pod*, brought to a momentary halt by its garish decorations, unlike those of any spaceship that Harry had ever seen before, he let the crippled robot take the lead. Dorry made short work of guiding him to the place where the two medirobots had been put away.

This was a short hallway intended primarily for the

use of maintenance and service machines, running between the galley and the dining room, kept air-filled because of frequent traffic between it and the dining room. The two coffin-sized, waist-high units had been shoved close against one wall, leaving only a narrow strip of passage open along the opposite one.

Dorry suggested that with the help of Perdix, the two medirobots with their unconscious burdens could be fairly quickly loaded into the ship's launch, or one of its lifeboats, assuming at least one of those small craft was still functional, and a quick getaway accomplished.

Thinking quickly, Harry decided against that plan. The best and simplest way would be to awaken and release the people first.

The robot could consider, or suggest to Harry, the possibility that Becky and Ethan would be in somewhat less danger staying where they were.

But Harry overruled the suggestion: in this situation the only path to real safety lay in escaping from the Gravel Pit entirely.

Bending over first one of the long boxes and then the other, Harry could see the small indicators showing that both devices were occupied, and in operation.

Suddenly the rogue's voice was once more an active presence in Harry's helmet, affecting to be surprised that the medirobots were here.

Harry growled back something nasty. "You didn't know that, I suppose. But when I got aboard this ship, you managed to locate me in a hurry."

"Of course, Harry Silver, when the *Chewing Pod* is this close to me as it is now, I find it relatively easy to establish communication with any entity aboard. Did you not know that this vessel was once my gift to your goodlife enemy? But that does not mean I constantly monitor the function of every device on board. And, as you must know, a human body in a state of suspended animation is not easily detected."

Harry only grunted, not wanting to waste time in argument.

He focused his attention on the pair of medirobots. Crippled Dorry knew where spacesuits were kept, and somewhat clumsily began the process of getting out a pair of them, one child-sized, and bringing them into the hallway.

Seizing the opportunity for a moment's private talk with the tame robot, Harry told Dorry that he wanted to keep watch on the inventor. "Also, I have my reasons for not wanting Mister G to be armed."

Dorijen accepted the idea calmly. "You are fearful that if he finds a ready means of escape he will immediately take it, without waiting for anyone else."

"Exactly. So do whatever you can to prevent that." He hesitated. "If you can come up with a spare weapon somewhere, better give it to Perdix. We can all feel a little safer that way."

If the readouts on the coffin-shaped boxes were to be believed, Harry's wife and child were both in good shape. Both faces were dimly visible, through semitransparent lids. Harry stared at each of them for only a moment. There was no time to spare.

Harry found the right control and started his son's revival process. But Becky had to be awakened first, if for no other reason than that her skills as a veteran spacer and combat veteran might be needed immediately. Harry wanted someone standing guard over the kid while he and Dorry finished checking out the *Pod*'s lifeboats and launch, to see what the prospects were for a quick, successful getaway.

Harry's armored fingers fumbled with the clasp. If there was a lock, it wasn't very formidable, and his powered gauntlets tore it free. In a moment he had unfastened the outer coffin lid and thumbed the EMERGENCY REVIVAL button.

This body also was nude, and Harry could see at a glance that all its major parts were still in place. As had been the case with the members of Cheng's family, there were no plugs stuck in their wrists and ankles.

The thick lid eased itself away. Becky's eyes opened slowly, and her voice lacked any urgency. "Harry. It's you."

"Who were you expecting?" Somehow his voice was warbling all up and down the scale. He heard himself say: "Damn it, woman, you knew me, even in this motherless suit."

The crease of a frown appeared in Becky's forehead. "Looks like someone's been using it for target practice. Of course I knew you, Harry, I've seen you in a lot of strange getups. Harry, don't cry, I'm all right, my God, where's Ethan?" Raising her head enough to look around a little, she goggled at the unfamiliar narrow corridor. "I can't remember anything. Where are we?"

"You always wanted to ride on a ship that was fixed up in real luxury. Well, see, this is it." Though she wouldn't be able to tell it from her immediate surroundings; no gaudy decorations had been wasted on this corridor. There was no time to waste, and Harry was lifting her out of the coffin, hoping she would be able to stand up.

"Where's Ethan?" More insistently this time; motherhood was awakening.

"He's right over here, in the other bin. His readings are fine, I'll get him out in a minute. Don't stand around like that with nothing on. Here's Dorry, a good robot, she's got a spacesuit ready for you. Get yourself into it. I'll do the kid."

"All right," said Becky doubtfully. "Dorry, you look like hell."

"Indeed I do, ma'am."

Becky was beginning to move, slowly. Harry remembered, all too well, how coming up suddenly out of that deep artificial sleep could hit you, like a combination of drunkenness with a bad hangover. His wife's voice was sleepy again, luxurious with blissful ignorance. Confusion persisted, but the peculiarity of her surroundings was beginning to sink in. "Harry, what happened to this poor robot? Is this your ship?"

"Yours and mine. For as long as we need it."

"All paid for?"

"Gods of deep space, is it paid for! I doubt any ship has ever cost like this one—but the rent's been paid, in advance. And a good down payment on something better."

At last Becky was starting to come fully awake, and alarm was naturally setting in. She turned back, resisting Dorry's gentle two-fingered tug.

"Harry, these are bloody motherless medirobots, what am I doing in a medirobot? I don't remember . . . you know what I think . . . ?"

"Tell me later. Or I'll tell you about it. Right now, will you just get moving?"

Harry turned to the other lifesaving device, saw

that EMERGENCY REVIVAL was having its effect, and in moments was reaching into the warm interior to deliver a smooth child-body back into the world.

"Daddy . . . are you the doctor?" came Ethan's sleepy murmur. And the five-year-old's arms went around Harry's armored neck. Ethan was just as quick at identification as his mother had been, though he could hardly have seen much more than a bulky shape in a strange suit. He must have heard Daddy's voice on the airspeakers.

"Today I am your doctor, kid. Daddy's checking you and taking you home. Got to get you right into your own suit." Not that the launch had children's sizes available, but an expert like Becky, once she got her mind together, would be able to fit a child into an adult size so it would at least serve as backup life support, even if the kid could hardly move. Under these conditions, cutting down the five-year-old's mobility, keeping him in one place, could be a definite advantage.

Becky wasn't up to full speed yet. But, working on instinct, she had managed to get her own suit on already. Now she was complaining. "Harry, this suit's not going to fit him. It's just way too loose."

"You take over, do the best you can. And tell him he'll grow into it. We're going home."

The five of them, four suited humans and Perdix, had just left the service hallway, passing through the doorway into the ornate dining salon, when an elaborate screen, part of the room's lush decoration, was knocked aside, revealing the asymmetrical body of Harry's dedicated assassin. The ring that the assassin had taken from him, days ago, was still visible on its right hand.

Professor Gianopolous squealed and turned to run. The berserker's monstrous other hand swung through the edge of the falling screen to pulp the inventor's skull before he had taken a full step, spattering its bone and clever brain over walls and floor and life-units alike.

TWENTY-FOUR

Gianopolous had gone down dead, the inadequate helmet of his simple suit completely shattered by the assassin's blow, his headless body twitching.

Harry had begun the act of swinging the carbine around—no need for an exact physical pointing of the muzzle, but he had to get within a certain angle of the target that his eyes were in the process of locking on. The tip of the muzzle had much less than a meter to go in its swift arc, and he was trying to swing it with all his might, but already he sensed that he was not likely to complete the move in time. Part of his mind noted, in the way it had of tallying useless things, the scars of fresh combat that marked the assassin's body and its ugly head.

At the same time, Perdix, reacting to a berserker's threat with his own robotic speed, had used his right

hand to hurl his primitive stanchion-club straight at
the killing machine's head. Before the streaking missile
reached its target the left hand of Perdix had drawn
from somewhere a heavy pistol—in the dreamlike
slowness in which these things seemed to be happening, Harry realized that Dorry must have dug out a
weapon from somewhere on the ship and given it to
Perdix just as he, Harry, had suggested.

Scattered around the room behind the assassin
were the helpless refugees, noncombatants, frozen
by slow time in a variety of awkward poses. All were
just starting to react.

The assassin's monstrous left hand came up with
speedy competence, to strike the thrown metal in
midflight, brushing it aside. In the same instant a
portal on the assassin's robust chest flicked open, not
far from the spot where a human heart would dwell
in living flesh. Fire came hammering out of the cavity
at the tame robot, cutting it down, the heavy-caliber
handgun spinning useless from the hand of Perdix to
go flying across the room, falling somewhere near the
entrance to the dining salon.

But the tame robot's effort had occupied the assassin for just long enough. The pieces of Perdix had
not had time to hit the deck, when Harry's swinging
weapon came within the proper angle of the target
picked by the direction of his gaze. The last half-
dozen forcepackets that his carbine's charge could
throw erupted from the muzzle. At point-blank range,
they were enough.

A few seconds later, Harry was shakily advancing
upon the shattered remnants of his fallen foe. The

assassin had been thoroughly mangled, brain and all. Harry was just in the act of reaching for the monster's right hand, which was still relatively intact, with some dazed purpose of retrieving his ring, when fresh sounds of movement caused him to look up in alarm.

But the small group of figures advancing toward him were only people, some of the prisoners that he had rescued. Claudia Cheng was walking carefully in their lead, with Winnie in his misfit suit hobbling beside her.

Fewer than a dozen people, actually, but they seemed to crowd the *Chewing Pod*'s dining salon, elbowing and almost trampling each other in a rush to what they must perceive as safety. Harry sighed and lowered the carbine's muzzle.

"We didn't know about your helper," someone commented brightly.

"Helper?" Harry's mind seemed to have gone blank.

And at the same moment, someone else: "He just joined us as we were coming in—"

"Drop the carbine, Silver," interrupted a taut, familiar voice. "Don't even think of turning round."

Satranji had entered the dining salon at the tail end of the line, joining it so smoothly and quietly that he seemed quite naturally to belong to it. He had Harry—as well as Becky and Ethan, Claudia and Winnie—covered with his own carbine before Harry even knew that he was there.

Remembering in time that his weapon's magazine was exhausted, Harry let it fall.

Satranji told him: "Now you can turn. Time we got acquainted, Silver. We're going to be taking a long, long trip together. Some of these other good people too—likely my partner will want them all. Oh, by all means you must bring the family. My partner has some special ideas about them." Then his head turned, with a nervous jerk as a figure appeared beside him.

The crippled robot Dorry had taken her position there, and, when her former master stared without recognition at her half-disassembled face and body, she addressed him in her usual cheerful voice.

"No doubt, sir, you would have been surprised to see me, had you recognized me in the other corridor just now."

"Gods of space, it's Dorijen." And Satranji, helping himself to a second look, then a third, at last seemed satisfied that this had been his robot. "I did just walk past you out there, didn't I? I thought you were a pile of junk." His voice turned ugly. "Actually, that's what you are."

Releasing one hand from his weapon, he swung the arm of his servo-powered combat suit, dealing Dorry a casual blow on the side of the head that sent her sprawling. It was a smashing impact that might have knocked bricks out of a wall.

"How in all the hells did you get here?" Satranji grumbled. He spoke to the robot, without taking his eyes away from Harry for a moment. "But it doesn't matter. What a ruin. Not worth a shit now. Turned into a piece of crap like all the other bitches."

This time Dorry needed longer to get up than she had the time when Harry knocked her down. But her voice still sounded cheerful. "That impact," she announced to the world, "seems to have clouded my optelectronic senses." Then she went down on her knees again, groping with her one crippled hand as if in search of something she had lost. "Sensory malfunction," she murmured softly.

Satranji still hadn't really taken his eyes off Harry. "Silver, it's time we had a little conversation, you and I."

"Why not?" Harry tried to sound as cheerful as the robot.

"Meanwhile you should get yourself out of that heavy suit. You always said the damned things made you uncomfortable."

"Sure," said Harry.

"Then do it!"

While checking as best he could as to where his people were, Harry started to release his metal gauntlets from the inside. That would be a reasonable first step in taking off the suit; it wouldn't look suspicious. The part of his mind that kept on scheming, no matter what, informed him that now he was going to have to throw one of the metal gloves, while he still had servo power in his arms. Not only throw it. He would have to hit the carbine in Satranji's grip and spoil his aim, or else hit his faceplate hard enough to cloud his vision for an instant. In that instant Harry would have to rush him . . . it might be a hundred-to-one shot, and that was being charitable. But it was better than nothing at all.

Some of the ship's automatic systems, evidently sensing that a small crowd had gathered, were coming on in the salon, and music tinkled in the background, sounding like an ancient piano with keys of ivory and ebony.

Satranji was still being very watchful. He said: "Now

we can have a little drink, and you can tell me about it. Hope you're not a sore loser, Silver. Someone told me that you like scotch."

Harry's first gauntlet fell to the deck. He was going to have to throw the second.

Becky, with Ethan suited and in tow, was edging, as if unconsciously, a little closer to her man. So were some of the other people, and Harry knew that in the next moment he was about to take his hopeless gamble, and Satranji's brain would pull the alphatrigger on the carbine, swift as thought, and many of the people in the room would die—

A fusillade of shots erupted, coming not from Satranji's weapon, but from behind the goodlife man, near the main entrance to the room.

The mass of Satranji's bulky figure was knocked forward, soaring in a low, involuntary leap, hurled in a tottering spin right past Harry before Harry could attempt to dodge. The suited form stopped when it hit a wall, then collapsed in smoking ruin. The third hit on the moving target had torn its armored backpack open, and a secondary interior explosion jerked Satranji's suit's four limbs to full extension, and momentarily lighted his faceplate with a baleful inner glow. Within seconds, the air in the room began to fill with smoke, the stench of burning chemicals and flesh.

From a spot near the main entrance, the slender figure of Dorry the robot came limping slowly forward. The heavy handgun that she had once given Perdix, who had not been able to draw it quite fast enough, was clamped solidly in the grip of her two remaining fingers and a thumb. Dorijen tilted her head as she drew near the fallen man, nearsightedly peering down at him with her one damaged eye.

Invisible environmental systems had already begun to work, patiently cleaning the large room's atmosphere, and faint tendrils of smoke were whisked away. There was near silence, broken only by some woman sobbing, and then the robot's usual cheery voice.

"It seems that I have killed a human being," Dorry announced brightly. "A clear case of sensory malfunction, as the result of trauma. Faulty perception assured me that I was firing at a berserker machine.

"The pistol is empty now, but still—" The weapon dropped from her crippled hand. In the quiet room, everyone heard clearly the soft thud of its landing. "Somehow I could not place Mister Satranji in the proper category. Perhaps in the circumstances you surviving humans will be safer if I no longer carry weapons." On her last cheerful word, Dorry suddenly sat down, as if her disorientation might be getting worse.

Harry choked out some response—later he could never remember just what he had said. He looked uncertainly about him, and blinked at the new weapon that had come into his own hands—by reflex he had already snatched up Satranji's carbine.

But there was nothing left to shoot.

TWENTY-FIVE

Harry at last had set his captured carbine down, laying the weapon close against the wall of the small control cabin in the *Chewing Pod*'s functional launch, where either he or Becky could grab it up in a hurry if need be. At the moment his wife was occupying the pilot's seat, in the last stages of running a quick checklist that so far indicated there was nothing wrong with the small vessel in which all the surviving humans were about to make their getaway. Harry had been concentrating on looking out for trouble, but now it appeared he would be able to give up riding shotgun.

The launch provided a comfortably furnished passenger space some fifteen meters long and four wide, which in happier times could have been quickly reconfigured to offer several distinctly different flavors of luxury. Now the only concern was that it afforded ample room, and speedy transportation.

Exchanging scraps of hasty conversation with his wife, while both were engaged in herding people into the launch, Harry had been reminded that she had seen genuine berserkers before. When the kidnappers came for her and Ethan, she had no doubt that she was seeing them again. "That was at first."

"At first?"

Becky went on: "You know, Harry? It was all so horrible . . . but there was a time when I began to suspect they weren't real berserkers."

"They were real enough. If they seemed a bit clumsy, that was probably just because they weren't used to trying to keep their victims alive."

"Ethan was screaming, just horribly, and then I was screaming too . . ."

"It's all right now, kid. That part's all over."

The robot Dorijen was still functioning, or at least capable of purposeful movement, having boarded the launch at the end of the line of surviving humans.

Ethan and Winnie, both children hampered in oversized spacesuits, had started some kind of game, withdrawing from the terrors of the adult world to something that perhaps made more sense to them.

Harry also had a short interlude of conversation with Claudia Cheng. While thanking him politely for all his trouble, she managed indirectly to convey her determination to fight any great change in the old man's will—though she remained amenable to buying her savior a new ship.

Half a minute later it was Becky who, having

already heard the story, remarked: "You could hire a lawyer, Harry. If there were any witnesses to what he said . . ."

Harry was shaking his head. "I've never had a lot of luck with witnesses. Or lawyers either."

Winnie had largely abandoned the game he had been playing, to eye the carbine that Harry had put down. Now he looked up to pester his mother for a gun of his own.

Harry had put his gauntlets on again, and had never taken his helmet off—it was going to stay on until he was sure they were safely away. Suddenly he started, abruptly distracted by the rogue's familiar radio voice.

"I am speaking to you, Harry Silver. Only to you. The life-units with you cannot hear me."

Harry was not at all surprised to hear the voice; the only surprise was that some perverse part of him seemed to be secretly pleased to have assurance that the damned rogue wasn't completely dead.

Something kept Harry from blurting out a general announcement that at least one of the berserkers still survived. Well, that probably would not be news to anyone.

"Rest easy, Harry Silver," said the small voice in his helmet. "You and I have reached a de facto truce, and today is not our day for fighting one another."

Mentally Harry made the adjustments that would allow him to subvocalize speech to the rogue, while remaining silent as far as the human company around him were aware. He had the feeling that this conversation could possibly take a turn that he wouldn't want them to hear . . .

Not even Becky?

Yes, for the moment, not even Becky.

"What do you want?" he demanded tersely.

"Only to maintain contact with my favorite experimental subject. I must congratulate you on your survival. And on the demise of your goodlife rival."

The rogue assured Harry that it had no need of the launch that he and his fellow humans were about to use. It also announced that it had attained all of its essential components, and was about to depart the Gravel Pit in its previously prepared escape module.

Harry wanted to ask the rogue if it had retained a few life-units to take with it as well, restocking its new laboratory; but whatever answer it gave to that question could be a lie.

Instead he asked: "You mean you've wiped out all of the assassin's units?"

"It would be unwise, would it not, to make any such assertion dogmatically?"

Whatever units of the assassin still survived would have no means of getting themselves away from this rock. But the prospect of ending their existence in this particular time and place would mean nothing to those machines. All that mattered to them would be their assigned missions, in order of priority.

When the voice of the rogue came back again, it was still mild, giving the impression of a lovely, balanced temperament, unshaken by anything that had ever happened, or ever would. "From now on, Harry Silver, you and I will remain closely associated."

"Up yours. You bloody, twisted . . ." When he remembered the body parts of people, still-living organs mounted on a wall for study, thoughts failed him, as did his extensive knowledge of bad language. Why couldn't life's enemy stay simply and dependably nasty? Be content to simply kill and have done with it?

"Defiant insult is not an unexpected response. I will continue to monitor your career as closely as possible—at times I will be much closer to you than you realize."

Harry's capacity to be frightened seemed to have been burned away, along with some other mental baggage. "I expect there's a rather large berserker task force on its way here even as we speak, dispatched by your own high command. I'm told your creators have decided you're a great disappointment, that putting you together was a ghastly blunder. I've never met a high command that could admit to making great mistakes, but maybe yours can do it. As soon as they catch you, they're going to hammer you into little bits of junk and lose the pieces."

Some of the people near Harry, unaware of the conversation he was having, were looking at him oddly. He smoothed out the expression on his face.

"Remember what I have told you, Harry Silver. Remember also that anger is irrational."

"I'm recording this, you obscenity. I'll spread the word about you to the Force, and to the Templars, and if you do somehow manage to get away from here I'll get all the help I need and we'll track you down."

Becky was through with the last details of the checklist, and the hatches closed. Without wasting any time on formalities, the lady was getting them free of the pileup of junked spaceships, and the berserker base.

"Tracking me down will not be necessary. Are you trying to frighten me, Harry Silver? It is interesting that you seek to frighten a machine."

After that there was a silence, long enough so that Harry began to wonder if the rogue was gone. But suddenly it was back. "I see that you have launched, and I will shortly do the same. I compute that you do not in fact have any intention of recording this—but know that I am doing so. You will want to destroy any record of it—but, of course, the record that I am making will never come within your reach. You will not want your Templars and your Space Force to see the evidence of our continuing close relationship."

Harry advised the rogue to perform an act of crude violence upon itself.

The other found that interesting too. "In your form of rhetoric, you attribute to me anatomical capabilities I do not possess. Goodbye for now, Harry Silver. I hope you are able to preserve your interesting life until we meet again. At some point in the future, I intend to carefully observe your death."

The signal had begun fading rapidly. The launch was picking up speed—and maybe the rogue was also, moving in some other direction.

Ethan was calling, looking for continued contact, reassurance: "Daddy? Who're you talking to?"

Five seconds passed before the question registered, and Harry could find an answer: "No one. No one at all."

AUTHOR'S NOTE

For information about Fred Saberhagen
and this series, see:

www.berserker.com

THE SF OF ERIC FLINT

MOTHER OF DEMONS
Humans stranded on an alien world precipitate a revolution.
Also available at the Baen Free Library, www.baen.com.

pb ◆ 0-671-87800-X ◆ $5.99

BOUNDARY with Ryk E. Spoor
A "funny" fossil is found in the American desert, and solving
the mystery of its origins takes paleontologist Helen Sutter all
the way to Mars. . . .

hc ◆1-4165-0932-1 ◆ $26.00

THE COURSE OF EMPIRE
with K.D. Wentworth
Conquered by the Jao twenty years ago, Earth is shackled
under alien tyranny—and threatened by the even more dangerous Ekhat. The humans will fight to the death, but the
battle to free the Earth may destroy it instead!

hc ◆ 0-7434-7154-7 ◆ $22.00
pb ◆ 0-7434-9893-3 ◆ $7.99

CROWN OF SLAVES with David Weber
A novel set in the *NY Times* best-selling Honor Harrington
universe. Sent on a mission to keep Erewhon from breaking with Manticore, the Star Kingdom's most able agent
and the Queen's niece may not even be able to escape
with their lives. . . .

pb ◆ 0-7434-9899-2 ◆ $7.99

A new Blackcollar novel by
TIMOTHY ZAHN

The legendary Blackcollar warriors were the only hope of a conquered Earth—if they still existed. Military SF by a *New York Times* best-selling author.

Blackcollar
Includes *The Blackcollar* and *Blackcollar: The Backlash Mission.*

1-4165-0925-9 • $25.00

Blackcollar: The Judas Solution
1-4165-2065-1 • $25.00

And don't miss:
The Cobra Trilogy
Trade pb • 1-4165-2067-8 • $14.00